LEO
TOLSTOY

THE COSSACKS

This novel of love, adventure, and male rivalry on the frontiers of nineteenth-century Russia – completed in 1862, when Tolstoy was in his early thirties – has always surprised readers who know Tolstoy best through the vast, panoramic fictions of his middle years. Unlike those works, THE COSSACKS is lean and supple, economical in design and execution. But Tolstoy could never touch a subject without imbuing it with his magnificent many-sidedness. And so this book bears witness almost in passing to the instinctive feeling for every level of human and natural life, the brilliant historical imagination, and the passionately alive spiritual awareness that characterize its author's genius.

EVERYMAN'S   LIBRARY

EVERYMAN,
I WILL GO WITH THEE,
AND BE THY GUIDE,
IN THY MOST NEED
TO GO BY THY SIDE

LEO TOLSTOY

The Cossacks

Translated by Louise and Aylmer Maude

with an Introduction by
John Bayley

EVERYMAN'S LIBRARY
Alfred A. Knopf New York Toronto

170

THIS IS A BORZOI BOOK

PUBLISHED BY ALFRED A. KNOPF, INC.

First included in Everyman's Library, 1994
Introduction, Bibliography and Chronology Copyright © 1994 by
David Campbell Publishers Ltd.
Typography by Peter B. Willberg

ISBN 0-679-43131-4
LC 93-81034

Book Design by Barbara de Wilde and Carol Devine Carson

Typeset in the UK by MS Filmsetting Limited, Frome, Somerset

Printed and bound in Germany by
Mohndruck Graphische Betriebe GmbH, Gütersloh

THE COSSACKS

INTRODUCTION

In World War II there was a famous British destroyer, one of the 'Tribal' class, named HMS Cossack. Her name recorded a common western misapprehension: that 'Cossacks', like Gurkhas or Afridis, were an exotic race, who happened to dwell within the wide borders of the Russian empire, and who served the Tsar in the same way that warlike local nationalities had come to serve the British Empire. In fact the word 'Cossack' ('Kazak' in Russian) carries no ethnic significance, but meant originally something like 'pieceworker', or one who works in his own time. The Cossacks were runaway serfs, outlaws, and adventurers, mostly from Great Russia, whom early Russian governments attempted to control and organize as frontier guards and farmer-soldiers living in the border regions.

The Cossack has always seemed a picturesque figure to the Russians themselves, though not an ethnic one. Asked by a western novelist whether anyone could become a Cossack, the novelist Sholokhov, who came from the Don region and claimed ancestry in the Cossack settlements there, replied that Turks and Poles and orientals might all become Cossacks, but not Jews. The writer had the sense to retort: 'But what about Isaac Babel?' – referring to the famous Jewish author of short stories, notably *Red Cavalry*, who had become an officer and commissar in a Cossack unit during the revolutionary war. Sholokhov's reply is not recorded, but his own status has now been shown to be an equivocal one. His epic novel *Quiet Don* (translated under the title *Quiet Flows the Don*), recording the troubled years of the revolution in the Cossack lands, may in fact have been plagiarized from the writings of an officer who was killed in that conflict, and had known it at first-hand as the younger Sholokhov did not.

The point is of some importance in the context of Tolstoy's own early masterpiece, *The Cossacks*, for Tolstoy cleverly arranged a scenario in which his young hero Olenin *thinks* he knows and understands about the Cossacks and their way of life whereas in fact he does not and cannot do so, a situation beautifully emphasized by the ending of the story.

Tolstoy has things both ways. He does all he can, and with all his amazing creative skill, to suggest the reality of the Cossack mode of life – the hard simple facts about it – while at the same time he can record through the eyes of his hero the full romantic impact, for his Russian readers, of that way of life, and the wild untamed beauty of the Caucasus and the River Terek. Tolstoy's 'realism' is never reductive, never seeks to show up a false exotic picture by presenting his own as the genuine accurate one. At the same time he was very conscious as a young author that 'my hero is truth', as he put it in his introduction to *Sevastopol Sketches*, his account of his own experiences at the front in the Crimean War. Both in this great early story, *The Cossacks*, and his last tale of all, *Hadji Murad*, which takes an historical episode from the same region, he presents a picture of sober factuality, observed with a masterfully neutral eye. In this he learnt much of course, and perhaps unconsciously, from his great predecessor, the poet Pushkin, who had written poems about the Cossacks (a phrase from one of which, *The Captive of the Caucasus*, was borrowed for his title by Sholokhov).

What has been called 'the anxiety of influence' is often found even in the greatest writers. There is no doubt that Tolstoy wished as a young man to add his own version of a work of art to those dramatic pictures of the Caucasus already created by Pushkin, and by Lermontov in *A Hero of Our Time*. The theme of the Caucasus presented, as it were, the stock challenge to an ambitious young Russian writer of the mid-nineteenth century. A sort of analogy in the twentieth century is to be found in Hemingway's development of the war stories of Stephen Crane, the predecessor who offered both a challenge and an example for his own genius.

The form of *The Cossacks* gave Tolstoy a great deal of trouble. He worked on it intermittently for ten years, between 1852 and 1862, interrupted by his service in the Crimea and his visits to Europe. (He had earlier served as a junior artillery officer in the campaign against the Caucasus tribesmen.) At one moment he even thought of attempting the subject as a poem, although so far as is known he only tried to write verses once in his life, and then only in a letter. The fact that he thought of it at all is none the less significant proof of the spell that the great poems earlier in the century, like Pushkin's *Captive*, and even more one of his narrative masterpieces, *The Gipsies*, had exercised on Russian readers. *The Gipsies* contrasts the simple heroic style of life of a wandering Gipsy tribe with the frivolous aristocratic outlook of a young Russian with a dubious past who hero-worships them and wishes to live among them. A tragic, even melodramatic, result ensues, when Aleko becomes insanely jealous of his Gipsy mistress and kills her and her new lover, and is left behind in broken solitude upon the steppe.

Tolstoy of course avoids any such dramatic outcome; but in the way in which he terminates his story, with Olenin tacitly snubbed and dismissed by his Cossack friends and the girl Maryanka, we can detect his subtle redeployment of the same kind of idea. It is in its way a version of the old cliché that east is east and west is west. The romantic young man who longs to join a different society, and become part of another way of life, finds out in the end that they are incompatible with his background and temperament. In terms of the development of romantic ideas and ideals since the late eighteenth century, when French authors had written hopeful and wildly popular novels about the Noble Savage, and the joys of abandoning civilized life for the American prairie or a tropic island, *The Cossacks*, like *The Gipsies* before it, presents a decidedly disillusioned picture. There is a great deal of *literature* at the back of *The Cossacks*, even though it gives us such an unsurpassably fresh and vivid picture of a natural setting, and of life in a Cossack community.

But even as a young man Tolstoy was always determined, as it were, to have his own say: to be dogmatic about experience, and to assert the truth as he himself is determined to see it. The dogmatist in him was always at war with the artist. And we can see the effects of this in the characterization and narrative pattern of *The Cossacks*. Although the subject was such a well-worn romantic one, and given a peculiarly Russian status by Pushkin and other Russian writers, Tolstoy is determined to add his own interpretation, as an author and an individual. He is determined to place his own experience in the most majestic form of literary context: not only the recent literary Russian one, but even that of Homer – whom he had come greatly to admire – and the tradition of the primitive epic.

And so, as frequently happens with this amazing author, several different and apparently incompatible literary forms and conventions – the romantic, the classical and epic, the personal – all come together in one brief and vivid 'novel'. (Tolstoy always claimed that Russian authors 'did not very well understand' the novel as practised conventionally in western Europe; and he said both of *The Cossacks* and of *War and Peace* that they were not novels in the western sense, but just works of art in the form in which the writer could 'most conveniently' say what he wanted.) In his early stories in the form of a memoir, *Childhood, Boyhood and Youth*, Tolstoy had used the models of Rousseau and Sterne, in which the author, the 'I', was securely built into a nominal hero, like Saint-Preux or Tristram Shandy. The epic form has of course no 'I' in this sense; and the novels of Scott, on which Russian prose romances had naturally come to be based, used a generally rather passive and even feeble hero, such as Waverley, who merely acted as the focus of the tale, the figure in its historically and geographically picturesque landscape.

A severe judge might say that Tolstoy's hero Olenin, in *The Cossacks*, has from this point of view the worst of all worlds. He is not very interesting in himself, as a personal hero should be, and he gets in the way of the epic and objective aspects of the story. That, roughly speaking, was the view of Tolstoy's older fellow-writer Turgenev, who admired his brilliant younger contemporary very much, but who was always shrewd and penetrating in his technical judgements. The matter resolves itself into the question: Are we to have 'The Cossacks', or 'The Cossacks as seen by Olenin?' – and that is the dilemma Tolstoy cannot be said to have satisfactorily settled, partly because in some degree, of course, he was himself Olenin. The time and trouble he took over the book shows how conscious he was of the problem. In his first sketch Olenin is a much more positive, even strong-minded figure, who has lost enormous sums at gambling, and whose departure for the Caucasus is correspondingly more urgent. This Olenin, indeed, is more like Tolstoy himself at the time, the young officer and gambler who lost large sums, while the final version of Olenin is more like the young, naive and idealistic Tolstoy still in his teens. Indeed it could be said to have an element of self-satire; to be a slightly comical version of the youthful author himself, by himself.

This childish quality engagingly appears in the description of the hero's setting out from Moscow, going past houses he had never seen before, so that 'it seemed to him that only travellers starting on a long journey went through those streets'. There is more than a touch of the child David Copperfield in this (Tolstoy much admired Dickens' novel), and Tolstoy seems almost deliberately to exaggerate the self-consciousness and self-absorption of the young. But Olenin is seen far less sentimentally than the young Copperfield; and Tolstoy never indicated both the magic and the absurdity of being young more memorably than in this passage:

Now and then he looked round at some house and wondered why it was so curiously built; sometimes he began wondering why the post-boy and Vanyusha, who were so different from himself, sat so near, and together with him were being jerked about and swayed by the tugs the side-horses gave at the frozen traces, and again he repeated: 'First rate . . . very fond!' and once he even said: 'And how it seizes one . . . excellent!' and wondered what made him say it. 'Dear me, am I drunk?' he asked himself. He had had a couple of bottles of wine, but it was not the wine alone that was having this effect on Olenin. He remembered all the words of friendship heartily, bashfully, spontaneously (as he believed) addressed to him on his departure. . . . He remembered his own deliberate frankness. And all this had a touching significance for him. . . . 'Perhaps I shall not return from the Caucasus', he thought. And he felt that he loved his friends and some one besides. He was sorry for himself. But it was not love for his friends that so stirred and uplifted his heart that he could not repress the meaningless words that seemed to rise of themselves to his lips; nor was it love for a woman (he had never yet been in love) that had brought on this mood. Love for himself, love full of hope – warm young love for all that was good in his own soul (and at that moment it seemed to him that there was nothing but good in it) – compelled him to weep and to utter incoherent words.

Olenin is one of those people whom we get to know so well so quickly that we are soon a bit bored by them. Amused and fond we may be, but is this the best company in which to meet the Cossacks? Perhaps it is, or at least Tolstoy makes it seem so, because of the very incongruity. We are aware, after all, that Olenin is not 'going anywhere'. He is not like the young Nicholas Rostov at the beginning of *War and Peace*, who exhibits in his homecoming, a similar incoherent ecstasy and self-satisfaction, but who is clearly destined for many other and further developments, as we can see from the number of pages stretching ahead. Olenin is the hero of a much briefer tale, which will abandon him on completion, just as the Cossacks themselves will do.

So why should he not, like the doomed Lensky in Pushkin's *Eugene Onegin*, be filled with romantic longings? He dreams of 'Circassian maidens, mountain precipices, terrible torrents, and perils.' And as he nears the Caucasus the confinement of our first over-intimacy with this young hero soon begins to lift. We catch our first glimpse of the great mountains of the region through his eyes; but beyond his view are the real mountains themselves, their objective presences, looming in epic grandeur. The difference between the subjective and the objective here is subtly conveyed by Tolstoy in his account of Olenin's own response. 'So this is where it begins,' he thinks, and he keeps expecting to see the mountains as he has read and heard of them, but anything he actually glimpses seems disappointing. 'He thought the special beauty of the snow peaks, of which he had so often been told, was as much an invention as Bach's music and the love of women, in which he did not believe. So he gave up looking forward to seeing the mountains.'

But then he *really* sees them. Gradually their majestic approach penetrates his callow, self-preoccupied consciousness, and he begins to *feel* them. 'From that moment all he saw, all he thought, all he felt, acquired for him a new character, sternly majestic like the mountains ... "Now it has begun," a solemn voice seemed to say to him.' And for the next paragraph every thought and impression ends for him with that awed and ecstatic refrain – one of the great bravura passages in Tolstoy's usually sober and factual prose ... 'And the mountains!'

To combine what seems the reality of them with his hero's first idea of them is a remarkable feat: probably no writer but Tolstoy could have so effectively made the two into one. And from now on in the story this dual vision becomes more emphatic, and yet more effective. Eroshka, the old Cossack, and Maryanka the Cossack girl, inhabit and obsess Olenin's consciousness; and yet they are also solid figures in their own right, whom we seem to see apart from him. Though very far from being the Circassian maiden of his dreams, Maryanka remains for Olenin on the same plane of enchantment and strangeness. Romance is inverted but retained. Coming and going on bare sinewy feet across the yard, her pink print smock clinging to her powerful chest and buttocks (we even seem to hear her peeing at one point: an extraordinary concession in the always prudish context of the Russian novel), Maryanka none the less remains a magical and unattainable figure, a *princesse lointaine*, although the detail of her physical being is as present as is the odour of 'vodka, sweat, gunpowder, wine, and congealed blood', which accompanies Uncle Eroshka.

Tolstoy is of course substituting as romantic object the full-bodied Maryanka for the conventional sloe-eyed Circassian maiden. Romance is adaptable; and in the work of a genius writing in poetry or in prose it is always capable of such adaptations: seventy years later Yeats was to substitute 'great-bladdered Emer' and her fancy man for the pallid and 'pearl-pale' Niamh and Deirdre. Indeed from the point of view of romantic techniques *The Cossacks* is probably the most influential of Tolstoy's works, and the tale which had most effect on later literary innovators. Hemingway revered it. And so odd can be the perspective of literary influences that we may have the feeling today, if we ourselves are reading *The Cossacks* for the first time, that its author has been reading Hemingway!

But Hemingway could not manage Tolstoy's humorously Russian – in a sense Pushkinian – approach to the consciousness of his hero. The hero of a *A Farewell to Arms*, for example, is not detached from the author in the way that Olenin is; and the heroine of that novel is not a patch – objectively speaking – on the sturdy Maryanka: she remains a passive dream princess at the beck and call of the hero. Tolstoy, even when young, was a deeply ironic as well as an analytic artist; and yet in *The Cossacks* this irony at the expense of his hero is not an unmixed blessing. It draws attention too often to the naivety of Olenin's outlook, and sometimes merges that naivety into the objective flow of the action itself. This is evident at the end of the tale, when a detachment of Cossacks have surrounded a party of *abreks*, the hostile tribesmen from across the river with whom they are permanently at war.

Olenin was much impressed by the place in which they sat. In reality it was very much like the rest of the steppe, but because the *abreks* sat there it seemed to detach itself from all the rest and to have become distinguished. Indeed it appeared to Olenin that it was the very spot for *abreks* to occupy.

This description is strangely akin to the young hero's naive and magical apprehension, as he started out from Moscow, that 'only travellers starting on a journey went through those streets'. We seem almost to be back where we started.

But in a sense this may be a part of Tolstoy's plan and purpose, which gives his *nouvelle* its strangely original, almost dreamlike quality. True, there are moments, perhaps left over from earlier drafts of the work, when Tolstoy seems to try to evade Olenin altogether, and to describe the Cossack settlement objectively, with the kind of epical simplicity which Pushkin used in his own historical *nouvelle*, *The Captain's Daughter*, and Gogol when he described the settlement of the Zaporozhe Cossacks in *Taras Bulba*. But Tolstoy cannot quite evade, as it were, the spell cast by his youthful hero's own naive and vivid awareness. So fastened to it is he that we seem to be seeing the Cossack village through Olenin's eyes, even though in the sequence of the narrative he has not yet arrived!

This *dual* outlook and method in the narrative, awkward as it undoubtedly can be, none the less contributes a great deal to the peculiar flavour of the tale. Take the fine set piece of the shooting of the *abrek* who is crossing the river. This is of course achieved in the absence of the hero by the alternative or epic

hero, the young Cossack Lukashka; but it is recounted with
the same detached, almost unearthly vividness with which it
might have been seen through the eyes of Olenin. Lukashka
goes on duty to the 'cordon', waits in ambush and shoots the
abrek; but the general context and logic of the sequence
remains largely unexplained. The extraordinary vividness of
the description, the night, the shooting, and Lukashka's
bringing in of the body as his spoil – all these epic details make
a sharp contrast with the lack of information about the
background. Their logic is that of Olenin's own vision: he is a
young man who responds all the more vividly to events
because he does not understand them, and because he is not
really interested in their sober and factual background.

Tolstoy always likes to appear omniscient; and in his later
work, and especially in his last story about the Caucasus, *Hadji
Murad*, he takes a great deal of trouble really to be so. But in
The Cossacks he cleverly conceals any shortcomings in knowledge behind his hero. Gogol, for instance, tells us that though
the Cossacks live for booty their way of life is so careless and
immediate that they often conceal their plunder, and then
forget all about it. Granted the difference in time and place,
this one touch tells us more about the Cossack mentality than
all Tolstoy's vividness of detail. The vividness can have too
much an air of artifice here, though Tolstoy's usual manner in
his big novels seems so natural. His Cossack village remains
strangely separated from the savage world of the Caucasus, as
if it belonged to a different world.

We may even have the feeling that the *abrek* who swims
across the river does so solely in order that the writer may
make a fine set piece out of his killing. And masterly as his
description of the dead *abrek* may be, Tolstoy seems to
concentrate more on the description than on the man. 'Under
the red trimmed moustache the fine lips, drawn at the corners,
seemed stiffened into a smile of good-natured subtle raillery.'
This comes near to the edge of 'fine writing' in a slightly
derogatory sense. Robert Louis Stevenson could have written
it, or Conrad. (It may remind us of the moment in *Heart of
Darkness* when the Negro helmsman, transfixed by a spear,
gives the narrator as he dies 'an extraordinarily profound

familiar look'.) After the final episode of the fight on the steppe one of the Cossacks, before coming to aid his friend, the wounded Lukashka, 'fumbled for some time, unable to put his sword in its sheath: it would not go the right way. The blade of the sword was blood-stained.' All telling details, but there is a kind of relish about them very unlike the mature Tolstoy's accounts of war, violence and suffering. There is a particularly strong contrast, which cannot fail to be of interest to Tolstoy's readers, between this account in *The Cossacks* and Tolstoy's description of the last fight of Hadji Murad, in the story he wrote in his old age.

But again it is important to remember that the method in *The Cossacks* centres on Olenin himself, and in the contrast between his youthful eagerness, and the Cossacks' indifferent acceptance of the routines of their life, and the way things are. When Olenin rides up, hoping to take part in the final attack, he asks some question which to the Cossacks 'appeared quite meaningless': from their point of view he understands nothing. Lukashka is wounded – perhaps fatally, we never find out – by the brother of the man he has killed – and this element of the blood feud and the hereditary enmities of the epic life passes Olenin by. This ignorance finally separates him from the Cossacks and from Maryanka, who are deeply concerned with these personal internal matters of grief, loss, and revenge. Ironically, too, the fight, and the violent rejection of him by Maryanka which follows it, cures Olenin of that eagerness for the really significant experience ('Now it has begun, a solemn voice seemed to say ...') which came from aimless living in the civilized world. She has flirted with the idea of him, but now the fight and the wounding of Lukashka have recalled her to the stern normalities of her existence. The daily realities of her world were for him romantic excitements which he felt might lead to 'the real thing'. And at the end he too sees this. He has learnt something at least.

Again as on the night of his departure from Moscow, a three-horsed conveyance stood waiting at the door. But Olenin did not confer with himself as he had done then, and did not say to himself that all he had thought and done here was 'not it'. He did not promise himself a new life.

Despite Olenin's disillusionment, and the fact that the tale itself is no idyll, there are wonderful things in the world of *The Cossacks*, out of which Tolstoy has made a fascinating and obsessively gripping narrative. What may move and appeal to us most in retrospect are the unforgettable character sketches: not only Maryanka and Eroshka, but the slighter ones which seem thrown off almost inadvertently in the course of the tale: Maryanka's friend Ustenka, Olenin's servant Vanyushka, Lukashka's dumb sister, the Cossack sergeant who spends all his time fishing. What they say and the kind of speech they use plays a large part in the story; and it is unfortunately here that we lose most in translation – perhaps more than we do in the larger and more leisurely world of the later novels. The portentous expression which the sergeant proudly displays before Olenin, can be rendered into English without much difficulty; but the Cossacks' speech among themselves, which in Russian contrasts sharply with that of Olenin and his fellow-officers, is another matter. That the Cossacks converse *merrily* and call each other *my lad* sounds pretty stilted now; but it is just as hard today to render their colloquial speech in a manner that sounds unselfconscious. The word *veselo*, which Tolstoy uses a great deal, still has to become 'merrily', 'gaily', or 'cheerfully' in English, although the connotations of such adverbs are rather different.

None the less Uncle Eroshka's manner comes over very well, perhaps because it is so simple and without significance. Olenin thinks that Eroshka must have some exciting philosophy of life that is probably IT at last! He is impressed when the old man tells him 'when you die the grass will grow on you and that's all'. Later Olenin repeats this phrase back to him admiringly, but the old man refuses to recognize it in his mouth. It turns out in any case to be something a Russian captain, killed long ago in Chechnya, used to say. The old boy will not even be the 'character' that Olenin wants him to be. He has no philosophy: he talks and exists without meaning, as Olenin understands it. '*Karga!*' he says to Olenin, who asks him what the word means. It seems to be a Tartar word meaning 'OK' – 'but I just say it,' laughs the old man. It is something meaning nothing but its own utterance, as

Eroshka's smell of vodka and sweat is simply him – nothing more. The nineteenth-century Russian critic Merezhkovsky called Tolstoy 'the seer of the flesh', as opposed to Dostoevsky, who was 'the seer of the spirit'. Certainly no other great writer conveys the reality of physical being more simply and more effectively than Tolstoy does; and *The Cossacks* is the first piece of writing in which his amazing gift is so strikingly apparent.

In *The Cossacks* this lordship of the flesh is at the root of the matter: the absolute separation between the down-to-earth way of life and Olenin's romantic admiration for it, and his attempt to become part of it. Such an attempt is itself unavailingly conscious and intellectual: it is an idea, a striving to identify with those who exist in the body, not in the head. When Olenin asks Maryanka to marry him she agrees because such an idea means nothing to her, and makes her burst out laughing. In the same spirit the Cossacks call Olenin their *kunak* – 'pal'. It means nothing to them, for it would not occur to them to address their real comrades in that way. But Olenin, taking it all seriously, writes in his diary.

Many things have I pondered over lately and much have I changed, and I have come back to the copybook maxim: The one way to be happy is to love ... to spread a web of love on all sides and to take all who come into it. In this way I caught Vanyusha, Daddy Eroshka, Lukashka, and Maryanka.

At this moment the old man himself comes in, urges Olenin to drink and sing instead of writing in a book, and eventually falls down dead drunk. Olenin feels depressed. Like E. M. Forster's great novel *A Passage to India*, *The Cossacks* ends on a note of total separation and uncomprehendingness. Tolstoy is brilliant at what has been called 'making strange': that is, using language so that words themselves reveal this kind of incompatibility. Olenin's servant, who prides himself on having picked up a bit of French from his master, uses it on Maryanka as she comes into the yard for the last time.

'*La fille!*' said Vanyushka, with a wink, and burst out into a silly laugh.
'Drive on!' shouted Olenin, angrily.

'Good-bye, my lad! Good-bye. I won't forget you!' shouted Eroshka.

Olenin turned round. Daddy Eroshka was talking to Maryanka, evidently about his own affairs, and neither the old man nor the girl looked at Olenin.

The idea of Maryanka as *la fille* – a girl in the sense in which Olenin and his kind understand the term – is as absurd as the hope that these Cossacks care about him and won't forget him. They return unthinking to their own lives. But though Olenin may be depressed by this the reader is not; for the book has been joyful throughout in its celebration of the flesh, of natural life and strength.

When it appeared many of its first readers, and Russian critics, were puzzled and even dissatisfied – as dissatisfied as the author was later to say he himself was with the book. But the clue the critics fastened on was – interestingly – Maryanka herself. She was the type of strong, honest, spontaneous Russian girl, in contrast to Olenin, the always evasive and uncertain intellectual who could not fit in anywhere, the 'superfluous man', as he had come to be called by those critics who were then questioning and analysing Russian literature. In the magazine *Fatherland Notes* E. L. Markov wrote a long review with the title 'National Types in our Literature' in which he praised Tolstoy's portrait of Maryanka, and suggested her role was not unlike that of Pushkin's Tatiana in *Eugene Onegin*; that is to say the natural and life-giving girl contrasted with the unnatural and 'superfluous' man. This common pattern of the time in Russian literature certainly fits *The Cossacks* in one sense. But what also puzzled and upset the critics was the element that today's reader may think the most successful in Tolstoy's treatment: the 'deromanticization' of a traditionally exotic and spectacular subject and place. Tolstoy tells the truth about his subject. The great Russian poet Tyutchev, a discerning and humorous man, recognized this in a comic epigram he wrote in first reading Tolstoy's novel when it appeared in 1863. The poet perceived that what had become that conventional Russian literary subject – the Caucasus – would never be quite the same again.

THE COSSACKS

The point of this story
We may determine thus:
Our good old Russian pigsty
Has been shifted to the Caucasus.

God bless the Russian pigsty, we might say, wherever Tolstoy
presents it to us!

John Bayley

SELECT BIBLIOGRAPHY

TRANSLATIONS
The admirable Centenary Edition of Tolstoy in 21 volumes, translated by LOUISE and AYLMER MAUDE (Oxford University Press, 1929–37), contains most of his important works, but excludes the diaries and letters.

The following comprehensive selection of Tolstoy's letters and diaries has been published jointly by the Athlone Press in London and Scribner's in New York: *Tolstoy's Letters*, edited and translated by R. F. CHRISTIAN, 2 volumes, 1978; *Tolstoy's Diaries*, edited and translated by R. F. CHRISTIAN, 2 volumes, 1985. Tolstoy's wife's diaries have been translated in full by CATHY PORTER: *The Diaries of Sofia Tolstaya*, Jonathan Cape, London, 1985.

REMINISCENCES
Most of Tolstoy's sons and daughters who survived him have written their reminiscences of their father, albeit of unequal value. The following are available in English: ILYA TOLSTOY, *Reminiscences of Tolstoy*, Chapman & Hall, London, 1914 (re-translated as *Tolstoy, My Father: Reminiscences*, Cowles, Chicago, 1971); LEON TOLSTOY, *The Truth About My Father*, John Murray, London and New York, 1924; SERGEI TOLSTOY, *Tolstoy Remembered By His Son Sergei Tolstoy*, Weidenfeld & Nicolson, London, 1961, Atheneum, New York, 1962; ALEXANDRA TOLSTOY, *Tolstoy, A Life of My Father*, Harper, New York, 1953; TATIANA SUKHOTIN-TOLSTOY, *The Tolstoy Home*, Harvill Press, London, 1950.

See also the memoirs of Tolstoy's sister-in-law, TATYANA KUZMINSKAYA, *Tolstoy as I Knew Him: My Life at Home and at Yasnaya Polyana*, Macmillan, London, 1948.

The following reminiscences by friends and acquaintances have been extensively drawn on by biographers: A. B. GOLDENWEISER, *Talks with Tolstoy*, translated by S. S. KOTELIANSKY and VIRGINIA WOOLF, Hogarth Press, London, 1923, New York, 1949, which, however, only contains about half of the Russian text; and MAXIM GORKY, *Reminiscences of Tolstoy, Chekhov and Andreyev*, translated by K. MANSFIELD, S. S. KOTELIANSKY and L. WOOLF, Hogarth Press, London, 1934, New York, 1959.

THE COSSACKS

BIOGRAPHY

Among biographies in general use, mention should be made (in alphabetical order) of:

AYLMER MAUDE, *The Life of Tolstoy*, 2 volumes, Oxford University Press, 1930 (revised version of 1908–10 edition). Maude was greatly assisted by Tolstoy himself, and although his own moral judgements sometimes intrude, and he was less than just to Tolstoy's wife, his biography is still widely and rightly regarded as the best in English.

E. J. SIMMONS, *Leo Tolstoy*, 2 volumes, Vintage Books, Boston, 1945–6 (Vintage paperback edition, 1960). Detailed, comprehensive and scholarly.

H. TROYAT, *Tolstoy*, Doubleday, New York, 1967, W. H. Allen, 1968 (first published in French, 1965). A popular bestseller; reads in places like a *vie romancée*, with embarrassing lapses into journalese and some factual errors. Good on the family tragedy, but has little on the impact or relevance of Tolstoy's thought. Bitterly criticized by Tolstoy's daughter, Alexandra.

A. N. WILSON, *Tolstoy*, Hamish Hamilton, London, 1988. Generous to Tolstoy the novelist, but highly critical of the man and the thinker. Entertaining and provocative; at times slipshod and colloquial.

CRITICISM

Any selection from the enormous secondary literature on Tolstoy is bound to be unsatisfactory. The fullest bibliographical aid in English is D. R. EGAN and M. A. EGAN, *Leo Tolstoy, an annotated bibliography of English language sources to 1978*, Scarecrow Press, New Jersey and London, 1979; but readers should also consult the comprehensive annotated list of titles in EDWARD WASIOLEK, *Tolstoy's Major Fiction*, pp. 227–51. The following critical works in English, listed alphabetically, which excludes articles and more specialized studies, may be of interest to the general reader:

JOHN BAYLEY, *Tolstoy and the Novel*, Chatto & Windus, London, 1966. Stimulating and original, draws on extensive knowledge of European literature. A subjective, appreciative approach, largely through the characters, with little to say on structure, language or genre.

R. F. CHRISTIAN, *Tolstoy: A Critical Introduction*, Cambridge University Press, 1969. Tries to show what is characteristic of Tolstoy's fiction. Minimum background and biographical information. Much space devoted to major novels, but most narrative and dramatic writings touched upon.

EDWARD CRANKSHAW, *Tolstoy. The Making of a Novelist*, Viking, New York, 1974. Well illustrated. Unduly harsh on Tolstoy the man, over-

SELECT BIBLIOGRAPHY

emphasizing the negative sides of his character and his alleged incapacity for logical thought.

BORIS EYKHENBAUM. The following translations of the works of this outstanding Russian scholar, written mostly in the 1920s and drawn on widely by later scholars, are particularly relevant to the major novels: *Tolstoi in the Sixties*, Ann Arbor, Michigan, 1982; and *Tolstoi in the Seventies*, Ann Arbor, Michigan, 1982.

HENRY GIFFORD, *Tolstoy*, Oxford University Press, 1982. Excellent introductory survey in 85 pages.

HENRY GIFFORD, ed., *Leo Tolstoy*, Penguin critical anthology, Harmondsworth, 1971. Admirably chosen selection of material from letters, diaries and articles, with extracts from longer works. In three parts: Contemporary Criticism, The Developing Debate, and Modern Views.

E. B. GREENWOOD, *Tolstoy: The Comprehensive Vision*, Dent, London, 1975. Thoughtful, lucid, well-written study of the artist and thinker. Uses Tolstoy as a pretext for thinking out for himself the fundamental problems of history, religion and art which exercised Tolstoy throughout his life.

EDWARD WASIOLEK, *Tolstoy's Major Fiction*, Chicago University Press, 1978. Penetrating and original, with some controversial judgements and minor factual errors, but overall one of the best critical studies of Tolstoy's fiction in English. Excellent bibliography.

CHRONOLOGY

DATE	AUTHOR'S LIFE	LITERARY CONTEXT
1825		Pushkin: *Boris Godunov.*
1826		
1828	Lev Nikolaevich Tolstoy born 28 August at Yasnaya Polyana, his mother's estate, eighty miles from Moscow.	Mickiewitz: *Konrad Wallenrod.*
1829		
1830		Stendhal: *Le Rouge et le Noir.*
1831	Death of his mother.	Death of Sir Walter Scott.
1832		George Sand: *Indiana.*
		Goethe: *Faust* (Part II).
1833		Pushkin: *Eugene Onegin.*
1835		Balzac: *Le Père Goriot.*
		Tocqueville: *De la Démocratie en Amérique* (Part I).
1836		Gogol: *The Government Inspector.*
		Pushkin: *The Captain's Daughter.*
1837	Death of his father.	Death of Pushkin in duel.
1838		Dickens: *Oliver Twist.*
1840		Lermontov: *A Hero of Our Time.*
		Poe: *Tales of the Grotesque and Arabesque.*
1841	Upon the death of their guardian Alexandra Osten-Saken, the Tolstoy children move to Kazan.	Death of Lermontov in duel.
1842		Gogol: *Dead Souls.*
1844	Tolstoy enters Kazan University, department of Eastern languages, but transfers to the faculty of Law the following year.	Dickens: *Martin Chuzzlewit.* Thackeray: *Barry Lyndon.*

Death of Alexander I. Accession of Nicholas I. Decembrist conspiracy crushed.
Notorious 'Third Section' under Count Benckendorff added to imperial chancery, soon assuming police functions: revolutionary movements suppressed, religious sectaries persecuted, censorship intensified, liberal newspapers closed and universities strictly supervised.
Russia and Turkey at war (to 1829).

By the Treaty of Adrianople Russia acquires the mouth of the Danube as well as free passage of Russian ships through the Dardanelles.
Revolution in Paris; accession of Louis Philippe. In Russia doctrine of 'Official Nationality' – Orthodoxy, Autocracy and Nationality – proclaimed by Uvarov, minister of education.
Suppression of uprising in Poland.
First Reform Act in Britain.

Slavery abolished throughout British Empire. Treaty of Unkiar-Skelessi between Russia and Turkey.
Speransky's codification of the law completed: the new code replaces the ancient *Ulozherue* of Tsar Alexis (1649) and lasts until 1917.

Accession of Queen Victoria.

1840s and 50s: Slavophile v Westernist debate amongst Russian intellectuals. The latter advocate progress by assimilating European nationalism and civic freedom. The former assert spiritual and moral superiority of Russia over the West and argue that future development should be based upon the traditions of the Orthodox Church and the peasant commune or *mir*.

xxvii

DATE	AUTHOR'S LIFE	LITERARY CONTEXT
1847	Leaves the University without graduating and returns to Yasnaya where he attempts a programme of social reform directed at the peasants.	Thackeray: *Vanity Fair*. Charlotte Brontë: *Jane Eyre*. Emily Brontë: *Wuthering Heights*. Herzen: *Who is to Blame?*
1848		Death of Belinsky.
1849		Petrashevsky circle disbanded; Dostoevsky arrested and sent into Siberian exile.
1851	Goes to the Caucasus with his eldest brother Nikolay to serve as a volunteer in the army.	Melville: *Moby-Dick*.
1852	Enlists officially in the army. *Childhood* published in *The Contemporary*.	Harriet Beecher Stowe: *Uncle Tom's Cabin*. Death of Gogol. Turgenev: *A Sportsman's Notebook*.
1853	Campaigning in the Caucasus. *The Raid* published.	Dickens: *Bleak House*.
1854	Tolstoy promoted to ensign and transferred to the Crimea. *Boyhood* published.	Dickens: *Hard Times*. Tyutchev's first volume of poetry published.
1855	Writes *Sevastopol Sketches*.	Trollope: *The Warden*.
1856	Death of his brother Dmitri. Tolstoy contemplates marrying Valerya Arseneva. Resigns from the army and returns to Yasnaya Polyana. Unsuccessful attempt to free his serfs. *Two Hussars* and *A Landowner's Morning* published.	Turgenev: *Rudin*. Sergey Aksakov: *A Family Chronicle*.
1857	Tolstoy visits western Europe; writes *Lucerne*. *Youth* in *The Contemporary*.	Flaubert: *Madame Bovary*. Conrad born. Trollope: *Barchester Towers*. Dickens: *Little Dorrit*.
1859	*Family Happiness* and *Three Deaths* published. Critical reception less enthusiastic than for his earlier works. Founds an experimental school for peasants at Yasnaya Polyana.	Darwin: *The Origin of Species*. Goncharov: *Oblomov*. George Eliot: *Adam Bede*.

CHRONOLOGY

DATE	AUTHOR'S LIFE	LITERARY CONTEXT
1860	Studies educational theory in Germany. Death of his brother Nikolay.	Turgenev: *On the Eve*. Dostoevsky: *House of the Dead*. George Eliot: *The Mill on the Floss*. Chekhov born.
1861	Quarrels with Turgenev, challenging him to a duel. Resumes school work at Yasnaya Polyana.	Dickens: *Great Expectations*. Herzen writes and publishes *My Past and Thoughts* (1861–7).
1862	Marries Sofya Andreyevna Behrs, daughter of a court physician. Educational journal *Yasnaya Polyana* published.	Turgenev: *Fathers and Children*. Hugo: *Les Misérables*. Flaubert: *Salammbô*.
1863	*The Cossacks*. First of his thirteen children born.	Dostoevsky: *The Gambler*. Chernyshevsky: *What is to be Done?* Death of Thackeray.
1864–9	Writes and publishes *War and Peace*.	Dostoevsky: *Notes from Underground* (1864). Dickens: *Our Mutual Friend* (1865). Leskov: *Lady Macbeth of Mtsensk* (1865). Dostoevsky: *Crime and Punishment* (1866). Marx: *Das Kapital*, vol 1 (1867). Turgenev: *Smoke* (1867). Zola: *Thérèse Raquin* (1867). Lavrov: *Historical Letters* (1868).
1870–72	Begins a novel about Peter the Great (never finished). Studies Greek. Works on a *Primer* for children.	Death of Dickens and Herzen (1870). Dostoevsky: *The Devils* (1871). George Eliot: *Middlemarch* (1872). Leskov: *Cathedral Folk* (1872).
1873–7	Writes *Anna Karenina*, serialized in the *Russian Herald*. Despite favourable critical response, Tolstoy expresses a deep dissatisfaction with the novel and confesses having great troubles writing it. Quarrels with publisher, Katkov, who refuses to print the epilogue to the novel because of its political content.	Hardy: *Far from the Madding Crowd* (1874). Henry James: *Roderick Hudson* (1876). Mark Twain: *Tom Sawyer* (1876). George Eliot: *Daniel Deronda* (1876). Turgenev: *Virgin Soil* (1877). Zola: *L'Assommoir* (1877).

CHRONOLOGY

HISTORICAL EVENTS

Garibaldi captures Naples and Sicily. Port of Vladivostock founded to serve
Russia's recent annexations from China.

Emancipation of the serfs (February), the climax of the Tsar's programme of
reform. While his achievement had great moral and symbolic significance,
many peasants felt themselves cheated by the terms of the complex
emancipation statute. Outbreak of American Civil War. Lincoln becomes
President of USA. Victor Emmanuel first King of Italy.
Bismarck becomes chief minister of Prussia. Financial reforms in Russia; a
ministry of finance and a state bank created. During 1860s and 70s 'nihilism',
a rationalist philosophy sceptical of all forms of established authority,
becomes widespread amongst young radical intellectuals in Russia.
Russia annexes Poland.

The first International. Establishment of the Zemstva, organs of rural self-
government and a significant liberal influence in Tsarist Russia (1864).
Reform of judiciary; trial by jury instituted and a Russian bar established
(1864). Slavery formally abolished in the USA (1865). Dmitri Karakozov, a
young nobleman, tries to assassinate the Tsar; he attributes his action to the
influence of the radical journal, *The Contemporary*, which is suppressed by the
government (1866). Second Pan-Slav congress in Moscow. Sale of Alaska to
USA (1867). Russian colonial expansion in Central Asia (1865–81).

Lenin born (1870). Franco-Prussian War. Paris commune set up and
suppressed. End of Second Empire in France; establishment of Third
Republic. Count Dmitri Tolstoy's reactionary educational reforms (1871).
Three Emperors' League between Germany, Austria and Russia (1872).
During the late 1860s and 1870s, Narodnik (Populist) 'going to the people'
campaign gathers momentum: young intellectuals incite peasantry to rebel
against autocracy.
Bulgarian Atrocities (Bulgarians massacred by Turks). Founding of Land and
Freedom, first Russian political party openly to advocate revolution (1876).
Official statute for Women's Higher Courses, whereby women able to study at
universities of St Petersburg, Moscow, Kiev and Kazan. By 1881 there are
2000 female students. Russia declares war on Turkey (conflict inspired by
Pan-Slavist movement). Queen Victoria proclaimed Empress of India (1877).

DATE	AUTHOR'S LIFE	LITERARY CONTEXT
1878	Reconciliation with Turgenev. Tolstoy's great moral crisis leads him into a period of intense theological studies.	Hardy: *The Return of the Native*.
1879		Ibsen: *A Doll's House*.
1880		Dostoevsky: *The Brothers Karamazov*.
1881	Letter to the Tsar.	Henry James: *The Portrait of a Lady*. Ibsen: *Ghosts*. Death of Dostoevsky.
1882	Publishes *Confession*.	Sergey Kravchinsky: *Underground Russia*.
1883	Writes *What I Believe*. Refuses to do jury service.	Death of Turgenev. Fet: *Evening Lights*. Maupassant: *Une Vie*.
1884	*What I Believe* banned. Takes up cobbling.	Strindberg: *Marriage*. Maupassant: *Miss Harriet*.
1885	Becomes a vegetarian and teetotaller.	Zola: *Germinal*.
1886	*Death of Ivan Ilych* published. Tolstoy's play *The Power of Darkness* offends the Tsar and is banned.	Henry James: *The Bostonians* and *The Princess Casamassima*. Chekhov publishes first volume of Stories. Stevenson: *Dr Jekyll and Mr Hyde*. Rimbaud: *Les Illuminations*.
1888		Matthew Arnold: *Essays in Criticism* (2nd volume, including an essay on Tolstoy). Strindberg: *Miss Julie*.
1889	*The Kreutzer Sonata*.	Kravchinsky: *The Career of a Nihilist*.

CHRONOLOGY

Russian forces reach gates of Constantinople. By the Treaty of San Stefano the Turks obliged to recognize independence of Slav nations in the Balkans. Congress of Berlin; with Bismarck acting as 'honest broker', the Great Powers modify the terms of San Stefano, increasing Austrian influence at the expense of Russia. Mass trial of Populist agitators in Russia ('The Trial of the 193'). Afghan War.

Birth of Stalin. The People's Will, terrorist offshoot of Land and Freedom, founded. Assassination of Prince Kropotkin, governor of Kharkov. During the 1880s organizations such as the Moscow Law Society and Committee for the Advancement of Literacy become centres for the discussion of political and social ideas amongst the intelligentsia.

Stalin born. Oil drilling begins in Azerbaidzhan; big programme of railway building begins.

Assassination of Alexander II by Ignatius Grinevitsky, a member of the People's Will, following which terrorist movement is crushed by the authorities. Revolutionary opposition goes underground until 1900. The new Tsar, Alexander III, is much influenced by his former tutor, the extreme conservativve Pobedonostsev, who becomes Chief Procurator of the Holy Synod. Loris-Melikov, architect of the reforms of Alexander II's reign, resigns. Jewish pogroms.

Censorship laws tightened. Student riots in Kazan and St Petersburg. Reactionary regime of Alexander III characterized by stagnation in agriculture, retrogression in education, russification of non-Russian section of the population, and narrow bureaucratic paternalism. Women's Property Act in England.

First Russian Marxist revolutionary organization, the Liberation of Labour, founded in Geneva by Georgi Plekhanov. Increased persecution of religious minorities.

New education minister, Delyanov, increases powers of inspectors; university appointments made directly by the ministry rather than academic councils; fees increased.

Murder of General Gordon in the Sudan. Anglo–Russian crisis over Afghanistan. William II becomes Emperor of Germany.

Some students hold a demonstration to commemorate 50th anniversary of the birth of Dobrolyubov. Several of them, disgusted by the brutal way in which the demonstration is suppressed, resolve to assassinate the Tsar; the plot is discovered and amongst those executed is Lenin's brother, Alexander Ulyanov, whose death he swears to avenge.

Land Captains introduced – powerful administrator magnates who increase control of the gentry over serfs, undermining previous judicial and local government reforms.

DATE	AUTHOR'S LIFE	LITERARY CONTEXT
1890		Birth of Pasternak. Ibsen: *Hedda Gabler*.
1891	Supervises famine relief.	Hardy: *Tess of the D'Urbervilles*. Birth of Bulgakov.
1893	*The Kingdom of God Is within You*.	Birth of Mayakovsky.
1894	*Master and Man, Christianity and Pacifism*.	Three collections of *The Russian Symbolists* brought out by poet Valery Bryusov. Konstantin Balmont: *Mountain Heights*; *Under Northern Skies*. Birth of Isaac Babel.
1898	Publishes *What is Art?*	Zola: *J'accuse*. Balmont: *Silence*.
1899	Publishes *Resurrection*, which he has been writing for ten years, to raise funds for emigration of Dukhobors.	Chekhov: *The Lady with the Little Dog; Uncle Vanya*. Gorky: *Foma Gordeev*. Kropotkin: *Memoirs of a Revolutionist*. Birth of Vladimir Nabokov.
1900		Freud: *The Interpretation of Dreams*.
1901	Excommunicated by the Holy Synod of the Russian Orthodox Church. *Reply to the Synod's Edict*. Starts to write *Hadji Murad*.	Chekhov: *Three Sisters*. Mann: *Buddenbrooks*. Alexander Blok: 'The Verses about the Beautiful Lady'.
1902		Gorky: *The Lower Depths*. Gide: *L'Immoraliste*. James: *The Wings of the Dove*. Merezhkovsky: 'Tolstoy and Dostoevsky'.
1903		Shaw: *Man and Superman*. Conrad: *Typhoon*. Balmont: *Let Us Be Like the Sun*. Bryusov: *Urbi et Orbis*.
1904	Publishes 'Bethink Yourselves!' a protest against the Japanese war.	Death of Chekhov. Bely: *Gold in Azure*.

CHRONOLOGY

HISTORICAL EVENTS

Bismarck dismissed. During the 1890s, growth rate for industrial output averages c. 8% per annum. Important development of coal mines in Southern European Russia. Industrial development backed up by growth of banking and joint Stock Companies, which begin to attract foreign, and later native, investment.

Work commences on Trans-Siberian railway. 20,000 Jews brutally evicted from Moscow. Franco-Russian Entente.

Independent Labour Party founded in England. Beginning of Armenian massacres.

Death of Alexander III; accession of Nicholas II.

Russian Social Democratic Workers' Party founded. Curies discover radium. Sergey Diaghilev and others found the *World of Art Society*, prominent members of which are Bakst and Benois; its most notable production is Diaghilev's *Ballet Russe*.

Student riots. All universities in Russia temperarily closed. Reactionary Sipyagin becomes Minister of the Interior. Russian industry enters period of depression. First peace conference at The Hague (attempt by the Tsar to halt the arms race in Europe).

Lenin allowed to leave Russia. Founds paper *Iskra* in Germany. Murder of education minister Bogolepov, by a student, marks the beginning of wave of political assassinations.

Death of Queen Victoria. Accession of Edward VII. Boxer rebellion in China.

Lenin's *What is to be Done?* provides blueprint for future Bolshevik party. Sipyagin, Minister of the Interior, assassinated by Socialist Revolutionaries.

Conflict between 'Bolsheviks' and 'Mensheviks' at 2nd Congress of Russian Social Democratic Workers' Party.

Russo–Japanese war (to 1905). Assassination of V. K. Pleve, Minister of the Interior, and notorious oppressor of minority peoples within the Empire.

DATE	AUTHOR'S LIFE	LITERARY CONTEXT
1905	*The One Thing Needful* and other articles seized by police.	Birth of Sholokhov. Nikolay Gumilev: *The Path of the Conquistadors*. Rainer Maria Rilke: *The Book of Hours*.
1906		
1907		Alexander Blok: *The Snow Mask*.
1908–9	Finishes *I Cannot Be Silent*, a protest against the hanging of the 1905 revolutionaries. Growing quarrels with his wife.	Andrei Bely: *The Silver Dove*. H. G. Wells: *Tono Bungay*.
1910	Tolstoy leaves his wife and is taken ill on a train. He dies on the platform of Astopovo railway station on 7 November.	Marina Tsvetsaeva: *Evening Album*. Rainer Maria Rilke: *Sketches of Malte Laurids Brigge*. Forster: *Howards End*. Ivan Bunin: *The Village*.

CHRONOLOGY

THE COSSACKS

★ ★ ★

A Tale of 1852

Chapter I

ALL IS quiet in Moscow. The squeak of wheels is seldom heard in the snow-covered street. There are no lights left in the windows and the street lamps have been extinguished. Only the sound of bells, borne over the city from the church towers, suggests the approach of morning. The streets are deserted. At rare intervals a night-cabman's sledge kneads up the snow and sand in the street as the driver makes his way to another corner where he falls asleep while waiting for a fare. An old woman passes by on her way to church, where a few wax candles burn with a red light reflected on the gilt mountings of the icons. Workmen are already getting up after the long winter night and going to their work – but for the gentlefolk it is still evening.

From a window in Chevalier's Restaurant a light – illegal at that hour – is still to be seen through a chink in the shutter. At the entrance a carriage, a sledge, and a cabman's sledge, stand close together with their backs to the curbstone. A three-horse sledge from the post-station is there also. A yard-porter muffled up and pinched with cold is sheltering behind the corner of the house.

'And what's the good of all this jawing?' thinks the footman who sits in the hall weary and haggard. 'This always happens when I'm on duty.' From the adjoining room are heard the voices of three young men, sitting there at a table on which are wine and the remains of supper. One, a rather plain, thin, neat little man, sits looking with tired kindly eyes at his friend, who is about to start on a journey. Another, a tall man, lies on a sofa beside a table on which are empty bottles, and plays with his watch-key. A third, wearing a short, fur-lined coat, is pacing up and down the room stopping now and then to crack an almond between his

strong, rather thick, but well-tended fingers. He keeps
smiling at something and his face and eyes are all aglow. He
speaks warmly and gesticulates, but evidently does not find
the words he wants and those that occur to him seem to him
inadequate to express what has risen to his heart.

'Now I can speak out fully,' said the traveller. 'I don't want
to defend myself, but I should like you at least to understand
me as I understand myself, and not look at the matter super-
ficially. You say I have treated her badly,' he continued, addressing the man with the kindly eyes who was watching him.

'Yes, you are to blame,' said the latter, and his look seemed
to express still more kindliness and weariness.

'I know why you say that,' rejoined the one who was leaving. 'To be loved is in your opinion as great a happiness as to
love, and if a man obtains it, it is enough for his whole life.'

'Yes, quite enough, my dear fellow, more than enough!'
confirmed the plain little man, opening and shutting his eyes.

'But why shouldn't the man love too?' said the traveller
thoughtfully, looking at his friend with something like pity.
'Why shouldn't one love? Because love doesn't come. . . .
No, to be beloved is a misfortune. It is a misfortune to feel
guilty because you do not give something you cannot give.
O my God!' he added, with a gesture of his arm. 'If it all
happened reasonably, and not all topsy-turvy – not in our
way but in a way of its own! Why, it's as if I had stolen that
love! You think so too, don't deny it. You must think so. But
will you believe it, of all the horrid and stupid things I have
found time to do in my life – and there are many – this is one
I do not and cannot repent of. Neither at the beginning nor
afterwards did I lie to myself or to her. It seemed to me that I
had at last fallen in love, but then I saw that it was an
involuntary falsehood, and that that was not the way to love,
and I could not go on, but she did. Am I to blame that I
couldn't? What was I to do?'

'Well, it's ended now!' said his friend, lighting a cigar to
master his sleepiness. 'The fact is that you have not yet loved
and do not know what love is.'

The man in the fur-lined coat was going to speak again, and put his hands to his head, but could not express what he wanted to say.

'Never loved! ... Yes, quite true, I never have! But after all, I have within me a desire to love, and nothing could be stronger than that desire! But then, again, does such love exist? There always remains something incomplete. Ah well! What's the use of talking? I've made an awful mess of life! But anyhow it's all over now; you are quite right. And I feel that I am beginning a new life.'

'Which you will again make a mess of,' said the man who lay on the sofa playing with his watch-key. But the traveller did not listen to him.

'I am sad and yet glad to go,' he continued. 'Why I am sad I don't know.'

And the traveller went on talking about himself, without noticing that this did not interest the others as much as it did him. A man is never such an egotist as at moments of spiritual ecstasy. At such times it seems to him that there is nothing on earth more splendid and interesting than himself.

'Dmítri Andréich!★ The coachman won't wait any longer!' said a young serf, entering the room in a sheepskin coat, with a scarf tied round his head. 'The horses have been standing since twelve, and it's now four o'clock!'

Dmítri Andréich looked at his serf, Vanyúsha. The scarf round Vanyúsha's head, his felt boots and sleepy face, seemed to be calling his master to a new life of labour, hardship, and activity.

'True enough! Good-bye!' said he, feeling for the un-fastened hook and eye on his coat.

In spite of advice to mollify the coachman by another tip, he put on his cap and stood in the middle of the room. The friends kissed once, then again, and after a pause, a third time. The man in the fur-lined coat approached the table and emptied a champagne glass, then took the plain little man's hand and blushed.

★Stress accents on proper names denote which syllable should be emphasized.

'Ah well, I will speak out all the same. . . . I must and will be frank with you because I am fond of you. . . . Of course you love her − I always thought so − don't you?'

'Yes,' answered his friend, smiling still more gently.

'And perhaps . . .'

'Please sir, I have orders to put out the candles,' said the sleepy attendant, who had been listening to the last part of the conversation and wondering why gentlefolk always talk about one and the same thing. 'To whom shall I make out the bill? To you, sir?' he added, knowing whom to address and turning to the tall man.

'To me,' replied the tall man. 'How much?'

'Twenty-six rubles.'

The tall man considered for a moment, but said nothing and put the bill in his pocket.

The other two continued their talk.

'Good-bye, you are a capital fellow!' said the short plain man with the mild eyes.

Tears filled the eyes of both. They stepped into the porch.

'Oh, by the by,' said the traveller, turning with a blush to the tall man, 'will you settle Chevalier's bill and write and let me know?'

'All right, all right!' said the tall man, pulling on his gloves. 'How I envy you!' he added quite unexpectedly when they were out in the porch.

The traveller got into his sledge, wrapped his coat about him, and said: 'Well then, come along!' He even moved a little to make room in the sledge for the man who said he envied him − his voice trembled.

'Good-bye, Mítya! I hope that with God's help you . . .' said the tall one. But his wish was that the other would go away quickly, and so he could not finish the sentence.

They were silent a moment. Then someone again said, 'Good-bye,' and a voice cried, 'Ready,' and the coachman touched up the horses.

'Hy, Elisár!' One of the friends called out, and the other coachman and the sledge-drivers began moving, clicking their tongues and pulling at the reins. Then the stiffened carriage-wheels rolled squeaking over the frozen snow.

'A fine fellow, that Olénin!' said one of the friends. 'But what an idea to go to the Caucasus – as a cadet, too! I wouldn't do it for anything. ... Are you dining at the club to-morrow?'

'Yes.'

They separated.

The traveller felt warm, his fur coat seemed too hot. He sat on the bottom of the sledge and unfastened his coat, and the three shaggy post-horses dragged themselves out of one dark street into another, past houses he had never before seen. It seemed to Olénin that only travellers starting on a long journey went through those streets. All was dark and silent and dull around him, but his soul was full of memories, love, regrets, and a pleasant tearful feeling.

Chapter II

'I'M FOND of them, very fond! ... First-rate fellows! ... Fine!' he kept repeating, and felt ready to cry. But why he wanted to cry, who were the first-rate fellows he was so fond of – was more than he quite knew. Now and then he looked round at some house and wondered why it was so curiously built; sometimes he began wondering why the post-boy and Vanyúsha, who were so different from himself, sat so near, and together with him were being jerked about and swayed by the tugs the side-horses gave at the frozen traces, and again he repeated: 'First rate ... very fond!' and once he even said: 'And how it seizes one ... excellent!' and wondered what made him say it. 'Dear me, am I drunk?' he asked himself. He had had a couple of bottles of wine, but it was not the wine alone that was having this effect on Olénin. He remembered all the words of friendship heartily, bashfully, spontaneously (as he believed) addressed to him on his departure. He remembered the clasp of hands, glances, the moments of silence, and the sound of a voice saying, *'Good-bye, Mítya!'* when he was already in the sledge. He remembered his own deliberate frankness. And all this had a touching significance for him. Not only friends and relatives, not only people who had been indifferent to him, but even those who did not like him, seemed to have agreed to become fonder of him, or to forgive him, before his departure, as people do before confession or death. 'Perhaps I shall not return from the Caucasus,' he thought. And he felt that he loved his friends and some one besides. He was sorry for himself. But it was not love for his friends that so stirred and uplifted his heart that he could not repress the meaningless words that seemed to rise of themselves to his lips; nor was it love for a woman (he had never yet been in love) that had brought on this mood. Love for himself, love full of hope — warm young love for all that was good in his own soul (and at that moment it seemed to him that there was nothing but good in it) — compelled him to weep and to mutter incoherent words.

Olénin was a youth who had never completed his university course, never served anywhere (having only a nominal post in some government office or other), who had squandered half his fortune and had reached the age of twenty-four without having done anything or even chosen a career. He was what in Moscow society is termed *un jeune homme*.

At the age of eighteen he was free — as only rich young Russians in the 'forties who had lost their parents at an early age could be. Neither physical nor moral fetters of any kind existed for him; he could do as he liked, lacking nothing and bound by nothing. Neither relatives, nor fatherland, nor religion, nor wants, existed for him. He believed in nothing and admitted nothing. But although he believed in nothing he was not a morose or blasé young man, nor self-opinionated, but on the contrary continually let himself be carried away. He had come to the conclusion that there is no such thing as love, yet his heart always overflowed in the presence of any young and attractive woman. He had long been aware that honours and position were nonsense, yet involuntarily he felt pleased when at a ball Prince Sergius came up and spoke to him affably. But he yielded to his impulses only in so far as they did not limit his freedom. As soon as he had yielded to any influence and became conscious of its leading on to labour and struggle, he instinctively hastened to free himself from the feeling or activity into which he was being drawn and to regain his freedom. In this way he experimented with society-life, the civil service, farming, music – to which at one time he intended to devote his life – and even with the love of women in which he did not believe. He meditated on the use to which he should devote that power of youth which is granted to man only once in a lifetime: that force which gives a man the power of making himself, or even – as it seemed to him – of making the universe, into anything he wishes: should it be to art, to science, to love of woman, or to practical activities? It is true that some people are devoid of this impulse, and on entering life at once place their necks under the first yoke that offers itself and honestly labour under it for the rest of their lives. But Olénin was too strongly conscious of the presence of that all-powerful God of Youth – of that capacity to be entirely transformed into an aspiration or idea – the capacity to wish and to do – to throw oneself headlong into a bottomless abyss without knowing why or wherefore. He bore this consciousness within himself, was proud of it and, without knowing it, was happy in that consciousness. Up to that time he had loved only himself, and could not help loving himself, for he expected nothing but good of himself and had not yet had time to be disillusioned. On leaving Moscow he was in that happy state of mind in which a young man, conscious of past mistakes, suddenly says to himself, 'That was not the real thing.' All that had gone before was accidental and unimportant. Till then he had not really tried to live, but now with his departure from Moscow a new life was beginning – a life in which there would be no mistakes, no remorse, and certainly nothing but happiness.

It is always the case on a long journey that till the first two or three stages have been passed imagination continues to dwell on the place left behind, but with the first morning on the road it leaps to the end of the journey and there begins building castles in the air. So it happened to Olénin.

After leaving the town behind, he gazed at the snowy fields and felt glad to be alone in their midst. Wrapping himself in his fur coat, he lay at the bottom of the sledge, became tranquil, and fell into a doze. The parting with his friends had touched him deeply, and memories of that last winter spent in Moscow and images of the past, mingled with vague thoughts and regrets, rose unbidden in his imagination.

He remembered the friend who had seen him off and his relations with the girl they had talked about. The girl was rich. 'How could he love her knowing that she loved me?' thought he, and evil suspicions crossed his mind. 'There is much dishonesty in men when one comes to reflect.' Then he was confronted by the question: 'But really, how is it I have never been in love? Every one tells me that I never have. Can it be that I am a moral monstrosity?' And he began to recall all his infatuations. He recalled his entry into society, and a friend's sister with whom he spent several evenings at a table with a lamp on it which lit up her slender fingers busy with needlework, and the lower part of her pretty delicate face. He recalled their conversations that dragged on like the game in which one passes on a stick which one keeps alight as long as possible, and the general awkwardness and restraint and his continual feeling of rebellion at all that conventionality. Some voice had always whispered: 'That's not it, that's not it,' and so it had proved. Then he remembered a ball and the mazurka he danced with the beautiful D——. 'How much in love I was that night and how happy! And how hurt and vexed I was next morning when I woke and felt myself still free! Why does not love come and bind me hand and foot?' thought he. 'No, there is no such thing as love! That neighbour who used to tell me, as she told Dubróvin and the Marshal, that she loved the stars, was not *it* either.' And now his farming and work in the country recurred to his mind, and in those recollections also there was nothing to dwell on with pleasure. 'Will they talk long of my departure?' came into his head; but who 'they' were he did not quite know. Next came a thought that made him wince and mutter incoherently. It was the recollection of M. Cappele the tailor, and the six hundred and seventy-eight rubles he still owed him, and he recalled the words in which he had begged him to wait another year, and the look of perplexity and resignation which had appeared on the tailor's face. 'Oh, my God, my God!' he repeated, wincing and trying to drive away the intolerable thought. 'All the same and in spite of everything she loved me,' thought he of the girl they had talked about at the farewell supper. 'Yes, had I married her I should not now be owing anything, and as it is I am in debt to Vasílyev.' Then he remembered the last night he had played with Vasílyev at the club (just after leaving her), and he recalled his humiliating requests for another game and the other's cold refusal. 'A year's economizing and they will all be paid, and the devil take them!' ... But despite this assurance he again began calculating his outstanding debts, their dates, and when he could hope to pay them off. 'And I owe something to Morell as well as to Chevalier,' thought he, recalling the night when he had run up so large a debt. It was at a carousel at the gipsies arranged by some fellows from Petersburg: Sáshka B——, an aide-de-camp to the Tsar, Prince D——, and that pompous old ——. 'How is it those gentlemen are so self-satisfied?' thought he, 'and by what right do they form a clique to which they think others must be highly flattered to be admitted? Can it be because they are on the Emperor's staff? Why, it's awful what fools and scoundrels they consider other people to be! But I showed them that I at any rate, on the contrary, do not at all want their intimacy. All the same, I fancy Andrew, the steward, would be amazed to know that I am on familiar terms with a man like Sáshka B——, a colonel and an aide-de-camp to the Tsar! Yes, and no one drank more than I did that evening, and I taught the gipsies a new song and everyone listened to it. Though I have done many foolish things, all the same I am a very good fellow,' thought he.

Morning found him at the third post-stage. He drank tea, and himself helped Vanyúsha to move his bundles and trunks and sat down among them, sensible, erect, and precise, knowing where all his belongings were, how much money he had and where it was, where he had put his passport and the post-horse requisition and toll-gate papers, and it all seemed to him so well arranged that he grew quite cheerful and the long journey before him seemed an extended pleasure-trip.

All that morning and noon he was deep in calculations of how many versts he had travelled, how many remained to the next stage, how many to the next town, to the place where he would dine, to the place where he would drink tea, and to Stavrópol, and what fraction of the whole journey was already accomplished. He also calculated how much money he had with him, how much would be left over, how much would pay off all his debts, and what proportion of his income he would spend each month. Towards evening, after tea, he calculated that to Stavrópol there still remained seven-elevenths of the whole journey, that his debts would require seven months' economy and one-eighth of his whole fortune; and then, tranquillized, he wrapped himself up, lay down in the sledge, and again dozed off. His imagination was now turned to the future: to the Caucasus. All his dreams of the future were mingled with pictures of Amalat-Beks, Circassian women, mountains, precipices, terrible torrents, and perils. All these things were vague and dim, but the love of fame and the danger of death furnished the interest of that future. Now, with unprecedented courage and a strength that amazed everyone, he slew and subdued an innumerable host of hillsmen; now he was himself a hillsman and with them was maintaining their independence against the Russians. As soon as he pictured anything definite, familiar Moscow figures always appeared on the scene. Sáshka B——fights with the Russians or the hillsmen against him. Even the tailor Cappele in some strange way takes part in the conqueror's triumph. Amid all this he remembered his former humiliations, weaknesses, and mistakes, and the recollection was not disagreeable. It was clear that there among the mountains, waterfalls, fair Circassians, and dangers, such mistakes could not recur. Having once made full confession to himself there was an end of it all. One other vision, the sweetest of them all, mingled with the young man's every thought of the future – the vision of a woman.

And there, among the mountains, she appeared to his imagination as a Circassian slave, a fine figure with a long plait of hair and deep submissive eyes. He pictured a lonely hut in the mountains, and on the threshold *she* stands awaiting him when, tired and covered with dust, blood, and fame, he returns to her. He is conscious of her kisses, her shoulders, her sweet voice, and her submissiveness. She is enchanting, but uneducated, wild, and rough. In the long winter evenings he begins her education. She is clever and gifted and quickly acquires all the knowledge essential. Why not? She can quite easily learn foreign languages, read the French masterpieces and understand them: *Notre Dame de Paris*, for instance, is sure to please her. She can also speak French. In a drawing-room she can show more innate dignity than a lady of the highest society. She can sing, simply, powerfully, and passionately. ... 'Oh, what nonsense!' said he to himself. But here they reached a post-station and he had to change into another sledge and give some tips. But his fancy again began searching for the 'nonsense' he had relinquished, and again fair Circassians, glory, and his return to Russia with an appointment as aide-de-camp and a lovely wife rose before his imagination. 'But there's no such thing as love,' said he to himself. 'Fame is all rubbish. But the six hundred and seventy-eight rubles? ... And the conquered land that will bring me more wealth than I need for a lifetime? It will not be right though to keep all that wealth for myself. I shall have to distribute it. But to whom? Well, six hundred and seventy-eight rubles to Cappele and then we'll see.' ... Quite vague visions now cloud his mind, and only Vanyúsha's voice and the interrupted motion of the sledge break his healthy youthful slumber. Scarcely conscious, he changes into another sledge at the next stage and continues his journey.

Next morning everything goes on just the same: the same kind of post-stations and tea-drinking, the same moving horses' cruppers, the same short talks with Vanyúsha, the same vague dreams and drowsiness, and the same tired, healthy, youthful sleep at night.

Chapter III

THE FARTHER Olénin travelled from Central Russia the farther he left his memories behind, and the nearer he drew to the Caucasus the lighter his heart became. 'I'll stay away for good and never return to show myself in society,' was a thought that sometimes occurred to him. 'These people whom I see here are *not* people. None of them know me and none of them can ever enter the Moscow society I was in or find out about my past. And no one in that society will ever know what I am doing, living among these people.' And quite a new feeling of freedom from his whole past came over him among the rough beings he met on the road whom he did not consider to be *people* in the sense that his Moscow acquaintances were. The rougher the people and the fewer the signs of civilization the freer he felt. Stavrópol, through which he had to pass, irked him. The signboards, some of them even in French, ladies in carriages, cabs in the market-place, and a gentleman wearing a fur cloak and tall hat who was walking along the boulevard and staring at the passers-by, quite upset him. 'Perhaps these people know some of my acquaintances,' he thought; and the club, his tailor, cards, society ... came back to his mind. But after Stavrópol everything was satisfactory – wild and also beautiful and warlike, and Olénin felt happier and happier. All the Cossacks, post-boys, and post-station masters seemed to him simple folk with whom he could jest and converse simply, without having to consider to what class they belonged. They all belonged to the human race which, without his thinking about it, all appeared dear to Olénin, and they all treated him in a friendly way.

Already in the province of the Don Cossacks his sledge had been exchanged for a cart, and beyond Stavrópol it became so warm that Olénin travelled without wearing his fur coat. It was already spring – an unexpected joyous spring for Olénin. At night he was no longer allowed to leave the Cossack villages, and they said it was dangerous to travel in the evening. Vanyúsha began to be uneasy, and they carried a loaded gun in the cart. Olénin became still happier. At one of the post-stations the post-master told of a terrible murder that had been committed recently on the high road. They began to meet armed men. 'So this is where it begins!' thought Olénin, and kept expecting to see the snowy mountains of which mention was so often made. Once, towards evening, the Nogáy driver pointed with his whip to the mountains shrouded in clouds. Olénin looked eagerly, but it was dull and the mountains were almost hidden by the clouds. Olénin made out something grey and white and fleecy, but try as he would he could find nothing beautiful in the mountains of which he had so often read and heard. The mountains and the clouds appeared to him quite alike, and he thought the special beauty of the snow peaks, of which he had so often been told, was as much an invention as Bach's music and the love of women, in which he did not believe. So he gave up looking forward to seeing the mountains. But early next morning, being awakened in his cart by the freshness of the air, he glanced carelessly to the right. The morning was perfectly clear. Suddenly he saw, about twenty paces away as it seemed to him at first glance, pure white gigantic masses with delicate contours, the distinct fantastic outlines of their summits showing sharply against the far-off sky. When he had realized the distance between himself and them and the sky and the whole immensity of the mountains, and felt the infinitude of all that beauty, he became afraid that it was but a phantasm or a dream. He gave himself a shake to rouse himself, but the mountains were still the same.

'What's that! What is it?' he said to the driver.

'Why, the mountains,' answered the Nogáy driver with indifference.

'And I too have been looking at them for a long while,' said Vanyúsha. 'Aren't they fine? They won't believe it at home.'

The quick progress of the three-horsed cart along the smooth road caused the mountains to appear to be running along the horizon, while their rosy crests glittered in the light of the rising sun. At first Olénin was only astonished at the sight, then gladdened by it; but later on, gazing more and more intently at that snow-peaked chain that seemed to rise not from among other black mountains, but straight out of the plain, and to glide away into the distance, he began by slow degrees to be penetrated by their beauty and at length to *feel* the mountains. From that moment all he saw, all he thought, and all he felt, acquired for him a new character, sternly majestic like the mountains! All his Moscow reminiscences, shame, and repentance, and his trivial dreams about the Caucasus, vanished and did not return. 'Now it has begun,' a solemn voice seemed to say to him. The road and the Térek, just becoming visible in the distance, and the Cossack villages and the people, all no longer appeared to him as a joke. He looked at himself or Vanyúsha, and again thought of the mountains. ... Two Cossacks ride by, their guns in their cases swinging rhythmically behind their backs, the white and bay legs of their horses mingling confusedly ... and the mountains! Beyond the Térek rises the smoke from a Tartar village ... and the mountains! The sun has risen and glitters on the Térek, now visible beyond the reeds ... and the mountains! From the village comes a Tartar wagon, and women, beautiful young women, pass by ... and the mountains! '*Abreks* canter about the plain, and here am I driving along and do not fear them! I have a gun, and strength, and youth ... and the mountains!'

Chapter IV

THAT WHOLE part of the Térek line (about fifty miles) along which lie the villages of the Grebénsk Cossacks is uniform in character both as to country and inhabitants. The Térek, which separates the Cossacks from the mountaineers, still flows turbid and rapid though already broad and smooth, always depositing greyish sand on its low reedy right bank and washing away the steep, though not high, left bank, with its roots of century-old oaks, its rotting plane trees, and young brushwood. On the right bank lie the villages of pro-Russian, though still somewhat restless, Tartars. Along the left bank, back half a mile from the river and standing five or six miles apart from one another, are Cossack villages. In olden times most of these villages were situated on the banks of the river; but the Térek, shifting northward from the mountains year by year, washed away those banks, and now there remain only the ruins of the old villages and of the gardens of pear and plum trees and poplars, all overgrown with blackberry bushes and wild vines. No one lives there now, and one only sees the tracks of the deer, the wolves, the hares, and the pheasants, who have learned to love these places. From village to village runs a road cut through the forest as a cannon-shot might fly. Along the roads are cordons of Cossacks and watch-towers with sentinels in them. Only a narrow strip about seven hundred yards wide of fertile wooded soil belongs to the Cossacks. To the north of it begin the sand-drifts of the Nogáy or Mozdók steppes, which fetch far to the north and run, Heaven knows where, into the Trukhmén, Astrakhán, and Kirghíz-Kaisátsk steppes. To the south, beyond the Térek, are the Great Chéchnya river, the Kochkálov range, the Black Mountains, yet another range, and at last the snowy mountains, which can just be seen but have never yet been scaled. In this fertile wooded strip, rich in vegetation, has dwelt as far back as memory runs the fine warlike and prosperous Russian tribe belonging to the sect of Old Believers, and called the Grebénsk Cossacks.

Long long ago their Old Believer ancestors fled from Russia and settled beyond the Térek among the Chéchens on the Grében, the first range of wooded mountains of Chéchnya. Living among the Chéchens the Cossacks intermarried with them and adopted the manners and customs of the hill tribes, though they still retained the Russian language in all its purity, as well as their Old Faith. A tradition, still fresh among them, declares that Tsar Iván the Terrible came to the

Térek, sent for their Elders, and gave them the land on this side of the river, exhorting them to remain friendly to Russia and promising not to enforce his rule upon them nor oblige them to change their faith. Even now the Cossack families claim relationship with the Chéchens, and the love of freedom, of leisure, of plunder and of war, still form their chief characteristics. Only the harmful side of Russian influence shows itself – by interference at elections, by confiscation of church bells, and by the troops who are quartered in the country or march through it. A Cossack is inclined to hate less the *dzhigit* hillsman who maybe has killed his brother, than the soldier quartered on him to defend his village, but who has defiled his hut with tobacco-smoke. He respects his enemy the hillsman and despises the soldier, who is in his eyes an alien and an oppressor. In reality, from a Cossack's point of view a Russian peasant is a foreign, savage, despicable creature, of whom he sees a sample in the hawkers who come to the country and in the Ukraínian immigrants whom the Cossack contemptuously calls 'wool-beaters'. For him, to be smartly dressed means to be dressed like a Circassian. The best weapons are obtained from the hillsmen and the best horses are bought, or stolen, from them. A dashing young Cossack likes to show off his knowledge of Tartar, and when carousing talks Tartar even to his fellow Cossack. In spite of all these things this small Christian clan stranded in a tiny corner of the earth, surrounded by half-savage Mohammedan tribes and by soldiers, considers itself highly advanced, acknowledges none but Cossacks as human beings, and despises everybody else. The Cossack spends most of his time in the cordon, in action, or in hunting and fishing. He hardly ever works at home. When he stays in the village it is an exception to the general rule and then he is holiday-making. All Cossacks make their own wine, and drunkenness is not so much a general tendency as a rite, the non-fulfilment of which would be considered apostasy. The Cossack looks upon a woman as an instrument for his welfare; only the unmarried girls are allowed to amuse themselves. A married woman has to work for her husband from youth to very old age: his demands on her are the Oriental ones of submission and labour. In consequence of this outlook women are strongly developed both physically and mentally, and though they are – as everywhere in the East – nominally in subjection, they possess far greater influence and importance in family-life than Western women. Their exclusion from public life and inurement to heavy male labour give the women all the more power and importance in the household. A Cossack, who before strangers considers it improper to speak affectionately or needlessly to his wife, when alone with her is involuntarily conscious of her superiority. His house and all his property, in fact the entire homestead, has been acquired and is kept together solely by her labour and care. Though firmly convinced that labour is degrading to a Cossack and is only proper for a Nogáy labourer or a woman, he is vaguely aware of the fact that all he makes use of and calls his own is the result of that toil, and that it is in the power of the woman (his mother or his wife) whom he considers his slave, to deprive him of all he possesses. Besides, the continuous performance of man's heavy work and the responsibilities entrusted to her have endowed the Grebénsk women with a peculiarly independent masculine character and have remarkably developed their physical powers, common sense, resolution, and stability. The women are in most cases stronger, more intelligent, more developed, and handsomer than the men. A striking feature of a Grebénsk woman's beauty is the combination of the purest Circassian type of face with the broad and powerful build of Northern women. Cossack women wear the Circassian dress – a Tartar smock, *beshmet*, and soft slippers – but they tie their kerchiefs round their heads in the Russian fashion. Smartness, cleanliness and elegance in dress and in the arrangement of their huts, are with them a custom and a necessity. In their relations with men the women, and especially the unmarried girls, enjoy perfect freedom.

Novomlínsk village was considered the very heart of Grebénsk Cossackdom. In it more than elsewhere the customs of the old Grebénsk population have been pre-served, and its women have from time immemorial been renowned all over the Caucasus for their beauty. A Cossack's livelihood is derived from vineyards, fruit-gardens, water melon and pumpkin plantations, from fishing, hunting, maize and millet growing, and from war plunder. Novomlínsk village lies about two and a half miles away from the Térek, from which it is separated by a dense forest. On one side of the road which runs through the village is the river; on the other, green vineyards and orchards, beyond which are seen the driftsands of the Nogáy Steppe. The village is surrounded by earth-banks and prickly bramble hedges, and is entered by tall gates hung between posts and covered with little reed-thatched roofs. Beside them on a wooden gun-carriage stands an unwieldy cannon captured by the Cossacks at some time or other, and which has not been fired for a hundred years. A uniformed Cossack sentinel with dagger and gun sometimes stands, and sometimes does not stand, on guard beside the gates, and sometimes presents arms to a passing officer and sometimes does not. Below the roof of the gateway is written in black letters on a white board: 'Houses 266: male inhabitants 897: female 1012.' The Cossacks' houses are all raised on pillars two and a half feet from the ground. They are carefully thatched with reeds and have large carved gables. If not new they are at least all straight and clean, with high porches of different shapes; and they are not built close together but have ample space around them, and are all picturesquely placed along broad streets and lanes. In front of the large bright windows of many of the houses, beyond the kitchen gardens, dark green poplars and acacias with their delicate pale verdure and scented white blossoms overtop the houses, and beside them grow flaunting yellow sunflowers, creepers, and grape vines. In the broad open square are three shops where drapery, sunflower and pump-kin seeds, locust beans and gingerbreads are sold; and surrounded by a tall fence, loftier and larger than the other houses, stands the Regimental Commander's dwelling with its casement windows, behind a row of tall poplars. Few people are to be seen in the streets of the village on weekdays, especially in summer. The young men are on duty in the cordons or on military expeditions; the old ones are fishing or helping the women in the orchards and gardens. Only the very old, the sick, and the children, remain at home.

Chapter V

IT WAS one of those wonderful evenings that occur only in the Caucasus. The sun had sunk behind the mountains but it was still light. The evening glow had spread over a third of the sky, and against its brilliancy the dull white immensity of the mountains was sharply defined. The air was rarefied, motionless, and full of sound. The shadow of the mountains reached for several miles over the steppe. The steppe, the opposite side of the river, and the roads, were all deserted. If very occasionally mounted men appeared, the Cossacks in the cordon and the Chéchens in their *aouls* (villages) watched them with surprised curiosity and tried to guess who those questionable men could be. At nightfall people from fear of one another flock to their dwellings, and only birds and beasts fearless of man prowl in those deserted spaces. Talking merrily, the women who have been tying up the vines hurry away from the gardens before sunset. The vineyards, like all the surrounding district, are deserted, but the villages become very animated at that time of the evening. From all sides, walking, riding, or driving in their creaking carts, people move towards the village. Girls with their smocks tucked up and twigs in their hands run chatting merrily to the village gates to meet the cattle that are crowding together in a cloud of dust and mosquitoes which they bring with them from the steppe. The well-fed cows and buffaloes disperse at a run all over the streets and Cossack women in coloured *beshmets* go to and fro among them. You can hear their merry laughter and shrieks mingling with the lowing of the cattle. There an armed and mounted Cossack, on leave from the cordon, rides up to a hut and, leaning towards the window, knocks. In answer to the knock the handsome head of a young woman appears at the window and you can hear caressing, laughing voices. There a tattered Nogáy labourer, with prominent cheekbones, brings a load of reeds from the steppes, turns his creaking cart into the Cossack captain's broad and clean courtyard, and lifts the yoke off the oxen that stand tossing their heads while he and his master shout to one another in Tartar. Past a puddle that reaches nearly across the street, a barefooted Cossack woman with a bundle of firewood on her back makes her laborious way by clinging to the fences, holding her smock high and exposing her white legs. A Cossack returning from shooting calls out in jest: 'Lift it higher, shameless thing!' and points his gun at her. The woman lets down her smock and drops the wood. An old Cossack, returning home from fishing with his trousers tucked up and his hairy grey chest uncovered, has a net across his shoulder containing silvery fish that are still struggling; and to take a short cut climbs over his neighbour's broken fence and gives a tug to his coat which has caught on the fence. There a woman is dragging a dry branch along and from round the corner comes the sound of an axe. Cossack children, spinning their tops wherever there is a smooth place in the street, are shrieking; women are climbing over fences to avoid going round. From every chimney rises the odorous *kisyak* smoke. From every homestead comes the sound of increased bustle, percursor to the stillness of night.

Granny Ulítka, the wife of the Cossack cornet who is also teacher in the regimental school, goes out to the gates of her yard like the other women, and waits for the cattle which her daughter Maryánka is driving along the street. Before she has had time fully to open the wattle gate in the fence, an enormous buffalo cow surrounded by mosquitoes rushes up bellowing and squeezes in. Several well-fed cows slowly follow her, their large eyes gazing with recognition at their mistress as they swish their sides with their tails. The beautiful and shapely Maryánka enters at the gate and throwing away her switch quickly slams the gate to and rushes with all the speed of her nimble feet to separate and drive the cattle into their sheds. 'Take off your slippers, you devil's wench!' shouts her mother, 'you've worn them into holes!' Maryánka is not at all offended at being called a 'devil's wench', but accepting it as a term of endearment cheerfully goes on with her task. Her face is covered with a kerchief tied round her head. She is wearing a pink smock and a green *beshmet*. She disappears inside the lean-to shed in the yard, following the big fat cattle; and from the shed comes her voice as she speaks gently and persuasively to the buffalo: 'Won't she stand still? What a creature! Come now, come old dear!' Soon the girl and the old woman pass from the shed to the dairy carrying two large pots of milk, the day's yield. From the dairy chimney rises a thin cloud of *kisyak* smoke: the milk is being used to make into clotted cream. The girl makes up the fire while her mother goes to the gate. Twilight has fallen on the village. The air is full of the smell of vegetables, cattle, and scented *kisyak* smoke. From the gates and along the streets Cossack women come running, carrying lighted rags. From the yards one hears the snorting and quiet chewing of the cattle eased of their milk, while in the street only the voices of women and children sound as they call to one another. It is rare on a week-day to hear the drunken voice of a man.

One of the Cossack wives, a tall, masculine old woman, approaches Granny Ulítka from the homestead opposite and asks her for a light. In her hand she holds a rag.

'Have you cleared up, Granny?'

'The girl is lighting the fire. Is it fire you want?' says Granny Ulítka, proud of being able to oblige her neighbour.

Both women enter the hut, and coarse hands unused to dealing with small articles tremblingly lift the lid of a match-box, which is a rarity in the Caucasus. The masculine-looking new-comer sits down on the doorstep with the evident intention of having a chat.

'And is your man at the school, Mother?' she asked.

'He's always teaching the youngsters, Mother. But he writes that he'll come home for the holidays,' said the cornet's wife.

'Yes, he's a clever man, one sees; it all comes useful.'

'Of course it does.'

'And my Lukáshka is at the cordon; they won't let him come home,' said the visitor, though the cornet's wife had known all this long ago. She wanted to talk about her Lukáshka whom she had lately fitted out for service in the Cossack regiment, and whom she wished to marry to the cornet's daughter, Maryánka.

'So he's at the cordon?'

'He is, Mother. He's not been home since last holidays. The other day I sent him some shirts by Fómushkin. He says he's all right, and that his superiors are satisfied. He says they are looking out for *abreks* again. Lukáshka is quite happy, he says.'

'Ah well, thank God,' said the cornet's wife. ' "Snatcher" is certainly the only word for him.' Lukáshka was surnamed 'the Snatcher' because of his bravery in snatching a boy from a watery grave, and the cornet's wife alluded to this, wishing in her turn to say something agreeable to Lukáshka's mother.

'I thank God, Mother, that he's a good son! He's a fine fellow, everyone praises him,' says Lukáshka's mother. 'All I wish is to get him married; then I could die in peace.'

'Well, aren't there plenty of young women in the village?' answered the cornet's wife slyly as she carefully replaced the lid of the match-box with her horny hands.

'Plenty, Mother, plenty,' remarked Lukáshka's mother, shaking her head. 'There's your girl now, your Maryánka – that's the sort of girl! You'd have to search through the whole place to find such another!'

The cornet's wife knows what Lukáshka's mother is after, but though she believes him to be a good Cossack she hangs back: first because she is a cornet's wife and rich, while Lukáshka is the son of a simple Cossack and fatherless, secondly because she does not want to part with her daughter yet, but chiefly because propriety demands it.

'Well, when Maryánka grows up she'll be marriageable too,' she answers soberly and modestly.

'I'll send the matchmakers to you – I'll send them! Only let me get the vineyard done and then we'll come and make our bows to you,' says Lukáshka's mother. 'And we'll make our bows to Elias Vasílich too.'

'Elias, indeed!' says the cornet's wife proudly. 'It's to me you must speak! All in its own good time.'

Lukáshka's mother sees by the stern face of the cornet's wife that it is not the time to say anything more just now, so she lights her rag with the match and says, rising: 'Don't refuse us, think of my words. I'll go, it is time to light the fire.'

As she crosses the road swinging the burning rag, she meets Maryánka, who bows.

'Ah, she's a regular queen, a splendid worker, that girl!' she thinks, looking at the beautiful maiden. 'What need for her to grow any more? It's time she was married and to a good home; married to Lukáshka!'

But Granny Ulítka had her own cares and she remained sitting on the threshold thinking hard about something, till the girl called her.

Chapter VI

THE MALE population of the village spend their time on military expeditions and in the cordon – or 'at their posts', as the Cossacks say. Towards evening, that same Lukáshka the Snatcher, about whom the old women had been talking, was standing on a watch-tower of the Nízhni-Prototsk post situated on the very banks of the Térek. Leaning on the railing of the tower and screwing up his eyes, he looked now far into the distance beyond the Térek, now down at his fellow Cossacks, and occasionally he addressed the latter. The sun was already approaching the snowy range that gleamed white above the fleecy clouds. The clouds undulating at the base of the mountains grew darker and darker. The clearness of evening was noticeable in the air. A sense of freshness came from the woods, though round the post it was still hot. The voices of the talking Cossacks vibrated more sonorously than before. The moving mass of the Térek's rapid brown waters contrasted more vividly with its motionless banks. The waters were beginning to subside and here and there the wet sands gleamed drab on the banks and in the shallows. The other side of the river, just opposite the cordon, was deserted; only an immense waste of low-growing reeds stretched far away to the very foot of the mountains. On the low bank, a little to one side, could be seen the flat-roofed clay houses and the funnel-shaped chimneys of a Chéchen village. The sharp eyes of the Cossack who stood on the watch-tower followed, through the evening smoke of the pro-Russian village, the tiny moving figures of the Chéchen women visible in the distance in their red and blue garments.

Although the Cossacks expected *abreks* to cross over and attack them from the Tartar side at any moment, especially as it was May when the woods by the Térek are so dense that it is difficult to pass through them on foot and the river is shallow enough in places for a horseman to ford it, and despite the fact that a couple of days before a Cossack had arrived with a circular from the commander of the regiment announcing that spies had reported the intention of a party of some eight men to cross the Térek, and ordering special vigilance – no special vigilance was being observed in the cordon. The Cossacks, unarmed and with their horses un-saddled just as if they were at home, spent their time some in fishing, some in drinking, and some in hunting. Only the horse of the man on duty was saddled, and with its feet hobbled was moving about by the brambles near the wood, and only the sentinel had his Circassian coat on and carried a gun and sword. The corporal, a tall thin Cossack with an exceptionally long back and small hands and feet, was sitting on the earth-bank of a hut with his *beshmet* unbuttoned. On his face was the lazy, bored expression of a superior, and having shut his eyes he dropped his head upon the palm first of one hand and then of the other. An elderly Cossack with a broad greyish-black beard was lying in his shirt, girdled with a black strap, close to the river and gazing lazily at the waves of the Térek as they monotonously foamed and swirled. Others, also overcome by the heat and half naked, were rinsing clothes in the Térek, plaiting a fishing line, or humming tunes as they lay on the hot sand of the river bank. One Cossack, with a thin face much burnt by the sun, lay near the hut evidently dead drunk, by a wall which though it had been in shadow some two hours previously was now exposed to the sun's fierce slanting rays.

Lukáshka, who stood on the watch-tower, was a tall handsome lad about twenty years old and very like his mother. His face and whole build, in spite of the angularity of youth, indicated great strength, both physical and moral. Though he had only lately joined the Cossacks at the front, it was evident from the expression of his face and the calm assurance of his attitude that he had already acquired the somewhat proud and warlike bearing peculiar to Cossacks and to men generally who continually carry arms, and that he felt he was a Cossack and fully knew his own value. His ample Circassian coat was torn in some places, his cap was on the back of his head Chéchen fashion, and his leggings had slipped below his knees. His clothing was not rich, but he wore it with that peculiar Cossack foppishness which consists in imitating the Chéchen brave. Everything on a real brave is ample, ragged, and neglected, only his weapons are costly. But these ragged clothes and these weapons are belted and worn with a certain air and matched in a certain manner, neither of which can be acquired by everybody and which at once strike the eye of a Cossack or a hillsman. Lukáshka had this resemblance to a brave. With his hands folded under his sword, and his eyes nearly closed, he kept looking at the distant Tartar village. Taken separately his features were not beautiful, but anyone who saw his stately carriage and his dark-browed intelligent face would involuntarily say, 'What a fine fellow!'

'Look at the women, what a lot of them are walking about in the village,' said he in a sharp voice, languidly showing his brilliant white teeth and not addressing anyone in particular.

Nazárka who was lying below immediately lifted his head and remarked:

'They must be going for water.'

'Supposing one scared them with a gun?' said Lukáshka, laughing, 'Wouldn't they be frightened?'

'It wouldn't reach.'

'What! Mine would carry beyond. Just wait a bit, and when their feast comes round I'll go and visit Giréy Khan and drink *buza* there,' said Lukáshka, angrily swishing away the mosquitoes which attached themselves to him.

A rustling in the thicket drew the Cossack's attention. A pied mongrel half-setter, searching for a scent and violently wagging its scantily furred tail, came running to the cordon. Lukáshka recognized the dog as one belonging to his neighbour, Uncle Eróshka, a hunter, and saw, following it through the thicket, the approaching figure of the hunter himself.

Uncle Eróshka was a gigantic Cossack with a broad, snow-white beard and such broad shoulders and chest that in the wood, where there was no one to compare him with, he did not look particularly tall, so well proportioned were his powerful limbs. He wore a tattered coat and, over the bands with which his legs were swathed, sandals made of undressed deer's hide tied on with strings; while on his head he had a rough little white cap. He carried over one shoulder a screen to hide behind when shooting pheasants, and a bag containing a hen for luring hawks, and a small falcon; over the other shoulder, attached by a strap, was a wild cat he had killed; and stuck in his belt behind were some little bags containing bullets, gunpowder, and bread, a horse's tail to swish away the mosquitoes, a large dagger in a torn scabbard smeared with old bloodstains, and two dead pheasants. Having glanced at the cordon he stopped.

'Hy, Lyam!' he called to the dog in such a ringing bass that it awoke an echo far away in the wood; and throwing over his shoulder his big gun, of the kind the Cossacks call a 'flint', he raised his cap.

'Had a good day, good people, eh?' he said, addressing the Cossacks in the same strong and cheerful voice, quite without effort, but as loudly as if he were shouting to someone on the other bank of the river.

'Yes, yes, Uncle!' answered from all sides the voices of the young Cossacks.

'What have you seen? Tell us!' shouted Uncle Eróshka, wiping the sweat from his broad red face with the sleeve of his coat.

'Ah, there's a vulture living in the plane tree here, Uncle. As soon as night comes he begins hovering round,' said Nazárka, winking and jerking his shoulder and leg.

'Come, come!' said the old man incredulously.

'Really, Uncle! You must keep watch,' replied Nazárka with a laugh.

The other Cossacks began laughing.

The wag had not seen any vulture at all, but it had long been the custom of the young Cossacks in the cordon to tease and mislead Uncle Eróshka every time he came to them.

'Eh, you fool, always lying!' exclaimed Lukáshka from the tower to Nazárka.

Nazárka was immediately silenced.

'It must be watched. I'll watch,' answered the old man to the great delight of all the Cossacks. 'But have you seen any boars?'

'Watching for boars, are you?' said the corporal, bending forward and scratching his back with both hands, very pleased at the chance of some distraction. 'It's *abreks* one has to hunt here and not boars! You've not heard anything, Uncle, have you?' he added, needlessly screwing up his eyes and showing his close-set white teeth.

'*Abreks*,' said the old man. 'No, I haven't. I say, have you any *chikhir*? Let me have a drink, there's a good man. I'm really quite done up. When the time comes I'll bring you some fresh meat, I really will. Give me a drink!' he added.

'Well, and are you going to watch?' inquired the corporal, as though he had not heard what the other said.

'I did mean to watch to-night,' replied Uncle Eróshka. 'Maybe, with God's help, I shall kill something for the holiday. Then you shall have a share, you shall indeed!'

'Uncle! Hallo, Uncle!' called out Lukáshka sharply from above, attracting everybody's attention. All the Cossacks

looked up at him. 'Just go to the upper water-course, there's
a fine herd of boars there. I'm not inventing, really! The
other day one of our Cossacks shot one there. I'm telling you
the truth,' added he, readjusting the musket at his back and in
a tone that showed he was not joking.

'Ah! Lukáshka the Snatcher is here!' said the old man,
looking up. 'Where has he been shooting?'

'Haven't you seen? I suppose you're too young!' said
Lukáshka. 'Close by the ditch,' he went on seriously with a
shake of the head. 'We were just going along the ditch when
all at once we heard something crackling, but my gun was in
its case. Elias fired suddenly. . . . But I'll show you the place,
it's not far. You just wait a bit. I know every one of their
footpaths. . . . Daddy Mósev,' said he, turning resolutely and
almost commandingly to the corporal, 'it's time to relieve
guard!' and holding aloft his gun he began to descend from
the watch-tower without waiting for the order.

'Come down!' said the corporal, after Lukáshka had
started, and glanced round. 'Is it your turn, Gúrka? Then go
. . . True enough your Lukáshka has become very skilful,' he
went on, addressing the old man. 'He keeps going about just
like you, he doesn't stay at home. The other day he killed a
boar.'

Chapter VII

THE SUN had already set and the shades of night were rapidly
spreading from the edge of the wood. The Cossacks finished
their task round the cordon and gathered in the hut for
supper. Only the old man still stayed under the plane tree
watching for the vulture and pulling the string tied to the
falcon's leg, but though a vulture was really perching on the
plane tree it declined to swoop down on the lure. Lukáshka,
singing one song after another, was leisurely placing nets
among the very thickest brambles to trap pheasants. In spite
of his tall stature and big hands every kind of work, both
rough and delicate, prospered under Lukáshka's fingers.

'Hallo, Luke!' came Nazárka's shrill, sharp voice calling

him from the thicket close by. 'The Cossacks have gone in to supper.'

Nazárka, with a live pheasant under his arm, forced his way through the brambles and emerged on the footpath.

'Oh!' said Lukáshka, breaking off in his song, 'where did you get that cock pheasant? I suppose it was in my trap?'

Nazárka was of the same age as Lukáshka and had also only been at the front since the previous spring.

He was plain, thin and puny, with a shrill voice that rang in one's ears. They were neighbours and comrades. Lukáshka was sitting on the grass crosslegged like a Tartar, adjusting his nets.

'I don't know whose it was – yours, I expect.'

'Was it beyond the pit by the plane tree? Then it is mine! I set the nets last night.'

Lukáshka rose and examined the captured pheasant. After stroking the dark burnished head of the bird, which rolled its eyes and stretched out its neck in terror, Lukáshka took the pheasant in his hands.

'We'll have it in a pilau to-night. You go and kill and pluck it.'

'And shall we eat it ourselves or give it to the corporal?'

'He has plenty!'

'I don't like killing them,' said Nazárka.

'Give it here!'

Lukáshka drew a little knife from under his dagger and gave it a swift jerk. The bird fluttered, but before it could spread its wings the bleeding head bent and quivered.

'That's how one should do it!' said Lukáshka, throwing down the pheasant. 'It will make a fat pilau.'

Nazárka shuddered as he looked at the bird.

'I say, Lukáshka, that fiend will be sending us to the ambush again to-night,' he said, taking up the bird. (He was alluding to the corporal.) 'He has sent Fómushkin to get wine, and it ought to be his turn. He always puts it on us.'

Lukáshka went whistling along the cordon.

'Take the string with you,' he shouted.

Nazárka obeyed.

'I'll give him a bit of my mind to-day, I really will,' continued Nazárka. 'Let's say we won't go; we're tired out and there's an end of it! No, really, you tell him, he'll listen to you. It's too bad!'

'Get along with you! What a thing to make a fuss about!' said Lukáshka, evidently thinking of something else. 'What bosh! If he made us turn out of the village at night now, that would be annoying: there one can have some fun, but here what is there? It's all one whether we're in the cordon or in ambush. What a fellow you are!'

'And are you going to the village?'

'I'll go for the holidays.'

'Gúrka says your Dunáyka is carrying on with Fómushkin,' said Nazárka suddenly.

'Well, let her go to the devil,' said Lukáshka, showing his regular white teeth, though he did not laugh. 'As if I couldn't find another!'

'Gúrka says he went to her house. Her husband was out and there was Fómushkin sitting and eating pie. Gúrka stopped awhile and then went away, and passing by the window he heard her say, "He's gone, the fiend. ... Why don't you eat your pie, my own? You needn't go home for the night," she says. And Gúrka under the window says to himself, "That's fine!"'

'You're making it up.'

'No, quite true, by Heaven!'

'Well, if she's found another let her go to the devil,' said Lukáshka, after a pause. 'There's no lack of girls and I was sick of her anyway.'

'Well, see what a devil you are!' said Nazárka. 'You should make up to the cornet's girl, Maryánka. Why doesn't she walk out with any one?'

Lukáshka frowned. 'What of Maryánka? They're all alike,' said he.

'Well, you just try ... '

'What do you think? Are girls so scarce in the village?'

And Lukáshka recommenced whistling, and went along the cordon pulling leaves and branches from the bushes as he went. Suddenly, catching sight of a smooth sapling, he drew the knife from the handle of his dagger and cut it down. 'What a ramrod it will make,' he said, swinging the sapling till it whistled through the air.

The Cossacks were sitting round a low Tartar table on the earthen floor of the clay-plastered outer room of the hut, when the question of whose turn it was to lie in ambush was raised. 'Who is to go to-night?' shouted one of the Cossacks through the open door to the corporal in the next room.

'Who is to go?' the corporal shouted back. 'Uncle Burlák has been and Fómushkin too,' said he, not quite confidently. 'You two had better go, you and Nazárka,' he went on, addressing Lukáshka. 'And Ergushóv must go too; surely he has slept it off?'

'You don't sleep it off yourself so why should he?' said Nazárka in a subdued voice.

The Cossacks laughed.

Ergushóv was the Cossack who had been lying drunk and asleep near the hut. He had only that moment staggered into the room rubbing his eyes.

Lukáshka had already risen and was getting his gun ready.

'Be quick and go! Finish your supper and go!' said the corporal; and without waiting for an expression of consent he shut the door, evidently not expecting the Cossack to obey. 'Of course,' thought he, 'if I hadn't been ordered to I wouldn't send anyone, but an officer might turn up at any moment. As it is, they say eight *abreks* have crossed over.'

'Well, I suppose I must go,' remarked Ergushóv, 'it's the regulation. Can't be helped! The times are such. I say, we must go.'

Meanwhile Lukáshka, holding a big piece of pheasant to his mouth with both hands and glancing now at Nazárka, now at Ergushóv, seemed quite indifferent to what passed and only laughed at them both. Before the Cossacks were ready to go into ambush, Uncle Eróshka, who had been vainly waiting under the plane tree till night fell, entered the dark outer room.

'Well, lads,' his loud bass resounded through the low-roofed room drowning all the other voices, 'I'm going with you. You'll watch for Chéchens and I for boars!'

Chapter VIII

IT WAS quite dark when Uncle Eróshka and the three Cossacks, in their cloaks and shouldering their guns, left the cordon and went towards the place on the Térek where they were to lie in ambush. Nazárka did not want to go at all, but Lukáshka shouted at him and they soon started. After they had gone a few steps in silence the Cossacks turned aside from the ditch and went along a path almost hidden by reeds till they reached the river. On its bank lay a thick black log cast up by the water. The reeds around it had been recently beaten down.

'Shall we lie here?' asked Nazárka.

'Why not?' answered Lukáshka. 'Sit down here and I'll be back in a minute. I'll only show Daddy where to go.'

'This is the best place; here we can see and not be seen,' said Ergushóv, 'so it's here we'll lie. It's a first-rate place!'

Nazárka and Ergushóv spread out their cloaks and settled down behind the log, while Lukáshka went on with Uncle Eróshka.

'It's not far from here, Daddy,' said Lukáshka, stepping softly in front of the old man; 'I'll show you where they've been – I'm the only one that knows, Daddy.'

'Show me! You're a fine fellow, a regular Snatcher!' replied the old man, also whispering.

Having gone a few steps Lukáshka stopped, stooped down over a puddle, and whistled. 'That's where they come to drink, d'you see?' He spoke in a scarcely audible voice, pointing to fresh hoof-prints.

'Christ bless you,' answered the old man. 'The boar will be in the hollow beyond the ditch,' he added. 'I'll watch, and you can go.'

Lukáshka pulled his cloak up higher and walked back alone, throwing swift glances now to the left at the wall of reeds, now to the Térek rushing by below the bank. 'I daresay he's watching or creeping along somewhere,' thought he of a possible Chéchen hillsman. Suddenly a loud rustling and a splash in the water made him start and seize his musket. From under the bank a boar leapt up – his dark outline showing for a moment against the glassy surface of the water and then disappearing among the reeds. Lukáshka pulled out his gun and aimed, but before he could fire the boar had disappeared in the thicket. Lukáshka spat with vexation and went on. On approaching the ambuscade he halted again and whistled softly. His whistle was answered and he stepped up to his comrades.

Nazárka, all curled up, was already asleep. Ergushóv sat with his legs crossed and moved slightly to make room for Lukáshka.

'How jolly it is to sit here! It's really a good place,' said he. 'Did you take him there?'

'Showed him where,' answered Lukáshka, spreading out his cloak. 'But what a big boar I roused just now close to the water! I expect it was the very one! You must have heard the crash?'

'I did hear a beast crashing through. I knew at once it was a beast. I thought to myself: "Lukáshka has roused a beast," ' Ergushóv said, wrapping himself up in his cloak. 'Now I'll go to sleep,' he added. 'Wake me when the cocks crow. We must have discipline. I'll lie down and have a nap, and then you will have a nap and I'll watch – that's the way.'

'Luckily I don't want to sleep,' answered Lukáshka.

The night was dark, warm, and still. Only on one side of the sky the stars were shining, the other and greater part was overcast by one huge cloud stretching from the mountain-tops. The black cloud, blending in the absence of any wind with the mountains, moved slowly onwards, its curved edges sharply defined against the deep starry sky. Only in front of him could the Cossack discern the Térek and the distance beyond. Behind and on both sides he was surrounded by a wall of reeds. Occasionally the reeds would sway and rustle against one another apparently without cause. Seen from down below, against the clear part of the sky, their waving tufts looked like the feathery branches of trees. Close in front at his very feet was the bank, and at its base the rushing torrent. A little farther on was the moving mass of glassy brown water which eddied rhythmically along the bank and round the shallows. Farther still, water, banks, and cloud all merged together in impenetrable gloom. Along the surface of the water floated black shadows, in which the experienced eyes of the Cossack detected trees carried down by the current. Only very rarely sheet-lightning, mirrored in the water as in a black glass, disclosed the sloping bank opposite. The rhythmic sounds of night – the rustling of the reeds, the snoring of the Cossacks, the hum of mosquitoes, and the rushing water, were every now and then broken by a shot fired in the distance, or by the gurgling of water when a piece of bank slipped down, the splash of a big fish, or the crashing of an animal breaking through the thick under-growth in the wood. Once an owl flew past along the Térek, flapping one wing against the other rhythmically at every second beat. Just above the Cossack's head it turned towards the wood and then, striking its wings no longer after every other flap but at every flap, it flew to an old plane tree where it rustled about for a long time before settling down among the branches. At every one of these unexpected sounds the watching Cossack listened intently, straining his hearing, and screwing up his eyes while he deliberately felt for his musket.

The greater part of the night was past. The black cloud that had moved westward revealed the clear starry sky from under its torn edge, and the golden upturned crescent of the moon shone above the mountains with a reddish light. The cold began to be penetrating. Nazárka awoke, spoke a little, and fell asleep again. Lukáshka feeling bored got up, drew the knife from his dagger-handle and began to fashion his stick into a ramrod. His head was full of the Chéchens who lived over there in the mountains, and of how their brave lads came across and were not afraid of the Cossacks, and might even now be crossing the river at some other spot. He thrust himself out of his hiding-place and looked along the river but could see nothing. And as he continued looking out at intervals upon the river and at the opposite bank, now dimly distinguishable from the water in the faint moonlight, he no longer thought about the Chéchens but only of when it would be time to wake his comrades, and of going home to the village. In the village he imagined Dunáyka, his 'little soul', as the Cossacks call a man's mistress, and thought of her with vexation. Silvery mists, a sign of coming morning, glittered white above the water, and not far from him young eagles were whistling and flapping their wings. At last the crowing of a cock reached him from the distant village, followed by the long-sustained note of another, which was again answered by yet other voices.

'Time to wake them,' thought Lukáshka, who had finished his ramrod and felt his eyes growing heavy. Turning to his comrades he managed to make out which pair of legs belonged to whom, when it suddenly seemed to him that he heard something splash on the other side of the Térek. He turned again towards the horizon beyond the hills, where day was breaking under the upturned crescent, glanced at the outline of the opposite bank, at the Térek, and at the now distinctly visible driftwood upon it. For one instant it seemed to him that he was moving and that the Térek with the drifting wood remained stationary. Again he peered out. One large black log with a branch particularly attracted his attention. The tree was floating in a strange way right down the middle of the stream, neither rocking nor whirling. It even appeared not to be floating altogether with the current, but to be crossing it in the direction of the shallows. Lukáshka stretching out his neck watched it intently. The tree floated to the shallows, stopped, and shifted in a peculiar manner. Lukáshka thought he saw an arm stretched out from beneath the tree. 'Supposing I killed an *abrek* all by myself!' he thought, and seized his gun with a swift, unhurried movement, putting up his gun-rest, placing the gun upon it, and holding it noiselessly in position. Cocking the trigger, with bated breath he took aim, still peering out intently. 'I won't wake them,' he thought. But his heart began beating so fast that he remained motionless, listening. Suddenly the trunk gave a plunge and again began to float across the stream towards our bank. 'Only not to miss ...' thought he, and now by the faint light of the moon he caught a glimpse of a Tartar's head in front of the floating wood. He aimed straight at the head which appeared to be quite near – just at the end of his rifle's barrel. He glanced across. 'Right enough it is an *abrek*!' he thought joyfully, and suddenly rising to his knees he again took aim. Having found the sight, barely visible at the end of the long gun, he said: 'In the name of the Father and of the Son,' in the Cossack way learnt in his childhood, and pulled the trigger. A flash of lightning lit up for an instant the reeds and the water, and the sharp, abrupt report of the shot was carried across the river, changing into a prolonged roll somewhere in the far distance. The piece of driftwood now floated not across, but with the current, rocking and whirling.

'Stop, I say!' exclaimed Ergushóv, seizing his musket and raising himself behind the log near which he was lying.

'Shut up, you devil!' whispered Lukáshka, grinding his teeth. *'Abreks!'*

'Whom have you shot?' asked Nazárka. 'Who was it, Lukáshka?'

Lukáshka did not answer. He was reloading his gun and watching the floating wood. A little way off it stopped on a sand-bank, and from behind it something large that rocked in the water came into view.

'What did you shoot? Why don't you speak?' insisted the Cossacks.

'*Abreks*, I tell you!' said Lukáshka.

'Don't humbug! Did the gun go off? ...'

'I've killed an *abrek*, that's what I fired at,' muttered Lukáshka in a voice choked by emotion, as he jumped to his feet. 'A man was swimming ...' he said, pointing to the sand-bank. 'I killed him. Just look there.'

'Have done with your humbugging!' said Ergushóv again, rubbing his eyes.

'Have done with what? Look there,' said Lukáshka, seizing

him by the shoulders and pulling him with such force that Ergushóv groaned.

He looked in the direction in which Lukáshka pointed, and discerning a body immediately changed his tone.

'O Lord! But I say, more will come! I tell you the truth,' said he softly, and began examining his musket. 'That was a scout swimming across: either the others are here already or are not far off on the other side – I tell you for sure!' Lukáshka was unfastening his belt and taking off his Circassian coat.

'What are you up to, you idiot?' exclaimed Ergushóv. 'Only show yourself and you've lost all for nothing, I tell you true! If you've killed him he won't escape. Let me have a little powder for my musket-pan – you have some? Nazárka, you go back to the cordon and look alive; but don't go along the bank or you'll be killed – I tell you true.'

'Catch me going alone! Go yourself!' said Nazárka angrily.

Having taken off his coat, Lukáshka went down to the bank.

'Don't go in, I tell you!' said Ergushóv, putting some powder on the pan. 'Look, he's not moving. I can see. It's nearly morning; wait till they come from the cordon. You go, Nazárka. You're afraid! Don't be afraid, I tell you.'

'Luke, I say, Lukáshka! Tell us how you did it!' said Nazárka.

Lukáshka changed his mind about going into the water just then. 'Go quick to the cordon and I will watch. Tell the Cossacks to send out the patrol. If the *abreks* are on this side they must be caught,' said he.

'That's what I say. They'll get off,' said Ergushóv, rising. 'True, they must be caught!'

Ergushóv and Nazárka rose and, crossing themselves, started off for the cordon – not along the riverbank but breaking their way through the brambles to reach a path in the wood.

'Now mind, Lukáshka – they may cut you down here, so you'd best keep a sharp look-out, I tell you!'

'Go along; I know,' muttered Lukáshka; and having examined his gun again he sat down behind the log.

He remained alone and sat gazing at the shallows and listening for the Cossacks; but it was some distance to the cordon and he was tormented by impatience. He kept thinking that the other *abreks* who were with the one he had killed would escape. He was vexed with the *abreks* who were going to escape just as he had been with the boar that had escaped the evening before. He glanced round and at the opposite bank, expecting every moment to see a man, and having arranged his gun-rest he was ready to fire. The idea that he might himself be killed never entered his head.

Chapter IX

IT WAS growing light. The Chéchen's body which was gently rocking in the shallow water was now clearly visible. Suddenly the reeds rustled not far from Luke and he heard steps and saw the feathery tops of the reeds moving. He set his gun at full cock and muttered: 'In the name of the Father and of the Son,' but when the cock clicked the sound of steps ceased.

'Hallo, Cossacks! Don't kill your Daddy!' said a deep bass voice calmly; and moving the reeds apart Daddy Eróshka came up close to Luke.

'I very nearly killed you, by God I did!' said Lukáshka.

'What have you shot?' asked the old man.

His sonorous voice resounded through the wood and downward along the river, suddenly dispelling the mysterious quiet of night around the Cossack. It was as if everything had suddenly become lighter and more distinct.

'There now, Uncle, you have not seen anything, but I've killed a beast,' said Lukáshka, uncocking his gun and getting up with unnatural calmness.

The old man was staring intently at the white back, now clearly visible, against which the Térek rippled.

'He was swimming with a log on his back. I spied him out! ... Look there. There! He's got blue trousers, and a gun I think. ... Do you see?' inquired Luke.

'How can one help seeing?' said the old man angrily, and a serious and stern expression appeared on his face. 'You've killed a brave,' he said, apparently with regret.

'Well, I sat here and suddenly saw something dark on the other side. I spied him when he was still over there. It was as if a man had come there and fallen in. Strange! And a piece of driftwood, a good-sized piece, comes floating, not with the stream but across it; and what do I see but a head appearing from under it! Strange! I stretched out of the reeds but could see nothing; then I rose and he must have heard, the beast, and crept out into the shallow and looked about. "No, you don't!" I said, as soon as he landed and looked round, "you won't get away!" Oh, there was something choking me! I got my gun ready but did not stir, and looked out. He waited a little and then swam out again; and when he came into the moonlight I could see his whole back. "In the name of the Father and of the Son and of the Holy Ghost" ... and through the smoke I see him struggling. He moaned, or so it seemed to me. "Ah," I thought, "the Lord be thanked, I've killed him!" And when he drifted onto the sand-bank I could see him distinctly: he tried to get up but couldn't. He struggled a bit and then lay down. Everything could be seen. Look, he does not move – he must be dead! The Cossacks have gone back to the cordon in case there should be any more of them.'

'And so you got him!' said the old man. 'He is far away now, my lad! ... ' And again he shook his head sadly.

Just then the sound reached them of breaking bushes and the loud voices of Cossacks approaching along the bank on horseback and on foot. 'Are you bringing the skiff?' shouted Lukáshka.

'You're a trump, Luke! Lug it to the bank!' shouted one of the Cossacks.

Without waiting for the skiff Lukáshka began to undress, keeping an eye all the while on his prey.

'Wait a bit, Nazárka is bringing the skiff,' shouted the corporal.

'You fool! Maybe he is alive and only pretending! Take your dagger with you!' shouted another Cossack.

'Get along,' cried Luke, pulling off his trousers. He quickly undressed and, crossing himself, jumped, plunging with a splash into the river. Then with long strokes of his white arms, lifting his back high out of the water and breathing deeply, he swam across the current of the Térek towards the shallows. A crowd of Cossacks stood on the bank talking loudly. Three horsemen rode off to patrol. The skiff appeared round a bend. Lukáshka stood up on the sandbank, leaned over the body, and gave it a couple of shakes. 'Quite dead!' he shouted in a shrill voice.

The Chéchen had been shot in the head. He had on a pair of blue trousers, a shirt, and a Circassian coat, and a gun and dagger were tied to his back. Above all these a large branch was tied, and it was this which at first had misled Lukáshka.

'What a carp you've landed!' cried one of the Cossacks who had assembled in a circle, as the body, lifted out of the skiff, was laid on the bank, pressing down the grass.

'How yellow he is!' said another.

'Where have our fellows gone to search? I expect the rest of them are on the other bank. If this one had not been a scout he would not have swum that way. Why else should he swim alone?' said a third.

'Must have been a smart one to offer himself before the others; a regular brave!' said Lukáshka mockingly, shivering as he wrung out his clothes that had got wet on the bank.

'His beard is dyed and cropped.'

'And he has tied a bag with a coat in it to his back.'

'That would make it easier for him to swim,' said some one.

'I say, Lukáshka,' said the corporal, who was holding the dagger and gun taken from the dead man. 'Keep the dagger for yourself and the coat too; but I'll give you three rubles for the gun. You see it has a hole in it,' said he, blowing into the muzzle. 'I want it just for a souvenir.'

Lukáshka did not answer. Evidently this sort of begging vexed him but he knew it could not be avoided.

'See, what a devil!' said he, frowning and throwing down the Chéchen's coat. 'If at least it were a good coat, but it's a mere rag.'

'It'll do to fetch firewood in,' said one of the Cossacks.

'Mósev, I'll go home,' said Lukáshka, evidently forgetting his vexation and wishing to get some advantage out of having to give a present to his superior.

'All right, you may go!'

'Take the body beyond the cordon, lads,' said the corporal, still examining the gun, 'and put a shelter over him from the sun. Perhaps they'll send from the mountains to ransom it.'

'It isn't hot yet,' said someone.

'And supposing a jackal tears him? Would that be well?' remarked another Cossack.

'We'll set a watch; if they should come to ransom him it won't do for him to have been torn.'

'Well, Lukáshka, whatever you do you must stand a pail of vodka for the lads,' said the corporal gaily.

'Of course! That's the custom,' chimed in the Cossacks. 'See what luck God has sent you! Without ever having seen anything of the kind before, you've killed a brave!'

'Buy the dagger and coat and don't be stingy, and I'll let you have the trousers too,' said Lukáshka. 'They're too tight for me; he was a thin devil.'

One Cossack bought the coat for a ruble and another gave the price of two pails of vodka for the dagger.

'Drink, lads! I'll stand you a pail!' said Luke. 'I'll bring it myself from the village.'

'And cut up the trousers into kerchiefs for the girls!' said Nazárka.

The Cossacks burst out laughing.

'Have done laughing!' said the corporal. 'And take the body away. Why have you put the nasty thing by the hut?'

'What are you standing there for? Haul him along, lads!' shouted Lukáshka in a commanding voice to the Cossacks, who reluctantly took hold of the body, obeying him as though he were their chief. After dragging the body along for a few steps the Cossacks let fall the legs, which dropped with a lifeless jerk, and stepping apart they then stood silent for a few moments. Nazárka came up and straightened the head, which was turned to one side so that the round wound above the temple and the whole of the dead man's face were visible. 'See what a mark he has made right in the brain,' he said. 'He won't get lost. His owners will always know him!' No one answered, and again the Angel of Silence flew over the Cossacks.

The sun had risen high and its diverging beams were lighting up the dewy grass. Near by, the Térek murmured in the awakened wood and, greeting the morning, the pheasants called to one another. The Cossacks stood still and silent around the dead man, gazing at him. The brown body, with nothing on but the wet blue trousers held by a girdle over the sunken stomach, was well shaped and handsome. The muscular arms lay stretched straight out by his sides; the blue, freshly shaven, round head with the clotted wound on one side of it was thrown back. The smooth tanned forehead contrasted sharply with the shaven part of the head. The open glassy eyes with lowered pupils stared upwards, seeming to gaze past everything. Under the red trimmed moustache the fine lips, drawn at the corners, seemed stiffened into a smile of good-natured subtle raillery. The fingers of the small hands covered with red hairs were bent inward, and the nails were dyed red.

Lukáshka had not yet dressed. He was wet. His neck was redder and his eyes brighter than usual, his broad jaws twitched, and from his healthy body a hardly perceptible steam rose in the fresh morning air.

'He too was a man!' he muttered, evidently admiring the corpse.

'Yes, if you had fallen into his hands you would have had short shrift,' said one of the Cossacks.

The Angel of Silence had taken wing. The Cossacks began bustling about and talking. Two of them went to cut brushwood for a shelter, others strolled towards the cordon. Luke and Nazárka ran to get ready to go to the village.

Half an hour later they were both on their way homewards, talking incessantly and almost running through the dense woods which separated the Térek from the village.

'Mind, don't tell her I sent you, but just go and find out if her husband is at home,' Luke was saying in his shrill voice.

'And I'll go round to Yámka too,' said the devoted Nazárka. 'We'll have a spree, shall we?'

'When should we have one if not to-day?' replied Luke.

When they reached the village the two Cossacks drank, and lay down to sleep till evening.

Chapter X

ON THE third day after the events above described, two companies of a Caucasian infantry regiment arrived at the Cossack village of Novomlínsk. The horses had been un-harnessed and the companies' wagons were standing in the square. The cooks had dug a pit, and with logs gathered from various yards (where they had not been sufficiently securely stored) were now cooking the food; the pay-sergeants were settling accounts with the soldiers. The Service Corps men were driving piles in the ground to which to tie the horses, and the quartermasters were going about the streets just as if they were at home, showing officers and men to their quarters. Here were green ammunition boxes in a line, the company's carts, horses, and cauldrons in which buckwheat porridge was being cooked. Here were the captain and the lieutenant and the sergeant-major, Onísim Mikháylovich, and all this was in the Cossack village where it was reported that the companies were ordered to take up their quarters: therefore they were at home here. But why they were stationed there, who the Cossacks were, and whether they wanted the troops to be there, and whether they were Old Believers or not – was all quite immaterial. Having received their pay and been dismissed, tired out and covered with dust, the soldiers noisily and in disorder, like a swarm of bees about to settle, spread over the squares and streets; quite regardless of the Cossacks' ill will, chattering merrily and with their muskets clinking, by twos and threes they entered the huts and hung up their accoutrements, unpacked their bags, and bantered the women. At their favourite spot, round the porridge-cauldrons, a large group of soldiers assembled and with little pipes between their teeth they gazed, now at the smoke which rose into the hot sky, becoming visible when it thickened into white clouds as it rose, and now at the camp fires which were quivering in the pure air like molten glass, and bantered and made fun of the Cossack men and women because they do not live at all like Russians. In all the yards one could see soldiers and hear their laughter and the exasperated and shrill cries of Cossack women defending their houses and refusing to give the soldiers water or cooking utensils. Little boys and girls, clinging to their mothers and to each other, followed all the movements of the troopers (never before seen by them) with frightened curiosity, or ran after them at a respectful distance. The old Cossacks came out silently and dismally and sat on the earthen embankments of their huts, and watched the soldiers' activity with an air of leaving it all to the will of God without understanding what would come of it.

Olénin, who had joined the Caucasian Army as a cadet three months before, was quartered in one of the best houses in the village, the house of the cornet, Elias Vasílich – that is to say at Granny Ulítka's.

'Goodness knows what it will be like, Dmítri Andréich,' said the panting Vanyúsha to Olénin, who, dressed in a Circassian coat and mounted on a Kabardá horse which he had bought in Gróznoe, was after a five-hours' march gaily entering the yard of the quarters assigned to him.

'Why, what's the matter?' he asked, caressing his horse and looking merrily at the perspiring, dishevelled, and worried Vanyúsha, who had arrived with the baggage wagons and was unpacking.

Olénin looked quite a different man. In place of his clean-shaven lips and chin he had a youthful moustache and a small beard. Instead of a sallow complexion, the result of nights turned into day, his cheeks, his forehead, and the skin behind his ears were now red with healthy sunburn. In place of a clean new black suit he wore a dirty white Circassian coat with a deeply pleated skirt, and he bore arms. Instead of a freshly starched collar, his neck was tightly clasped by the red band of his silk *beshmet*. He wore Circassian dress but did not wear it well, and anyone would have known him for a Russian and not a Tartar brave. It was the thing – but not the real thing. But for all that, his whole person breathed health, joy, and satisfaction.

'Yes, it seems funny to you,' said Vanyúsha, 'but just try to talk to these people yourself: they set themselves against one and there's an end of it. You can't get as much as a word out of them.' Vanyúsha angrily threw down a pail on the threshold. 'Somehow they don't seem like Russians.'

'You should speak to the Chief of the Village!'

'But I don't know where he lives,' said Vanyúsha in an offended tone.

'Who has upset you so?' asked Olénin, looking round.

'The devil only knows. Faugh! There is no real master here. They say he has gone to some kind of *kriga*, and the old woman is a real devil. God preserve us!' answered Vanyúsha, putting his hands to his head. 'How we shall live here I don't know. They are worse than Tartars, I do declare – though they consider themselves Christians! A Tartar is bad enough, but all the same he is more noble. Gone to the *kriga* indeed! What this *kriga* they have invented is, I don't know!' concluded Vanyúsha, and turned aside.

'It's not as it is in the serfs' quarters at home, eh?' chaffed Olénin without dismounting.

'Please sir, may I have your horse?' said Vanyúsha, evidently perplexed by this new order of things but resigning himself to his fate.

'So a Tartar is more noble, eh, Vanyúsha?' repeated Olénin, dismounting and slapping the saddle.

'Yes, you're laughing! You think it funny,' muttered Vanyúsha angrily.

'Come, don't be angry, Vanyúsha,' replied Olénin, still smiling. 'Wait a minute, I'll go and speak to the people of the house; you'll see I shall arrange everything. You don't know what a jolly life we shall have here. Only don't get upset.'

Vanyúsha did not answer. Screwing up his eyes he looked contemptuously after his master, and shook his head. Vanyúsha regarded Olénin as only his master, and Olénin regarded Vanyúsha as only his servant; and they would both have been much surprised if anyone had told them that they were friends, as they really were without knowing it themselves. Vanyúsha had been taken into his proprietor's house when he was only eleven and when Olénin was the same age. When Olénin was fifteen he gave Vanyúsha lessons for a time and taught him to read French, of which the latter was inordinately proud; and when in specially good spirits he still let off French words, always laughing stupidly when he did so.

Olénin ran up the steps of the porch and pushed open the door of the hut. Maryánka, wearing nothing but a pink smock, as all Cossack women do in the house, jumped away from the door, frightened, and pressing herself against the wall covered the lower part of her face with the broad sleeve of her Tartar smock. Having opened the door wider, Olénin in the semi-darkness of the passage saw the whole tall, shapely figure of the young Cossack girl. With the quick and eager curiosity of youth he involuntarily noticed the firm maidenly form revealed by the fine print smock, and the beautiful black eyes fixed on him with childlike terror and wild curiosity. 'This is *she*,' thought Olénin. 'But there will be many others like her' came at once into his head, and he opened the inner door. Old Granny Ulítka, also dressed only in a smock, was stooping with her back turned to him, sweeping the floor.

'Good-day to you, Mother! I've come about my lodgings,' he began.

The Cossack woman, without unbending, turned her severe but still handsome face towards him.

'What have you come here for? Want to mock at us, eh? I'll teach you to mock; may the black plague seize you!' she shouted, looking askance from under her frowning brow at the new-comer.

Olénin had at first imagined that the way-worn, gallant Caucasian Army (of which he was a member) would be everywhere received joyfully, and especially by the Cossacks, our comrades in the war; and he therefore felt perplexed by this reception. Without losing presence of mind however he tried to explain that he meant to pay for his lodgings, but the old woman would not give him a hearing.

'What have you come for? Who wants a pest like you, with your scraped face? You just wait a bit; when the master returns he'll show you your place. I don't want your dirty money! A likely thing – just as if we had never seen any! You'll stink the house out with your beastly tobacco and want to put it right with money! Think we've never seen a pest! May you be shot in your bowels and your heart!' shrieked the old woman in a piercing voice, interrupting Olénin.

'It seems Vanyúsha was right!' thought Olénin. "A Tartar would be nobler",' and followed by Granny Ulítka's abuse he went out of the hut. As he was leaving, Maryánka, still wearing only her pink smock, but with her forehead covered down to her eyes by a white kerchief, suddenly slipped out from the passage past him. Pattering rapidly down the steps with her bare feet she ran from the porch, stopped, and looking round hastily with laughing eyes at the young man, vanished round the corner of the hut.

Her firm youthful step, the untamed look of the eyes glistening from under the white kerchief, and the firm stately build of the young beauty, struck Olénin even more powerfully than before. 'Yes, it must be *she*,' he thought, and troubling his head still less about the lodgings, he kept looking round at Maryánka as he approached Vanyúsha.

'There you see, the girl too is quite savage, just like a wild filly!' said Vanyúsha, who though still busy with the luggage wagon had now cheered up a bit. '*La fame!*' he added in a loud triumphant voice and burst out laughing.

Chapter XI

TOWARDS evening the master of the house returned from his fishing, and having learnt that the cadet would pay for the lodging, pacified the old woman and satisfied Vanyúsha's demands.

Everything was arranged in the new quarters. Their hosts moved into the winter hut and let their summer hut to the cadet for three rubles a month. Olénin had something to eat and went to sleep. Towards evening he woke up, washed and made himself tidy, dined, and having lit a cigarette sat down by the window that looked onto the street. It was cooler. The slanting shadow of the hut with its ornamental gables fell across the dusty road and even bent upwards at the base of the wall of the house opposite. The steep reed-thatched roof of that house shone in the rays of the setting sun. The air grew fresher. Everything was peaceful in the village. The soldiers had settled down and become quiet. The herds had not yet been driven home and the people had not returned from their work.

Olénin's lodging was situated almost at the end of the village. At rare intervals, from somewhere far beyond the Térek in those parts whence Olénin had just come (the Chéchen or the Kumýtsk plain), came muffled sounds of firing. Olénin was feeling very well contented after three months of bivouac life. His newly washed face was fresh and his powerful body clean (an unaccustomed sensation after the campaign) and in all his rested limbs he was conscious of a feeling of tranquillity and strength. His mind, too, felt fresh and clear. He thought of the campaign and of past dangers. He remembered that he had faced them no worse than other men, and that he was accepted as a comrade among valiant Caucasians. His Moscow recollections were left behind Heaven knows how far! The old life was wiped out and a quite new life had begun in which there were as yet no mistakes. Here as a new man among new men he could gain a new and good reputation. He was conscious of a youthful and unreasoning joy of life. Looking now out of the window at the boys spinning their tops in the shadow of the house, now round his neat new lodging, he thought how pleasantly he would settle down to this new Cossack village life. Now and then he glanced at the mountains and the blue sky, and an appreciation of the solemn grandeur of nature mingled with his reminiscences and dreams. His new life had begun, not as he imagined it would when he left Moscow, but unexpectedly well. 'The mountains, the mountains, the mountains!' they permeated all his thoughts and feelings.

'He's kissed his dog and licked the jug! . . . Daddy Eróshka has kissed his dog!' suddenly the little Cossacks who had been spinning their tops under the window shouted, looking towards the side street. 'He's drunk his bitch, and his dagger!' shouted the boys, crowding together and stepping backwards.

These shouts were addressed to Daddy Eróshka, who with his gun on his shoulder and some pheasants hanging at his girdle was returning from his shooting expedition.

'I have done wrong, lads, I have!' he said, vigorously swinging his arms and looking up at the windows on both sides of the street. 'I have drunk the bitch; it was wrong,' he repeated, evidently vexed but pretending not to care.

Olénin was surprised by the boys' behavior towards the old hunter, but was still more struck by the expressive, intelligent face and the powerful build of the man whom they called Daddy Eróshka.

'Here Daddy, here Cossack!' he called. 'Come here!'

The old man looked into the window and stopped.

'Good evening, good man,' he said, lifting his little cap off his cropped head.

'Good evening, good man,' replied Olénin. 'What is it the youngsters are shouting at you?'

Daddy Eróshka came up to the window. 'Why, they're teasing the old man. No matter, I like it. Let them joke about their old daddy,' he said with those firm musical intonations with which old and venerable people speak. 'Are you an army commander?' he added.

'No, I am a cadet. But where did you kill those pheasants?' asked Olénin.

'I dispatched these three hens in the forest,' answered the old man, turning his broad back towards the window to show the hen pheasants which were hanging with their heads tucked into his belt and staining his coat with blood. 'Haven't you seen any?' he asked. 'Take a brace if you like! Here you are,' and he handed two of the pheasants in at the window. 'Are you a sportsman yourself?' he asked.

'I am. During the campaign I killed four myself.'

'Four? What a lot!' said the old man sarcastically. 'And are you a drinker? Do you drink *chikhir?*'

'Why not? I like a drink.'

'Ah, I see you are a trump! We shall be *kunaks*, you and I,' said Daddy Eróshka.

'Step in,' said Olénin. 'We'll have a drop of *chikhir.*'

'I might as well,' said the old man, 'but take the pheasants.' The old man's face showed that he liked the cadet. He had seen at once that he could get free drinks from him, and that therefore it would be all right to give him a brace of pheasants.

Soon Daddy Eróshka's figure appeared in the doorway of the hut, and it was only then that Olénin became fully conscious of the enormous size and sturdy build of this man, whose red-brown face with its perfectly white broad beard was all furrowed by deep lines produced by age and toil. For an old man, the muscles of his legs, arms, and shoulders were quite exceptionally large and prominent. There were deep scars on his head under the short-cropped hair. His thick sinewy neck was covered with deep intersecting folds like a bull's. His horny hands were bruised and scratched. He stepped lightly and easily over the threshold, unslung his gun and placed it in a corner, and casting a rapid glance round the room noted the value of the goods and chattels deposited in the hut, and with out-turned toes stepped softly, in his sandals of raw hide, into the middle of the room. He brought with him a penetrating but not unpleasant smell of *chikhir* wine, vodka, gunpowder, and congealed blood.

Daddy Eróshka bowed down before the icons, smoothed his beard, and approaching Olénin held out his thick brown hand. '*Koshkildy*,' said he; 'That is Tartar for "Good-day" – "Peace be unto you," it means in their tongue.'

'*Koshkildy*, I know,' answered Olénin, shaking hands.

'Eh, but you don't, you won't know the right order! Fool!' said Daddy Eróshka, shaking his head reproachfully. 'If anyone says "*Koshkildy*" to you, you must say "*Allah rasi bo sun*," that is, "God save you." That's the way, my dear fellow, and not "*Koshkildy*." But I'll teach you all about it. We had a fellow here, Elias Mosévich, one of your Russians, he and I were *kunaks*. He was a trump, a drunkard, a thief, a sportsman – and what a sportsman! I taught him everything.'

'And what will you teach me?' asked Olénin, who was becoming more and more interested in the old man.

'I'll take you hunting and teach you to fish. I'll show you Chéchens and find a girl for you, if you like – even that! That's the sort I am! I'm a wag!' – and the old man laughed. 'I'll sit down. I'm tired. *Karga?*' he added inquiringly.

'And what does "*Karga*" mean?' asked Olénin.

'Why, that means "All right" in Georgian. But I say it just so. It is a way I have, it's my favourite word. *Karga, Karga*. I say it just so; in fun I mean. Well, lad, won't you order the *chikhir*? You've got an orderly, haven't you? Hey, Iván!' shouted the old man. 'All your soldiers are Iváns. Is yours Iván?'

'True enough, his name is Iván – Vanyúsha. Here Vanyúsha! Please get some *chikhir* from our landlady and bring it here.'

'Iván or Vanyúsha, that's all one. Why are all your soldiers Iváns? Iván, old fellow,' said the old man, 'you tell them to give you some from the barrel they have begun. They have the best *chikhir* in the village. But don't give more than thirty kopeks for the quart, mind, because that witch would be only too glad. ... Our people are anathema people; stupid people,' Daddy Eróshka continued in a confidential tone after Vanyúsha had gone out. 'They do not look upon you as on men, you are worse than a Tartar in their eyes. "Worldly

Russians" they say. But as for me, though you are a soldier
you are still a man, and have a soul in you. Isn't that right?
Elias Mosévich was a soldier, yet what a treasure of a man he
was! Isn't that so, my dear fellow? That's why our people
don't like me; but I don't care! I'm a merry fellow, and I like
everybody. I'm Eróshka; yes, my dear fellow.'

And the old Cossack patted the young man affectionately
on the shoulder.

Chapter XII

VANYÚSHA, who meanwhile had finished his housekeeping
arrangements and had even been shaved by the company's
barber and had pulled his trousers out of his high boots as a
sign that the company was stationed in comfortable quarters,
was in excellent spirits. He looked attentively but not
benevolently at Eróshka, as at a wild beast he had never seen
before, shook his head at the floor which the old man had
dirtied and, having taken two bottles from under a bench,
went to the landlady.

'Good evening, kind people,' he said, having made up his
mind to be very gentle. 'My master has sent me to get some
chikhir. Will you draw some for me, good folk?'

The old woman gave no answer. The girl, who was
arranging the kerchief on her head before a little Tartar
mirror, looked round at Vanyúsha in silence.

'I'll pay money for it, honoured people,' said Vanyúsha,
jingling the coppers in his pocket. 'Be kind to us and we, too
will be kind to you,' he added.

'How much?' asked the old woman abruptly.

'A quart.'

'Go, my own, draw some for them,' said Granny Ulítka to
her daughter. 'Take it from the cask that's begun, my
precious.'

The girl took the keys and a decanter and went out of the
hut with Vanyúsha.

'Tell me, who is that young woman?' asked Olénin,
pointing to Maryánka, who was passing the window. The

old man winked and nudged the young man with his elbow.

'Wait a bit,' said he and reached out of the window.
'Khm,' he coughed, and bellowed, 'Maryánka dear. Hallo,
Maryánka, my girlie, won't you love me, darling? I'm a
wag,' he added in a whisper to Olénin. The girl, not turning
her head and swinging her arms regularly and vigorously,
passed the window with the peculiarly smart and bold gait of
a Cossack woman and only turned her dark shaded eyes
slowly towards the old man.

'Love me and you'll be happy,' shouted Eróshka, winking,
and he looked questioningly at the cadet.

'I'm a fine fellow, I'm a wag!' he added. 'She's a regular
queen, that girl. Eh?'

'She is lovely,' said Olénin. 'Call her here!'

'No, no,' said the old man. 'For that one a match is being
arranged with Lukáshka, Luke, a fine Cossack, a brave, who
killed an *abrek* the other day. I'll find you a better one. I'll
find you one that will be all dressed up in silk and silver.
Once I've said it I'll do it. I'll get you a regular beauty!'

'You, an old man – and say such things,' replied Olénin.
'Why, it's a sin!'

'A sin? Where's the sin?' said the old man emphatically. 'A
sin to look at a nice girl? A sin to have some fun with
her? Or is it a sin to love her? Is that so in your parts? ...
No, my dear fellow, it's not a sin, it's salvation! God made
you and God made the girl too. He made it all; so it is no sin
to look at a nice girl. That's what she was made for; to be
loved and to give joy. That's how I judge it, my good
fellow.'

Having crossed the yard and entered a cool dark store-
room filled with barrels, Maryánka went up to one of them
and repeating the usual prayer plunged a dipper into it.
Vanyúsha standing in the doorway smiled as he looked at
her. He thought it very funny that she had only a smock on,
close-fitting behind and tucked up in front, and still funnier
that she wore a necklace of silver coins. He thought this quite
un-Russian and that they would all laugh in the serfs'
quarters at home if they saw a girl like that. '*La fille comme*

c'est tres bien, for a change,' he thought. 'I'll tell that to my master.'

'What are you standing in the light for, you devil!' the girl suddenly shouted. 'Why don't you pass me the decanter!'

Having filled the decanter with cool red wine, Maryánka handed it to Vanyúsha.

'Give the money to Mother,' she said, pushing away the hand in which he held the money.

Vanyúsha laughed.

'Why are you so cross, little dear?' he said good-naturedly, irresolutely shuffling with his feet while the girl was covering the barrel.

She began to laugh.

'And you! Are you kind?'

'We, my master and I, are very kind,' Vanyúsha answered decidedly. 'We are so kind that wherever we have stayed our hosts were always very grateful. It's because he's generous.'

The girl stood listening.

'And is your master married?' she asked.

'No. The master is young and unmarried, because noble gentlemen can never marry young,' said Vanyúsha didactically.

'A likely thing! See what a fed-up buffalo he is – and too young to marry! Is he the chief of you all?' she asked.

'My master is a cadet; that means he's not yet an officer, but he's more important than a general – he's an important man! Because not only our colonel, but the Tsar himself, knows him,' proudly explained Vanyúsha. 'We are not like those other beggars in the line regiment, and our papa himself was a Senator. He had more than a thousand serfs, all his own, and they send us a thousand rubles at a time. That's why everyone likes us. Another may be a captain but have no money. What's the use of that?'

'Go away. I'll lock up,' said the girl, interrupting him.

Vanyúsha brought Olénin the wine and announced that '*La fille c'est tres joulie*,' and, laughing stupidly, at once went out.

Chapter XIII

MEANWHILE the tattoo had sounded in the village square. The people had returned from their work. The herd lowed as in clouds of golden dust it crowded at the village gate. The girls and the women hurried through the streets and yards, turning in their cattle. The sun had quite hidden itself behind the distant snowy peaks. One pale bluish shadow spread over land and sky. Above the darkened gardens stars just discernible were kindling, and the sounds were gradually hushed in the village. The cattle having been attended to and left for the night, the women came out and gathered at the corners of the streets and, cracking sunflower seeds with their teeth, settled down on the earthen embankments of the houses. Later on Maryánka, having finished milking the buffalo and the other two cows, also joined one of these groups.

The group consisted of several women and girls and one old Cossack man.

They were talking about the *abrek* who had been killed.

The Cossack was narrating and the women questioning him.

'I expect he'll get a handsome reward,' said one of the women.

'Of course. It's said that they'll send him a cross.'

'Mósev did try to wrong him. Took the gun away from him, but the authorities at Kizlyár heard of it.'

'A mean creature that Mósev is!'

'They say Lukáshka has come home,' remarked one of the girls.

'He and Nazárka are merry-making at Yámka's.' (Yámka was an unmarried, disreputable Cossack woman who kept an illicit pot-house.) 'I heard say they had drunk half a pailful.'

'What luck that Snatcher has,' somebody remarked. 'A real snatcher. But there's no denying he's a fine lad, smart enough for anything, a right-minded lad! His father was just such another, Daddy Kiryák was: he takes after his father. When he was killed the whole village howled. Look, there they are,' added the speaker, pointing to the Cossacks who were coming down the street towards them.

'And Ergushóv has managed to come along with them too! The drunkard!'

Lukáshka, Nazárka, and Ergushóv, having emptied half a pail of vodka, were coming towards the girls. The faces of all three, but especially that of the old Cossack, were redder than usual. Ergushóv was reeling and kept laughing and nudging Nazárka in the ribs.

'Why are you not singing?' he shouted to the girls. 'Sing to our merry-making, I tell you!'

They were welcomed with the words, 'Had a good day? Had a good day?'

'Why sing? It's not a holiday,' said one of the women. 'You're tight, so you go and sing.'

Ergushóv roared with laughter and nudged Nazárka. 'You'd better sing. And I'll begin too. I'm clever, I tell you.'

'Are you asleep, fair ones?' said Nazárka. 'We've come from the cordon to drink your health. We've already drunk Lukáshka's health.'

Lukáshka, when he reached the group, slowly raised his cap and stopped in front of the girls. His broad cheekbones and neck were red. He stood and spoke softly and sedately, but in his tranquillity and sedateness there was more of animation and strength than in all Nazárka's loquacity and bustle. He reminded one of a playful colt that with a snort and a flourish of its tail suddenly stops short and stands as though nailed to the ground with all four feet. Lukáshka stood quietly in front of the girls, his eyes laughed, and he spoke but little as he glanced now at his drunken companions and now at the girls. When Maryánka joined the group he raised his cap with a firm deliberate movement, moved out of her way and then stepped in front of her with one foot a little forward and with his thumbs in his belt, fingering his dagger. Maryánka answered his greeting with a leisurely bow of her head, settled down on the earth-bank, and took some seeds out of the bosom of her smock. Lukáshka, keeping his eyes fixed on Maryánka, slowly cracked seeds and spat out the shells. All were quiet when Maryánka joined the group.

'Have you come for long?' asked a woman, breaking the silence.

'Till to-morrow morning,' quietly replied Lukáshka.

'Well, God grant you get something good,' said the Cossack; 'I'm glad of it, as I've just been saying.'

'And I say so too,' put in the tipsy Ergushóv, laughing. 'What a lot of visitors have come,' he added, pointing to a soldier who was passing by. 'The soldiers' vodka is good – I like it.'

'They've sent three of the devils to us,' said one of the women. 'Grandad went to the village Elders, but they say nothing can be done.'

'Ah, ha! Have you met with trouble?' said Ergushóv.

'I expect they have smoked you out with their tobacco?' asked another woman. 'Smoke as much as you like in the yard, I say, but we won't allow it inside the hut. Not if the Elder himself comes, I won't allow it. Besides, they may rob you. He's not quartered any of them on himself, no fear, that devil's son of an Elder.'

'You don't like it?' Ergushóv began again.

'And I've also heard say that the girls will have to make the soldiers' beds and offer them *chikhir* and honey,' said Nazárka, putting one foot forward and tilting his cap like Lukáshka.

Ergushóv burst into a roar of laughter, and seizing the girl nearest to him, he embraced her. 'I tell you true.'

'Now then, you black pitch!' squealed the girl, 'I'll tell your old woman.'

'Tell her,' shouted he. 'That's quite right what Nazárka says; a circular has been sent round. He can read, you know. Quite true!' And he began embracing the next girl.

'What are you up to, you beast?' squealed the rosy, round-faced Ústenka, laughing and lifting her arm to hit him.

The Cossack stepped aside and nearly fell.

'There, they say girls have no strength, and you nearly killed me.'

'Get away, you black pitch, what devil has brought you from the cordon?' said Ústenka, and turning away from him she again burst out laughing. 'You were asleep and missed the *abrek*, didn't you? Suppose he had done for you it would have been all the better.'

'You'd have howled, I expect,' said Nazárka, laughing.

'Howled! A likely thing.'

'Just look, she doesn't care. She'd howl, Nazárka, eh? Would she?' said Ergushóv.

Lukáshka all this time had stood silently looking at Maryánka. His gaze evidently confused the girl.

'Well, Maryánka! I hear they've quartered one of the chiefs on you?' he said, drawing nearer.

Maryánka, as was her wont, waited before she replied, and slowly raising her eyes looked at the Cossack. Lukáshka's eyes were laughing as if something special, apart from what was said, was taking place between himself and the girl.

'Yes, it's all right for them as they have two huts,' replied an old woman on Maryánka's behalf, 'but at Fómushkin's now they also have one of the chiefs quartered on them and they say one whole corner is packed full with his things, and the family have no room left. Was such a thing ever heard of as that they should turn a whole horde loose in the village?' she said. 'And what the plague are they going to do here?'

'I've heard say they'll build a bridge across the Térek,' said one of the girls.

'And I've been told that they will dig a pit to put the girls in because they don't love the lads,' said Nazárka, approaching Ústenka; and he again made a whimsical gesture which set everybody laughing, and Ergushóv, passing by Maryánka, who was next in turn, began to embrace an old woman.

'Why don't you hug Maryánka? You should do it to each in turn,' said Nazárka.

'No, my old one is sweeter,' shouted the Cossack, kissing the struggling old woman.

'You'll throttle me,' she screamed, laughing.

The tramp of regular footsteps at the other end of the

street interrupted their laughter. Three soldiers in their cloaks, with their muskets on their shoulders, were marching in step to relieve guard by the ammunition wagon.

The corporal, an old cavalry man, looked angrily at the Cossacks and led his men straight along the road where Lukáshka and Nazárka were standing, so that they should have to get out of the way. Nazárka moved, but Lukáshka only screwed up his eyes and turned his broad back without moving from his place.

'People are standing here, so you go round,' he muttered, half turning his head and tossing it contemptuously in the direction of the soldiers.

The soldiers passed by in silence, keeping step regularly along the dusty road.

Maryánka began laughing and all the other girls chimed in.

'What swells!' said Nazárka, 'Just like long-skirted choristers,' and he walked a few steps down the road imitating the soldiers.

Again everyone broke into peals of laughter.

Lukáshka came slowly up to Maryánka.

'And where have you put up the chief?' he asked.

Maryánka thought for a moment.

'We've let him have the new hut,' she said.

'And is he old or young,' asked Lukáshka, sitting down beside her.

'Do you think I've asked?' answered the girl. 'I went to get him some *chikhir* and saw him sitting at the window with Daddy Eróshka. Red-headed he seemed. They've brought a whole cartload of things.'

And she dropped her eyes.

'Oh, how glad I am that I got leave from the cordon!' said Lukáshka, moving closer to the girl and looking straight in her eyes all the time.

'And have you come for long?' asked Maryánka, smiling slightly.

'Till the morning. Give me some sunflower seeds,' he said, holding out his hand.

Maryánka now smiled outright and unfastened the neckband of her smock.

'Don't take them all,' she said.

'Really I felt so dull all the time without you, I swear I did,' he said in a calm, restrained whisper, helping himself to some seeds out of the bosom of the girl's smock, and stooping still closer over her he continued with laughing eyes to talk to her in low tones.

'I won't come, I tell you,' Maryánka suddenly said aloud, leaning away from him.

'No really ... what I wanted to say to you, ...' whispered Lukáshka. 'By the Heavens! Do come!'

Maryánka shook her head, but did so with a smile.

'Nursey Maryánka! Hallo Nursey! Mammy is calling! Supper time!' shouted Maryánka's little brother, running towards the group.

'I'm coming,' replied the girl. 'Go, my dear, go alone – I'll come in a minute.'

Lukáshka rose and raised his cap.

'I expect I had better go home too, that will be best,' he said, trying to appear unconcerned but hardly able to repress a smile, and he disappeared behind the corner of the house.

Meanwhile night had entirely enveloped the village. Bright stars were scattered over the dark sky. The streets became dark and empty. Nazárka remained with the women on the earth-bank and their laughter was still heard, but Lukáshka, having slowly moved away from the girls, crouched down like a cat and then suddenly started running lightly, holding his dagger to steady it: not homeward, however, but towards the cornet's house. Having passed two streets he turned into a lane and lifting the skirt of his coat sat down on the ground in the shadow of a fence. 'A regular cornet's daughter!' he thought about Maryánka. 'Won't even have a lark – the devil! But just wait a bit.'

The approaching footsteps of a woman attracted his attention. He began listening, and laughed all by himself. Maryánka with bowed head, striking the pales of the fences with a switch, was walking with rapid regular strides straight towards him. Lukáshka rose. Maryánka started and stopped.

'What an accursed devil! You frightened me! So you have not gone home?' she said, and laughed aloud.

Lukáshka put one arm round her and with the other hand raised her face. 'What I wanted to tell you, by Heaven!' his voice trembled and broke.

'What are you talking of, at night time!' answered Maryánka. 'Mother is waiting for me, and you'd better go to your sweetheart.'

And freeing herself from his arms she ran away a few steps. When she had reached the wattle fence of her home she stopped and turned to the Cossack who was running beside her and still trying to persuade her to stay a while with him.

'Well, what do you want to say, midnight-gadabout?' and she again began laughing.

'Don't laugh at me, Maryánka! By the Heaven! Well, what if I have a sweetheart? May the devil take her! Only say the word and now I'll love *you* – I'll do anything you wish. Here they are!' and he jingled the money in his pocket. 'Now we can live splendidly. Others have pleasures, and I? I get no pleasure from you, Maryánka dear!'

The girl did not answer. She stood before him breaking her switch into little bits with a rapid movement of her fingers.

Lukáshka suddenly clenched his teeth and fists.

'And why keep waiting and waiting? Don't I love you, darling? You can do what you like with me,' said he suddenly, frowning angrily and seizing both her hands.

The calm expression of Maryánka's face and voice did not change.

'Don't bluster, Lukáshka, but listen to me,' she answered, not pulling away her hands but holding the Cossack at arm's length. 'It's true I am a girl, but you listen to me! It does not depend on me, but if you love me I'll tell you this. Let go my hands, I'll tell you without. – I'll marry you, but you'll never get any nonsense from me,' said Maryánka without turning her face.

'What, you'll marry me? Marriage does not depend on us. Love me yourself, Maryánka dear,' said Lukáshka, from sullen and furious becoming again gentle, submissive, and tender, and smiling as he looked closely into her eyes.

Maryánka clung to him and kissed him firmly on the lips.

'Brother dear!' she whispered, pressing him convulsively to her. Then, suddenly tearing herself away, she ran into the gate of her house without looking round.

In spite of the Cossack's entreaties to wait another minute to hear what he had to say, Maryánka did not stop.

'Go,' she cried, 'you'll be seen! I do believe that devil, our lodger, is walking about the yard.'

'Cornet's daughter,' thought Lukáshka. 'She will marry me. Marriage is all very well, but you just love me!'

He found Nazárka at Yámka's house, and after having a spree with him went to Dunáyka's house, where, in spite of her not being faithful to him, he spent the night.

Chapter XIV

IT WAS quite true that Olénin had been walking about the yard when Maryánka entered the gate, and had heard her say, 'That devil, our lodger, is walking about.' He had spent that evening with Daddy Eróshka in the porch of his new lodging. He had had a table, a samovar, wine, and a candle brought out, and over a cup of tea and a cigar he listened to the tales the old man told seated on the threshold at his feet. Though the air was still, the candle dripped and flickered: now lighting up the post of the porch, now the table and crockery, now the cropped white head of the old man. Moths circled round the flame and, shedding the dust of their wings, fluttered on the table and in the glasses, flew into the candle flame, and disappeared in the black space beyond. Olénin and Eróshka had emptied five bottles of *chikhir*. Eróshka filled the glasses every time, offering one to Olénin, drinking his health, and talking untiringly. He told of Cossack life in the old days: of his father, 'The Broad', who alone had carried on his back a boar's carcass weighing three hundredweight, and drank two pails of *chikhir* at one sitting. He told of his own days and his chum Gírchik, with whom during the plague he used to smuggle felt cloaks across the Térek. He told how one morning he had killed two deer, and about his 'little soul' who used to run to him at the cordon at night. He told all this so eloquently and picturesquely that Olénin did not notice how time passed. 'Ah yes, my dear fellow, you did not know me in my golden days; then I'd have shown you things. To-day it's "Eróshka licks the jug", but then Eróshka was famous in the whole regiment. Whose was the finest horse? Who had a Gurda sword? To whom should one go to get a drink? With whom go on the spree? Who should be sent to the mountains to kill Ahmet Khan? Why, always Eróshka! Whom did the girls love? Always Eróshka had to answer for it. Because I was a real brave: a drinker, a thief (I used to seize herds of horses in the mountains), a singer; I was a master of every art! There are no Cossacks like that nowadays. It's disgusting to look at them. When they're that high [Eróshka held his hand three feet from the ground] they put on idiotic boots and keep looking at them — that's all the pleasure they know. Or they'll drink themselves foolish, not like men but all wrong. And who was I? I was Eróshka, the thief; they knew me not only in this village but up in the mountains. Tartar princes, my *kunaks*, used to come to see me! I used to be everybody's *kunak*. If he was a Tartar — with a Tartar; an Armenian — with an Armenian; a soldier — with a soldier; an officer — with an officer! I didn't care as long as he was a drinker. He says you should cleanse yourself from intercourse with the world, not drink with soldiers, not eat with a Tartar.'

'Who says all that?' asked Olénin.

'Why, our teacher! But listen to a Mullah or a Tartar Cadi. He says, "You unbelieving Giaours, why do you eat pig?" That shows that everyone has his own law. But I think it's all one. God has made everything for the joy of man. There is no sin in any of it. Take example from an animal. It lives in the Tartar's reeds or in ours. Wherever it happens to go, there is its home! Whatever God gives it, that it eats! But our people say we have to lick red-hot plates in hell for that. And I think it's all a fraud,' he added after a pause.

'What is a fraud?' asked Olénin.

'Why, what the preachers say. We had an army captain in Chervlëna who was my *kunak*: a fine fellow just like me. He was killed in Chéchnya. Well, he used to say that the preachers invent all that out of their own heads. "When you die the grass will grow on your grave and that's all!"' The old man laughed. 'He was a desperate fellow.'

'And how old are you?' asked Olénin.

'The Lord only knows! I must be about seventy. When a Tsaritsa reigned in Russia I was no longer very small. So you can reckon it out. I must be seventy.'

'Yes you must, but you are still a fine fellow.'

'Well, thank Heaven I am healthy, quite healthy, except that a woman, a witch, has harmed me. . . .'

'How?'

'Oh, just harmed me.'

'And so when you die the grass will grow?' repeated Olénin.

Eróshka evidently did not wish to express his thought clearly. He was silent for a while.

'And what did you think? Drink!' he shouted suddenly, smiling and handing Olénin some wine.

Chapter XV

'WELL, what was I saying?' he continued, trying to remember. 'Yes, that's the sort of man I am. I am a hunter. There is no hunter to equal me in the whole army. I will find and show you any animal and any bird, and what and where. I know it all! I have dogs, and two guns, and nets, and a screen and a hawk. I have everything, thank the Lord! If you are not bragging but are a real sportsman, I'll show you everything. Do you know what a man I am? When I have found a track – I know the animal. I know where he will lie down and where he'll drink or wallow. I make myself a perch and sit there all night watching. What's the good of staying at home? One only gets into mischief, gets drunk. And here women come and chatter, and boys shout at me –

enough to drive one mad. It's a different matter when you go out at nightfall, choose yourself a place, press down the reeds and sit there and stay waiting, like a jolly fellow. One knows everything that goes on in the woods. One looks up at the sky: the stars move, you look at them and find out from them how the time goes. One looks round – the wood is rustling; one goes on waiting, now there comes a crackling – a boar comes to rub himself; one listens to hear the young eaglets screech and then the cocks give voice in the village, or the geese. When you hear the geese you know it is not yet midnight. And I know all about it! Or when a gun is fired somewhere far away, thoughts come to me. One thinks, who is that firing? Is it another Cossack like myself who has been watching for some animal? And has he killed it? Or only wounded it so that now the poor thing goes through the reeds smearing them with its blood all for nothing? I don't like that! Oh, how I dislike it! Why injure a beast? You fool, you fool! Or one thinks, "Maybe an *abrek* has killed some silly little Cossack." All this passes through one's mind. And once as I sat watching by the river I saw a cradle floating down. It was sound except for one corner which was broken off. Thoughts did come that time! I thought some of your soldiers, the devils, must have got into a Tartar village and seized the Chéchen women, and one of the devils has killed the little one: taken it by its legs, and hit its head against a wall. Don't they do such things? Sh! Men have no souls! And thoughts came to me that filled me with pity. I thought: they've thrown away the cradle and driven the wife out, and her brave has taken his gun and come across to our side to rob us. One watches and thinks. And when one hears a litter breaking through the thicket, something begins to knock inside one. Dear one, come this way! "They'll scent me," one thinks; and one sits and does not stir while one's heart goes dun! dun! dun! and simply lifts you. Once this spring a fine litter came near me, I saw something black. "In the name of the Father and of the Son," and I was just about to fire when she grunts to her pigs: "Danger, children," she says, "there's a man here," and off they all ran, breaking through the bushes. And she had been so close I could almost have bitten her.'

'How could a sow tell her brood that a man was there?' asked Olénin.

'What do you think? You think the beast's a fool? No, he is wiser than a man though you do call him a pig! He knows everything. Take this for instance. A man will pass along your track and not notice it; but a pig as soon as it gets onto your track turns and runs at once: that shows there is wisdom in him, since he scents your smell and you don't. And there is this to be said too: you wish to kill it and it wishes to go about the woods alive. You have one law and it has another. It is a pig, but it is no worse than you – it too is God's creature. Ah, dear! Man is foolish, foolish, foolish!' The old man repeated this several times and then, letting his head drop, he sat thinking.

Olénin also became thoughtful, and descending from the porch with his hands behind his back began pacing up and down the yard.

Eróshka, rousing himself, raised his head and began gazing intently at the moths circling round the flickering flame of the candle and burning themselves in it.

'Fool, fool!' he said. 'Where are you flying to? Fool, fool!' He rose and with his thick fingers began to drive away the moths.

'You'll burn, little fool! Fly this way, there's plenty of room.' He spoke tenderly, trying to catch them delicately by their wings with his thick fingers and then letting them fly again. 'You are killing yourself and I am sorry for you!'

He sat a long time chattering and sipping out of the bottle. Olénin paced up and down the yard. Suddenly he was struck by the sound of whispering outside the gate. Involuntarily holding his breath, he heard a woman's laughter, a man's voice, and the sound of a kiss. Intentionally rustling the grass under his feet he crossed to the opposite side of the yard, but after a while the wattle fence creaked. A Cossack in a dark Circassian coat and a white sheepskin cap passed along the other side of the fence (it was Luke), and a tall woman with a white kerchief on her head went past Olénin. 'You and I have nothing to do with one another' was what Maryánka's firm step gave him to understand. He followed her with his eyes to the porch of the hut, and he even saw her through the window take off her kerchief and sit down. And suddenly a feeling of lonely depression and some vague longings and hopes, and envy of someone or other, overcame the young man's soul.

The last lights had been put out in the huts. The last sounds had died away in the village. The wattle fences and the cattle gleaming white in the yards, the roofs of the houses and the stately poplars, all seemed to be sleeping the labourers' healthy peaceful sleep. Only the incessant ringing voices of frogs from the damp distance reached the young man. In the east the stars were growing fewer and fewer and seemed to be melting in the increasing light, but overhead they were denser and deeper than before. The old man was dozing with his head on his hand. A cock crowed in the yard opposite, but Olénin still paced up and down thinking of something. The sound of a song sung by several voices reached him and he stepped up to the fence and listened. The voices of several young Cossacks carolled a merry song, and one voice was distinguishable among them all by its firm strength.

'Do you know who is singing there?' said the old man, rousing himself. 'It is the Brave, Lukáshka. He has killed a Chéchen and now he rejoices. And what is there to rejoice at? ... The fool, the fool!'

'And have you ever killed people?' asked Olénin.

'You devil!' shouted the old man. 'What are you asking? One must not talk so. It is a serious thing to destroy a human being. ... Ah, a very serious thing! Good-bye, my dear fellow. I've eaten my fill and am drunk,' he said rising. 'Shall I come to-morrow to go shooting?'

'Yes, come!'

'Mind, get up early; if you oversleep you will be fined!'

'Never fear, I'll be up before you,' answered Olénin.

The old man left. The song ceased, but one could hear footsteps and merry talk. A little later the singing broke out again but farther away, and Eróshka's loud voice chimed in with the other. 'What people, what a life!' thought Olénin with a sigh as he returned alone to his hut.

Chapter XVI

DADDY ERÓSHKA was a superannuated and solitary Cossack: twenty years ago his wife had gone over to the Orthodox Church and run away from him and married a Russian sergeant-major, and he had no children. He was not bragging when he spoke of himself as having been the boldest dare-devil in the village when he was young. Everybody in the regiment knew of his old-time prowess. The death of more than one Russian, as well as Chéchen, lay on his conscience. He used to go plundering in the mountains, and robbed the Russians too; and he had twice been in prison. The greater part of his life was spent in the forests, hunting. There he lived for days on a crust of bread and drank nothing but water. But on the other hand, when he was in the village he made merry from morning to night. After leaving Olénin he slept for a couple of hours and awoke before it was light. He lay on his bed thinking of the man he had become acquainted with the evening before. Olénin's 'simplicity' (simplicity in the sense of not grudging him a drink) pleased him very much, and so did Olénin himself. He wondered why the Russians were all 'simple' and so rich, and why they were educated, and yet knew nothing. He pondered on these questions and also considered what he might get out of Olénin.

Daddy Eróshka's hut was of a good size and not old, but the absence of a woman was very noticeable in it. Contrary to the usual cleanliness of the Cossacks, the whole of this hut was filthy and exceedingly untidy. A blood-stained coat had been thrown on the table, half a dough-cake lay beside a plucked and mangled crow with which to feed the hawk. Sandals of raw hide, a gun, a dagger, a little bag, wet clothes, and sundry rags lay scattered on the benches. In a corner stood a tub with stinking water, in which another pair of sandals were being steeped, and near by was a gun and a hunting-screen. On the floor a net had been thrown down and several dead pheasants lay there, while a hen tied by its leg was walking about near the table pecking among the dirt. In the unheated oven stood a broken pot with some kind of milky liquid. On the top of the oven a falcon was screeching and trying to break the cord by which it was tied, and a moulting hawk sat quietly on the edge of the oven, looking askance at the hen and occasionally bowing its head to right and left. Daddy Eróshka himself, in his shirt, lay on his back on a short bed rigged up between the wall and the oven, with his strong legs raised and his feet on the oven. He was picking with his thick fingers at the scratches left on his hands by the hawk, which he was accustomed to carry without wearing gloves. The whole room, especially near the old man, was filled with that strong but not unpleasant mixture of smells that he always carried about with him.

'*Uyde-ma*, Daddy?' (Is Daddy in?) came through the window in a sharp voice, which he at once recognized as Lukáshka's.

'*Uyde, Uyde, Uyde*. I am in!' shouted the old man. 'Come in, neighbour Mark, Luke Mark. Come to see Daddy? On your way to the cordon?'

At the sound of his master's shout the hawk flapped his wings and pulled at his cord.

The old man was fond of Lukáshka, who was the only man he excepted from his general contempt for the younger generation of Cossacks. Besides that, Lukáshka and his mother, as near neighbours, often gave the old man wine, clotted cream, and other home produce which Eróshka did not possess. Daddy Eróshka, who all his life had allowed himself to get carried away, always explained his infatuations from a practical point of view. 'Well, why not?' he used to say to himself. 'I'll give them some fresh meat, or a bird, and they won't forget Daddy: they'll sometimes bring a cake or a piece of pie.'

'Good morning, Mark! I am glad to see you,' shouted the old man cheerfully, and quickly putting down his bare feet he jumped off his bed and walked a step or two along the creaking floor, looked down at his out-turned toes, and suddenly, amused by the appearance of his feet, smiled, stamped with his bare heel on the ground, stamped again, and then performed a funny dance-step. 'That's clever, eh?' he asked, his small eyes glistening. Lukáshka smiled faintly. 'Going back to the cordon?' asked the old man.

'I have brought the *chikhir* I promised you when we were at the cordon.'

'May Christ save you!' said the old man, and he took up the extremely wide trousers that were lying on the floor, and his *beshmet*, put them on, fastened a strap round his waist, poured some water from an earthenware pot over his hands, wiped them on the old trousers, smoothed his beard with a bit of comb, and stopped in front of Lukáshka. 'Ready,' he said.

Lukáshka fetched a cup, wiped it and filled it with wine, and then handed it to the old man.

'Your health! To the Father and the Son!' said the old man, accepting the wine with solemnity. 'May you have what you desire, may you always be a hero, and obtain a cross.'

Lukáshka also drank a little after repeating a prayer, and then put the wine on the table. The old man rose and brought out some dried fish which he laid on the threshold, where he beat it with a stick to make it tender; then, having put it with his horny hands on a blue plate (his only one), he placed it on the table.

'I have all I want. I have victuals, thank God!' he said proudly. 'Well, and what of Mósev?' he added.

Lukáshka, evidently wishing to know the old man's opinion, told him how the officer had taken the gun from him.

'Never mind the gun,' said the old man. 'If you don't give the gun you will get no reward.'

'But they say, Daddy, it's little reward a fellow gets when he is not yet a mounted Cossack; and the gun is a fine one, a Crimean, worth eighty rubles.'

'Eh, let it go! I had a dispute like that with an officer, he

wanted my horse. "Give it me and you'll be made a cornet,"
says he. I wouldn't, and I got nothing!'

'Yes, Daddy, but you see I have to buy a horse; and they
say you can't get one the other side of the river under fifty
rubles, and mother has not yet sold our wine.'

'Eh, we didn't bother,' said the old man; 'when Daddy
Eróshka was your age he already stole herds of horses from
the Nogáy folk and drove them across the Térek. Sometimes
we'd give a fine horse for a quart of vodka or a cloak.'

'Why so cheap?' asked Lukáshka.

'You're a fool, a fool, Mark,' said the old man contemptuously. 'Why, that's what one steals for, so as not to be
stingy! As for you, I suppose you haven't so much as seen
how one drives off a herd of horses? Why don't you speak?'

'What's one to say, Daddy?' replied Lukáshka. 'It seems
we are not the same sort of men as you were.'

'You're a fool, Mark, a fool! "Not the same sort of
men!"' retorted the old man, mimicking the Cossack lad. 'I
was not that sort of Cossack at your age.'

'How's that?' asked Lukáshka.

The old man shook his head contemptuously.

'Daddy Eróshka was *simple*; he did not grudge anything!
That's why I was *kunak* with all Chéchnya. A *kunak* would
come to visit me and I'd make him drunk with vodka and
make him happy and put him to sleep with me, and when I
went to see him I'd take him a present – a dagger! That's the
way it is done, and not as you do nowadays: the only
amusement lads have now is to crack seeds and spit out the
shells!' the old man finished contemptuously, imitating the
present-day Cossacks cracking seeds and spitting out the
shells.

'Yes, I know,' said Lukáshka; 'that's so!'

'If you wish to be a fellow of the right sort, be a brave and
not a peasant! Because even a peasant can buy a horse – pay
the money and take the horse.'

They were silent for a while.

'Well, of course it's dull both in the village and the cordon,
Daddy: but there's nowhere one can go for a bit of sport. All

our fellows are so timid. Take Nazárka. The other day when
we went to the Tartar village, Giréy Khan asked us to come
to Nogáy to take some horses, but no one went, and how
was I to go alone?'

'And what of Daddy? Do you think I am quite dried
up? . . . No, I'm not dried up. Let me have a horse and I'll be
off to Nogáy at once.'

'What's the good of talking nonsense!' said Luke. 'You'd
better tell me what to do about Giréy Khan. He says, "Only
bring horses to the Térek, and then even if you bring a whole
stud I'll find a place for them." You see he's also a shaven-
headed Tartar – how's one to believe him?'

'You may trust Giréy Khan, all his kin were good people.
His father too was a faithful *kunak*. But listen to Daddy and I
won't teach you wrong: make him take an oath, then it will
be all right. And if you go with him, have your pistol ready
all the same, especially when it comes to dividing up the
horses. I was nearly killed that way once by a Chéchen. I
wanted ten rubles from him for a horse. Trusting is all right,
but don't go to sleep without a gun.' Lukáshka listened
attentively to the old man.

'I say, Daddy, have you any stone-break grass?' he asked
after a pause.

'No, I haven't any, but I'll teach you how to get it. You're
a good lad and won't forget the old man. . . . Shall I tell you?'

'Tell me, Daddy.'

'You know a tortoise? She's a devil, the tortoise is!'

'Of course I know!'

'Find her nest and fence it round so that she can't get in.
Well, she'll come, go round it, and then will go off to find
the stone-break grass and will bring some along and destroy
the fence. Anyhow next morning come in good time, and
where the fence is broken there you'll find the stone-break
grass lying. Take it wherever you like. No lock and no bar
will be able to stop you.'

'Have you tried it yourself, Daddy?'

'As for trying, I have not tried it, but I was told of it by
good people. I used only one charm: that was to repeat the

Pilgrim rhyme when mounting my horse; and no one ever killed me!'

'What is the Pilgrim rhyme, Daddy?'

'What, don't you know it? Oh, what people! You're right to ask Daddy. Well, listen, and repeat after me:

> 'Hail! Ye, living in Sion,
> This is your King,
> Our steeds we shall sit on,
> Sophonius is weeping.
> Zacharias is speaking,
> Father Pilgrim,
> Mankind ever loving.'

'Kind ever loving,' the old man repeated. 'Do you know it now? Try it.'

Lukáshka laughed.

'Come, Daddy, was it that that hindered their killing you? Maybe it just happened so!'

'You've grown too clever! You learn it all, and say it. It will do you no harm. Well, suppose you have sung "Pilgrim", it's all right,' and the old man himself began laughing. 'But just one thing, Luke, don't you go to Nogáy!'

'Why?'

'Times have changed. You are not the same men. You've become rubbishy Cossacks! And see how many Russians have come down on us! You'd get to prison. Really, give it up! Just as if you could! Now Gírchik and I, we used ... '

And the old man was about to begin one of his endless tales, but Lukáshka glanced at the window and interrupted him.

'It is quite light, Daddy. It's time to be off. Look us up some day.'

'May Christ save you! I'll go to the officer; I promised to take him out shooting. He seems a good fellow.'

Chapter XVII

FROM ERÓSHKA'S hut Lukáshka went home. As he

returned, the dewy mists were rising from the ground and enveloped the village. In various places the cattle, though out of sight, could be heard beginning to stir. The cocks called to one another with increasing frequency and insistence. The air was becoming more transparent, and the villagers were getting up. Not till he was close to it could Lukáshka discern the fence of his yard, all wet with dew, the porch of the hut, and the open shed. From the misty yard he heard the sound of an axe chopping wood. Lukáshka entered the hut. His mother was up, and stood at the oven throwing wood into it. His little sister was still lying in bed asleep.

'Well, Lukáshka, had enough holiday-making?' asked his mother softly. 'Where did you spend the night?'

'I was in the village,' replied her son reluctantly, reaching for his musket, which he drew from its cover and examined carefully.

His mother swayed her head.

Lukáshka poured a little gunpowder onto the pan, took out a little bag from which he drew some empty cartridge cases which he began filling, carefully plugging each one with a ball wrapped in a rag. Then, having tested the loaded cartridges with his teeth and examined them, he put down the bag.

'I say, Mother, I told you the bags wanted mending; have they been done?' he asked.

'Oh yes, our dumb girl was mending something last night. Why, is it time for you to be going back to the cordon? I haven't seen anything of you!'

'Yes, as soon as I have got ready I shall have to go,' answered Lukáshka, tying up the gunpowder. 'And where is our dumb one? Outside?'

'Chopping wood, I expect. She kept fretting for you. "I shall not see him at all!" she said. She puts her hand to her face like this, and clicks her tongue and presses her hands to her heart as much as to say – "sorry." Shall I call her in? She understood all about the *abrek*.'

'Call her,' said Lukáshka. 'And I had some tallow there; bring it: I must grease my sword.'

The old woman went out, and a few minutes later Lukáshka's dumb sister came up the creaking steps and entered the hut. She was six years older than her brother and would have been extremely like him had it not been for the dull and coarsely changeable expression (common to all deaf and dumb people) of her face. She wore a coarse smock all patched; her feet were bare and muddy, and on her head she had an old blue kerchief. Her neck, arms, and face were sinewy like a peasant's. Her clothing and her whole appearance indicated that she always did the hard work of a man. She brought in a heap of logs which she threw down by the oven. Then she went up to her brother, and with a joyful smile which made her whole face pucker up, touched him on the shoulder and began making rapid signs to him with her hands, her face, and whole body.

'That's right, that's right, Stëpka is a trump!' answered the brother, nodding. 'She's fetched everything and mended everything, she's a trump! Here, take this for it!' He brought out two pieces of gingerbread from his pocket and gave them to her.

The dumb woman's face flushed with pleasure, and she began making a weird noise for joy. Having seized the gingerbread she began to gesticulate still more rapidly, frequently pointing in one direction and passing her thick finger over her eyebrows and her face. Lukáshka understood her and kept nodding, while he smiled slightly. She was telling him to give the girls dainties, and that the girls liked him, and that one girl, Maryánka – the best of them all – loved him. She indicated Maryánka by rapidly pointing in the direction of Maryánka's home and to her own eyebrows and face, and by smacking her lips and swaying her head. 'Loves' she expressed by pressing her hands to her breast, kissing her hand, and pretending to embrace someone. Their mother returned to the hut, and seeing what her dumb daughter was saying, smiled and shook her head. Her daughter showed her the gingerbread and again made the noise which expressed joy.

'I told Ulítka the other day that I'd send a matchmaker to

them,' said the mother. 'She took my words well.'

Lukáshka looked silently at his mother.

'But how about selling the wine, mother? I need a horse.'

'I'll cart it when I have time. I must get the barrels ready,' said the mother, evidently not wishing her son to meddle in domestic matters. 'When you go out you'll find a bag in the passage. I borrowed from the neighbours and got something for you to take back to the cordon; or shall I put it in your saddle-bag?'

'All right,' answered Lukáshka. 'And if Giréy Khan should come across the river send him to me at the cordon, for I shan't get leave again for a long time now; I have some business with him.'

He began to get ready to start.

'I will send him on,' said the old women. 'It seems you have been spreeing at Yámka's all the time. I went out in the night to see the cattle, and I think it was your voice I heard singing songs.'

Lukáshka did not reply, but went out into the passage, threw the bags over his shoulder, tucked up the skirts of his coat, took his musket, and then stopped for a moment on the threshold.

'Good-bye, mother!' he said as he closed the gate behind him. 'Send me a small barrel with Nazárka. I promised it to the lads, and he'll call for it.'

'May Christ keep you, Lukáshka. God be with you! I'll send you some, some from the new barrel,' said the old woman, going to the fence: 'But listen,' she added, leaning over the fence.

The Cossack stopped.

'You've been making merry here; well, that's all right. Why should not a young man amuse himself? God has sent you luck and that's good. But now look out and mind, my son. Don't you go and get into mischief. Above all, satisfy your superiors: one has to! And I will sell the wine and find money for a horse and will arrange a match with the girl for you.'

'All right, all right!' answered her son, frowning.

His deaf sister shouted to attract his attention. She pointed to her head and the palm of her hand, to indicate the shaved head of a Chéchen. Then she frowned, and pretending to aim with a gun, she shrieked and began rapidly humming and shaking her head. This meant that Lukáshka should kill another Chéchen.

Lukáshka understood. He smiled, and shifting the gun at his back under his cloak stepped lightly and rapidly, and soon disappeared in the thick mist.

The old woman, having stood a little while at the gate, returned silently to the hut and immediately began working.

Chapter XVIII

LUKÁSHKA returned to the cordon and at the same time Daddy Eróshka whistled to his dogs and, climbing over his wattle fence, went to Olénin's lodging, passing by the back of the houses (he disliked meeting women before going out hunting or shooting). He found Olénin still asleep, and even Vanyúsha, though awake, was still in bed and looking round the room considering whether it was not time to get up, when Daddy Eróshka, gun on shoulder and in full hunter's trappings, opened the door.

'A cudgel!' he shouted in his deep voice. 'An alarm! The Chéchens are upon us! Iván! get the samovar ready for your master, and get up yourself – quick,' cried the old man. 'That's our way, my good man! Why even the girls are already up! Look out of the window. See, she's going for water and you're still sleeping!'

Olénin awoke and jumped up, feeling fresh and light-hearted at the sight of the old man and at the sound of his voice.

'Quick, Vanyúsha, quick!' he cried.

'Is that the way you go hunting?' said the old man. 'Others are having their breakfast and you are asleep! Lyam! Here!' he called to his dog. 'Is your gun ready?' he shouted, as loud as if a whole crowd were in the hut.

'Well, it's true I'm guilty, but it can't be helped! The powder, Vanyúsha, and the wads!' said Olénin.

'A fine!' shouted the old man.

'*Du tay voulay vou?*' asked Vanyúsha, grinning.

'You're not one of us – your gabble is not like our speech, you devil!' the old man shouted at Vanyúsha, showing the stumps of his teeth.

'A first offence must be forgiven,' said Olénin playfully, drawing on his high boots.

'The first offence shall be forgiven,' answered Eróshka, 'but if you oversleep another time you'll be fined a pail of *chikhir*. When it gets warmer you won't find the deer.'

'And even if we do find him he is wiser than we are,' said Olénin, repeating the words spoken by the old man the evening before, 'and you can't deceive him!'

'Yes, laugh away! You kill one first, and then you may talk. Now then, hurry up! Look, there's the master himself coming to see you,' added Eróshka, looking out of the window. 'Just see how he's got himself up. He's put on a new coat so that you should see that he's an officer. Ah, these people, these people!'

Sure enough Vanyúsha came in and announced that the master of the house wished to see Olénin.

'*L'arjan!*' he remarked profoundly, to forewarn his master of the meaning of this visitation. Following him, the master of the house in a new Circassian coat with an officer's stripes on the shoulders and with polished boots (quite exceptional among Cossacks) entered the room, swaying from side to side, and congratulated his lodger on his safe arrival.

The cornet, Elias Vasílich, was an *educated* Cossack. He had been to Russia proper, was a regimental schoolteacher, and above all he was noble. He wished to appear noble, but one could not help feeling beneath his grotesque pretence of polish, his affectation, his self-confidence, and his absurd way of speaking, he was just the same as Daddy Eróshka. This could also be clearly seen by his sunburnt face and his hands and his red nose. Olénin asked him to sit down.

'Good morning, Father Elias Vasílich,' said Eróshka, rising

with (or so it seemed to Olénin) an ironically low bow.

'Good morning, Daddy. So you're here already,' said the cornet, with a careless nod.

The cornet was a man of about forty, with a grey pointed beard, skinny and lean, but handsome and very fresh-looking for his age. Having come to see Olénin he was evidently afraid of being taken for an ordinary Cossack, and wanted to let Olénin feel his importance from the first.

'That's our Egyptian Nimrod,' he remarked, addressing Olénin and pointing to the old man with a self-satisfied smile. 'A mighty hunter before the Lord! He's our foremost man on every hand. You've already been pleased to get acquainted with him.'

Daddy Eróshka gazed at his feet in their shoes of wet raw hide and shook his head thoughtfully at the cornet's ability and learning, and muttered to himself: 'Gyptian Nimvrod! What things he invents!'

'Yes, you see we mean to go hunting,' answered Olénin.

'Yes, sir, exactly,' said the cornet, 'but I have a small business with you.'

'What do you want?'

'Seeing that you are a gentleman,' began the cornet, 'and as I may understand myself to be in the rank of an officer too, and therefore we may always progressively negotiate, as gentlemen do.' (He stopped and looked with a smile at Olénin and at the old man.) 'But if you have the desire with my consent, then, as my wife is a foolish woman of our class, she could not quite comprehend your words of yesterday's date. Therefore my quarters might be let for six rubles to the Regimental Adjutant, without the stables; but I can always avert that from myself free of charge. But, as you desire, therefore I, being myself of an officer's rank, can come to an agreement with you in everything personally, as an inhabitant of this district, not according to our customs, but can maintain the conditions in every way. . . .'

'Speaks clearly!' muttered the old man.

The cornet continued in the same strain for a long time. At last, not without difficulty, Olénin gathered that the cornet wished to let his rooms to him, Olénin, for six rubles a month. The latter gladly agreed to this, and offered his visitor a glass of tea. The cornet declined it.

'According to our silly custom we consider it a sort of sin to drink out of a "worldly" tumbler,' he said. 'Though, of course, with my education I may understand, but my wife from her human weakness . . .'

'Well then, will you have some tea?'

'If you will permit me, I will bring my own particular glass,' answered the cornet, and stepped out into the porch.

'Bring me my glass!' he cried.

In a few minutes the door opened and a young sunburnt arm in a print sleeve thrust itself in, holding a tumbler in the hand. The cornet went up, took it, and whispered something to his daughter. Olénin poured tea for the cornet into the latter's own 'particular' glass, and for Eróshka into a 'worldly' glass.

'However, I do not desire to detain you,' said the cornet, scalding his lips and emptying his tumbler. 'I too have a great liking for fishing, and I am here, so to say, only on leave of absence for recreation from my duties. I too have the desire to tempt fortune and see whether some *Gifts of the Térek* may not fall to my share. I hope you too will come and see us and have a drink of our wine, according to the custom of our village,' he added.

The cornet bowed, shook hands with Olénin, and went out. While Olénin was getting ready, he heard the cornet giving orders to his family in an authoritative and sensible tone, and a few minutes later he saw him pass by the window in a tattered coat with his trousers rolled up to his knees and a fishing net over his shoulder.

'A rascal!' said Daddy Eróshka, emptying his 'worldly' tumbler. 'And will you really pay him six rubles? Was such a thing ever heard of? They would let you the best hut in the village for two rubles. What a beast! Why, I'd let you have mine for three!'

'No, I'll remain here,' said Olénin.

'Six rubles! . . . Clearly it's a fool's money. Eh, eh, eh!'

answered the old man. 'Let's have some *chikhir*, Iván!'

Having had a snack and a drink of vodka to prepare themselves for the road, Olénin and the old man went out together before eight o'clock.

At the gate they came up against a wagon to which a pair of oxen were harnessed. With a white kerchief tied round her head down to her eyes, a coat over her smock, and wearing high boots, Maryánka with a long switch in her hand was dragging the oxen by a cord tied to their horns.

'Mammy,' said the old man, pretending that he was going to seize her.

Maryánka flourished her switch at him and glanced merrily at them both with her beautiful eyes.

Olénin felt still more light-hearted.

'Now then, come on, come on,' he said, throwing his gun on his shoulder and conscious of the girl's eyes upon him.

'Gee up!' sounded Maryánka's voice behind them, followed by the creak of the moving wagon.

As long as their road lay through the pastures at the back of the village Eróshka went on talking. He could not forget the cornet and kept on abusing him.

'Why are you so angry with him?' asked Olénin.

'He's stingy. I don't like it,' answered the old man. 'He'll leave it all behind when he dies! Then who's he saving up for? He's built two houses, and he's got a second garden from his brother by a law-suit. And in the matter of papers what a dog he is! They come to him from other villages to fill up documents. As he writes it out, exactly so it happens. He gets it quite exact. But who is he saving for? He's only got one boy and the girl; when she's married who'll be left?'

'Well then, he's saving up for her dowry,' said Olénin.

'What dowry? The girl is sought after, she's a fine girl. But he's such a devil that he must yet marry her to a rich fellow. He wants to get a big price for her. There's Luke, a Cossack, a neighbour and a nephew of mine, a fine lad. It's he who killed the Chéchen – he has been wooing her for a long time, but he hasn't let him have her. He's given one excuse, and another, and a third. "The girl's too young," he says. But I know what he is thinking. He wants to keep them bowing to him. He's been acting shamefully about that girl. Still, they will get her for Lukáshka, because he is the best Cossack in the village, a brave, who has killed an *abrek* and will be rewarded with a cross.'

'But how about this? When I was walking up and down the yard last night, I saw my landlord's daughter and some Cossack kissing,' said Olénin.

'You're pretending!' cried the old man, stopping.

'On my word,' said Olénin.

'Women are the devil,' said Eróshka pondering. 'But what Cossack was it?'

'I couldn't see.'

'Well, what sort of a cap had he, a white one?'

'Yes.'

'And a red coat? About your height?'

'No, a bit taller.'

'It's he!' and Eróshka burst out laughing. 'It's himself, it's Mark. He is Luke, but I call him Mark for a joke. His very self! I love him. I was just such a one myself. What's the good of minding them? My sweetheart used to sleep with her mother and her sister-in-law, but I managed to get in. She used to sleep upstairs; that witch her mother was a regular demon; it's awful how she hated me. Well, I used to come with a chum, Gírchik his name was. We'd come under her window and I'd climb on his shoulders, push up the window and begin groping about. She used to sleep just there on a bench. Once I woke her up and she nearly called out. She hadn't recognized me. "Who is there?" she said, and I could not answer. Her mother was even beginning to stir, but I took off my cap and shoved it over her mouth; and she at once knew it by a seam in it, and ran out to me. I used not to want anything then. She'd bring along clotted cream and grapes and everything,' added Eróshka (who always explained things practically), 'and she wasn't the only one. It was a life!'

'And what now?'

'Now we'll follow the dog, get a pheasant to settle on a tree, and then you may fire.'

'Would you have made up to Maryánka?'

'Attend to the dogs. I'll tell you tonight,' said the old man, pointing to his favourite dog, Lyam.

After a pause they continued talking, while they went about a hundred paces. Then the old man stopped again and pointed to a twig that lay across the path.

'What do you think of that?' he said. 'You think it's nothing? It's bad that this stick is lying so.'

'Why is it bad?'

He smiled.

'Ah, you don't know anything. Just listen to me. When a stick lies like that don't you step across it, but go round it or throw it off the path this way, and say "Father and Son and Holy Ghost," and then go on with God's blessing. Nothing will happen to you. That's what the old men used to teach me.'

'Come, what rubbish!' said Olénin. 'You'd better tell me more about Maryánka. Does she carry on with Lukáshka?'

'Hush, . . . be quiet now!' the old man again interrupted in a whisper: 'just listen, we'll go round through the forest.'

And the old man, stepping quietly in his soft shoes, led the way by a narrow path leading into the dense, wild, over-grown forest. Now and again with a frown he turned to look at Olénin, who rustled and clattered with his heavy boots and, carrying his gun carelessly, several times caught the twigs of trees that grew across the path.

'Don't make a noise. Step softly, soldier!' the old man whispered angrily.

There was a feeling in the air that the sun had risen. The mist was dissolving but it still enveloped the tops of the trees. The forest looked terribly high. At every step the aspect changed: what had appeared like a tree proved to be a bush, and a reed looked like a tree.

Chapter XIX

THE MIST had partly lifted, showing the wet reed thatches, and was now turning into dew that moistened the road and the grass beside the fence. Smoke rose everywhere in clouds from the chimneys. The people were going out of the village, some to their work, some to the river, and some to the cordon. The hunters walked together along the damp, grass-grown path. The dogs, wagging their tails and looking at their masters, ran on both sides of them. Myriads of gnats hovered in the air and pursued the hunters, covering their backs, eyes, and hands. The air was fragrant with the grass and with the dampness of the forest. Olénin continually looked round at the ox-cart in which Maryánka sat urging on the oxen with a long switch.

It was calm. The sounds from the village, audible at first, now no longer reached the sportsmen. Only the brambles cracked as the dogs ran under them, and now and then birds called to one another. Olénin knew that danger lurked in the forest, that *abreks* always hid in such places. But he knew too that in the forest, for a man on foot, a gun is a great protection. Not that he was afraid, but he felt that another in his place might be; and looking into the damp misty forest and listening to the rare and faint sounds with strained attention, he changed his hold on his gun and experienced a pleasant feeling that was new to him. Daddy Eróshka went in front, stopping and carefully scanning every puddle where an animal had left a double track, and pointing it out to Olénin. He hardly spoke at all and only occasionally made remarks in a whisper. The track they were following had once been made by wagons, but the grass had long over-grown it. The elm and plane-tree forest on both sides of them was so dense and overgrown with creepers that it was impossible to see anything through it. Nearly every tree was enveloped from top to bottom with wild grape vines, and dark bramble bushes covered the ground thickly. Every little glade was overgrown with blackberry bushes and grey feathery reeds. In places, large hoof-prints and small funnel-shaped pheasant-trails led from the path into the thicket. The vigour of the growth of this forest, untrampled by cattle, struck Olénin at every turn, for he had never seen anything like it. This forest, the danger, the old man and his mysterious whispering, Maryánka with her virile upright bearing, and the mountains — all this seemed to him like a dream.

'A pheasant has settled,' whispered the old man, looking round and pulling his cap over his face — 'Cover your mug! A pheasant!' he waved his arm angrily at Olénin and pushed forward almost on all fours. 'He don't like a man's mug.'

Olénin was still behind him when the old man stopped and began examining a tree. A cock-pheasant on the tree clucked at the dog that was barking at it, and Olénin saw the pheasant; but at that moment a report, as of a cannon, came from Eróshka's enormous gun, the bird fluttered up and, losing some feathers, fell to the ground. Coming up to the old man Olénin disturbed another, and raising his gun he aimed and fired. The pheasant flew swiftly up and then, catching at the branches as he fell, dropped like a stone to the ground.

'Good man!' the old man (who could not hit a flying bird) shouted, laughing.

Having picked up the pheasants they went on. Olénin, excited by the exercise and the praise, kept addressing remarks to the old man.

'Stop! Come this way,' the old man interrupted. 'I noticed the track of deer here yesterday.'

After they had turned into the thicket and gone some three hundred paces they scrambled through into a glade overgrown with reeds and partly under water. Olénin failed to keep up with the old huntsman and presently Daddy Eróshka, some twenty paces in front, stooped down, nodding and beckoning with his arm. On coming up with him Olénin saw a man's footprint to which the old man was pointing.

'D'you see?'

'Yes, well?' said Olénin, trying to speak as calmly as he could. 'A man's footstep!'

Involuntarily a thought of Cooper's *Pathfinder* and of *abreks* flashed through Olénin's mind, but noticing the mysterious manner with which the old man moved on, he hesitated to question him and remained in doubt whether this mysteriousness was caused by fear of danger or by the sport.

'No, it's my own footprint,' the old man said quietly, and pointed to some grass under which the track of an animal was just perceptible.

The old man went on, and Olénin kept up with him.

Descending to lower ground some twenty paces farther on they came upon a spreading pear-tree, under which, on the black earth, lay the fresh dung of some animal.

The spot, all covered over with wild vines, was like a cosy arbour, dark and cool.

'He's been here this morning,' said the old man with a sigh; 'the lair is still damp, quite fresh.'

Suddenly they heard a terrible crash in the forest some ten paces from where they stood. They both started and seized their guns, but they could see nothing and only heard the branches breaking. The rhythmical rapid thud of galloping was heard for a moment and then changed into a hollow rumble which resounded farther and farther off, re-echoing in wider and wider circles through the forest. Olénin felt as though something had snapped in his heart. He peered carefully but vainly into the green thicket and then turned to the old man. Daddy Eróshka with his gun pressed to his breast stood motionless; his cap was thrust backwards, his eyes gleamed with an unwonted glow, and his open mouth, with its worn yellow teeth, seemed to have stiffened in that position.

'A horned stag!' he muttered, and throwing down his gun in despair he began pulling at his grey beard, 'Here it stood. We should have come round by the path. . . . Fool! fool!' and he gave his beard an angry tug. 'Fool! Pig!' he repeated, pulling painfully at his own beard. Through the forest something seemed to fly away in the mist, and ever farther and farther off was heard the sound of the flight of the stag.

It was already dusk when, hungry, tired, but full of vigour, Olénin returned with the old man. Dinner was ready. He ate and drank with the old man till he felt warm and merry. Olénin then went out into the porch. Again, to the west, the mountains rose before his eyes. Again the old man told his endless stories of hunting, of *abreks*, of sweethearts, and of all that free and reckless life. Again the fair Maryánka went in and out and across the yard, her beautiful powerful form outlined by her smock.

Chapter XX

THE NEXT day Olénin went alone to the spot where he and the old man startled the stag. Instead of passing round through the gate he climbed over the prickly hedge, as everybody else did, and before he had had time to pull out the thorns that had caught in his coat, his dog, which had run on in front, started two pheasants. He had hardly stepped among the briers when the pheasants began to rise at every step (the old man had not shown him that place the day before as he meant to keep it for shooting from behind the screen). Olénin fired twelve times and killed five pheasants, but clambering after them through the briers he got so fatigued that he was drenched with perspiration. He called off his dog, uncocked his gun, put in a bullet above the small shot, and brushing away the mosquitoes with the wide sleeve of his Circassian coat he went slowly to the spot where they had been the day before. It was however impossible to keep back the dog, who found trails on the very path, and Olénin killed two more pheasants, so that after being detained by this it was getting towards noon before he began to find the place he was looking for.

The day was perfectly clear, calm, and hot. The morning moisture had dried up even in the forest, and myriads of mosquitoes literally covered his face, his back, and his arms. His dog had turned from black to grey, its back being covered with mosquitoes, and so had Olénin's coat through which the insects thrust their stings. Olénin was ready to run

away from them and it seemed to him that it was impossible
to live in this country in the summer. He was about to go
home, but remembering that other people managed to
endure such pain he resolved to bear it and gave himself up to
be devoured. And strange to say, by noontime the feeling
became actually pleasant. He even felt that without this
mosquito-filled atmosphere around him, and that mosquito-
paste mingled with perspiration which his hand smeared
over his face, and that unceasing irritation all over his body,
the forest would lose for him some of its character and
charm. These myriads of insects were so well suited to that
monstrously lavish wild vegetation, these multitudes of birds
and beasts which filled the forest, this dark foliage, this hot
scented air, these runlets filled with turbid water which
everywhere soaked through from the Térek and gurgled
here and there under the overhanging leaves, that the very
thing which had at first seemed to him dreadful and intolerable now seemed pleasant. After going round the place
where yesterday they had found the animal and not finding
anything, he felt inclined to rest. The sun stood right above
the forest and poured its perpendicular rays down on his back
and head whenever he came out into a glade or onto the
road. The seven heavy pheasants dragged painfully at his
waist. Having found the traces of yesterday's stag he crept
under a bush into the thicket just where the stag had lain, and
lay down in its lair. He examined the dark foliage around
him, the place marked by the stag's perspiration and yesterday's dung, the imprint of the stag's knees, the bit of black
earth it had kicked up, and his own footprints of the day
before. He felt cool and comfortable and did not think of or
wish for anything. And suddenly he was overcome by such a
strange feeling of causeless joy and of love for everything,
that from an old habit of his childhood he began crossing
himself and thanking someone. Suddenly, with extraordinary clearness, he thought: 'Here am I, Dmítri Olénin, a
being quite distinct from every other being, now lying all
alone Heaven only knows where – where a stag used to live –
an old stag, a beautiful stag who perhaps had never seen a

man, and in a place where no human being has ever sat or thought these thoughts. Here I sit, and around me stand old and young trees, one of them festooned with wild grape vines, and pheasants are fluttering, driving one another about and perhaps scenting their murdered brothers.' He felt his pheasants, examined them, and wiped the warm blood off his hand onto his coat. 'Perhaps the jackals scent them and with dissatisfied faces go off in another direction: above me, flying in among the leaves which to them seem enormous islands, mosquitoes hang in the air and buzz: one, two, three, four, a hundred, a thousand, a million mosquitoes, and all of them buzz something or other and each one of them is separate from all else and is just such a separate Dmítri Olénin as I am myself.' He vividly imagined what the mosquitoes buzzed: 'This way, this way, lads! Here's some one we can eat!' They buzzed and stuck to him. And it was clear to him that he was not a Russian nobleman, a member of Moscow society, the friend and relation of so-and-so and so-and-so, but just such a mosquito, or pheasant, or deer, as those that were now living all around him. 'Just as they, just as Daddy Eróshka, I shall live awhile and die, and as he says truly: "grass will grow and nothing more".

'But what though the grass does grow?' he continued thinking. 'Still I must live and be happy, because happiness is all I desire. Never mind what I am – an animal like all the rest, above whom the grass will grow and nothing more; or a frame in which a bit of the one God has been set, – still I must live in the very best way. How then must I live to be happy, and why was I not happy before?' And he began to recall his former life and he felt disgusted with himself. He appeared to himself to have been terribly exacting and selfish, though he now saw that all the while he really needed nothing for himself. And he looked round at the foliage with the light shining through it, at the setting sun and the clear sky, and he felt just as happy as before. 'Why am I happy, and what used I to live for?' thought he. 'How much I exacted for myself; how I schemed and did not manage to gain anything but shame and sorrow! and, there now, I require nothing to be happy;' and suddenly a new light seemed to reveal itself to him. 'Happiness is this!' he said to himself. 'Happiness lies in living for others. That is evident. The desire for happiness is innate in every man; therefore it is legitimate. When trying to satisfy it selfishly – that is, by seeking for oneself riches, fame, comforts, or love – it may happen that circumstances arise which make it impossible to satisfy these desires. It follows that it is these desires that are illegitimate, but not the need for happiness. But what desires can always be satisfied despite external circumstances? What are they? Love, self-sacrifice.' He was so glad and excited when he had discovered this, as it seemed to him, new truth, that he jumped up and began impatiently seeking some one to sacrifice himself for, to do good to and to love. 'Since one wants nothing for oneself,' he kept thinking, 'why not live for others?' He took up his gun with the intention of returning home quickly to think this out and to find an opportunity of doing good. He made his way out of the thicket. When he had come out into the glade he looked around him; the sun was no longer visible above the tree-tops. It had grown cooler and the place seemed to him quite strange and not like the country round the village. Everything seemed changed – the weather and the character of the forest; the sky was wrapped in clouds, the wind was rustling in the tree-tops, and all around nothing was visible but reeds and dying broken-down trees. He called to his dog who had run away to follow some animal, and his voice came back as in a desert. And suddenly he was seized with a terrible sense of weirdness. He grew frightened. He remembered the *abreks* and the murders he had been told about, and he expected every moment that an *abrek* would spring from behind every bush and he would have to defend his life and die, or be a coward. He thought of God and of the future life as for long he had not thought about them. And all around was that same gloomy stern wild nature. 'And is it worth while living for oneself,' thought he, 'when at any moment you may die, and die without having done any good, and so that no one will know of it?' He went in the direction where he fancied the village lay. Of his shooting he had no further thought; but he felt tired to death and peered round at every bush and tree with particular attention and almost with terror, expecting every moment to be called to account for his life. After having wandered about for a considerable time he came upon a ditch down which was flowing cold sandy water from the Térek, and, not to go astray any longer, he decided to follow it. He went on without knowing where the ditch would lead him. Suddenly the reeds behind him crackled. He shuddered and seized his gun, and then felt ashamed of himself: the over-excited dog, panting hard, had thrown itself into the cold water of the ditch and was lapping it!

He too had a drink, and then followed the dog in the direction it wished to go, thinking it would lead him to the village. But despite the dog's company everything around him seemed still more dreary. The forest grew darker and the wind grew stronger and stronger in the tops of the broken old trees. Some large birds circled screeching round their nests in those trees. The vegetation grew poorer and he came oftener and oftener upon rustling reeds and bare sandy spaces covered with animal footprints. To the howling of the wind was added another kind of cheerless monotonous roar. Altogether his spirits became gloomy. Putting his hand behind him he felt his pheasants, and found one missing. It had broken off and was lost, and only the bleeding head and beak remained sticking in his belt. He felt more frightened than he had ever done before. He began to pray to God, and feared above all that he might die without having done anything good or kind; and he so wanted to live, and to live so as to perform a feat of self-sacrifice.

Chapter XXI

SUDDENLY it was as though the sun had shone into his soul. He heard Russian being spoken, and also heard the rapid smooth flow of the Térek, and a few steps farther in front of him saw the brown moving surface of the river, with the dim-coloured wet sand of its banks and shallows, the distant steppe, the cordon watch-tower outlined above the water, a saddled and hobbled horse among the brambles, and then the mountains opening out before him. The red sun appeared for an instant from under a cloud and its last rays glittered brightly along the river over the reeds, on the watch-tower, and on a group of Cossacks, among whom Lukáshka's vigorous figure attracted Olénin's involuntary attention.

Olénin felt that he was again, without any apparent cause, perfectly happy. He had come upon the Nízhni-Protótsk post on the Térek, opposite a pro-Russian Tartar village on the other side of the river. He accosted the Cossacks, but not finding as yet any excuse for doing anyone a kindness, he entered the hut; nor in the hut did he find any such opportunity. The Cossacks received him coldly. On entering the mud hut he lit a cigarette. The Cossacks paid little attention to him, first because he was smoking a cigarette, and secondly because they had something else to divert them that evening. Some hostile Chéchens, relatives of the *abrek* who had been killed, had come from the hills with a scout to ransom the body; and the Cossacks were waiting for their Commanding Officer's arrival from the village. The dead man's brother, tall and well shaped with a short cropped beard which was dyed red, despite his very tattered coat and cap was calm and majestic as a king. His face was very like that of the dead *abrek*. He did not deign to look at anyone, and never once glanced at the dead body, but sitting on his heels in the shade he spat as he smoked his short pipe, and occasionally uttered some few guttural sounds of command, which were respectfully listened to by his companion. He was evidently a brave who had met Russians more than once before in quite other circumstances, and nothing about them could astonish or even interest him. Olénin was about to approach the dead body and had begun to look at it when the brother, looking up at him from under his brows with calm contempt, said something sharply and angrily. The scout hastened to cover the dead man's face with his coat. Olénin was struck by the dignified and stern expression of the brave's face. He began to speak to him, asking from what village he came, but the Chéchen, scarcely giving him a glance, spat contemptuously and turned away. Olénin was so surprised at the Chéchen not being interested in him that he could only put it down to the man's stupidity or ignorance of Russian; so he turned to the scout, who also acted as interpreter. The scout was as ragged as the other, but instead of being red-haired he was black-haired, restless, with extremely white gleaming teeth and sparkling black eyes. The scout willingly entered into conversation and asked for a cigarette.

'There were five brothers,' began the scout in his broken Russian. 'This is the third brother the Russians have killed, only two are left. He is a brave, a great brave!' he said, pointing to the Chéchen. 'When they killed Ahmet Khan (the dead brave) this one was sitting on the opposite bank among the reeds. He saw it all. Saw him laid in the skiff and brought to the bank. He sat there till the night and wished to kill the old man, but the others would not let him.'

Lukáshka went up to the speaker, and sat down.

'Of what village?' asked he.

'From there in the hills,' replied the scout, pointing to the misty bluish gorge beyond the Térek. 'Do you know Suuk-su? It is about eight miles beyond that.'

'Do you know Giréy Khan in Suuk-su?' asked Lukáshka, evidently proud of the acquaintance. 'He is my *kunak.*'

'He is my neighbour,' answered the scout.

'He's a trump!' and Lukáshka, evidently much interested, began talking to the scout in Tartar.

Presently a Cossack captain, with the head of the village, arrived on horseback with a suite of two Cossacks. The captain – one of the new type of Cossack officers – wished the Cossacks 'Good health,' but no one shouted in reply, 'Hail! Good health to your honour,' as is customary in the Russian Army, and only a few replied with a bow. Some, and among them Lukáshka, rose and stood erect. The corporal replied that all was well at the outposts. All this seemed ridiculous: it was as if these Cossacks were playing at being soldiers. But these formalities soon gave place to ordinary ways of behaviour, and the captain, who was a smart Cossack just like the others, began speaking fluently in Tartar to the interpreter. They filled in some document, gave it to the scout, and received from him some money. Then they approached the body.

'Which of you is Luke Gavrílov?' asked the captain.

Lukáshka took off his cap and came forward.

'I have reported your exploit to the Commander. I don't know what will come of it. I have recommended you for a cross; you're too young to be made a sergeant. Can you read?'

'I can't.'

'But what a fine fellow to look at!' said the captain, again playing the commander. 'Put on your cap. Which of the Gavrílovs does he come of? . . . the Broad, eh?'

'His nephew,' replied the corporal.

'I know, I know. Well, lend a hand, help them,' he said, turning to the Cossacks.

Lukáshka's face shone with joy and seemed handsomer than usual. He moved away from the corporal, and having put on his cap sat down beside Olénin.

When the body had been carried to the skiff the brother Chéchen descended to the bank. The Cossacks involuntarily stepped aside to let him pass. He jumped into the boat and pushed off from the bank with his powerful leg, and now, as Olénin noticed, for the first time threw a rapid glance at all the Cossacks and then abruptly asked his companion a question. The latter answered something and pointed to Lukáshka. The Chéchen looked at him and, turning slowly away, gazed at the opposite bank. That look expressed not hatred but cold contempt. He again made some remark.

'What is he saying?' Olénin asked of the fidgety scout.

'Yours kill ours, ours slay yours. It's always the same,' replied the scout, evidently inventing, and he smiled, showing his white teeth, as he jumped into the skiff.

The dead man's brother sat motionless, gazing at the opposite bank. He was so full of hatred and contempt that there was nothing on this side of the river that moved his curiosity. The scout, standing up at one end of the skiff and dipping his paddle now on one side now on the other, steered skilfully while talking incessantly. The skiff became smaller and smaller as it moved obliquely across the stream, the voices became scarcely audible, and at last, still within sight, they landed on the opposite bank where their horses stood waiting. There they lifted out the corpse and (though the horse shied) laid it across one of the saddles, mounted, and rode at a foot-pace along the road past a Tartar village from which a crowd came out to look at them. The Cossacks on the Russian side of the river were highly satisfied and jovial. Laughter and jokes were heard on all sides. The captain and the head of the village entered the mud hut to regale themselves. Lukáshka, vainly striving to impart a sedate expression to his merry face, sat down with his elbows on his knees beside Olénin and whittled away at a stick.

'Why do you smoke?' he said with assumed curiosity. 'Is it good?'

He evidently spoke because he noticed Olénin felt ill at ease and isolated among the Cossacks.

'It's just a habit,' answered Olénin. 'Why?'

'H'm, if one of us were to smoke there would be a row! Look there now, the mountains are not far off,' continued Lukáshka, 'yet you can't get there! How will you get back alone? It's getting dark. I'll take you, if you like. You ask the corporal to give me leave.'

'What a fine fellow!' thought Olénin, looking at the Cossack's bright face. He remembered Maryánka and the kiss he had heard by the gate, and he was sorry for Lukáshka and his want of culture. 'What confusion it is,' he thought. 'A man kills another and is happy and satisfied with himself as if he had done something excellent. Can it be that nothing tells him that it is not a reason for any rejoicing, and that happiness lies not in killing, but in sacrificing oneself?'

'Well, you had better not meet him again now, mate!' said one of the Cossacks who had seen the skiff off, addressing Lukáshka. 'Did you hear him asking about you?'

Lukáshka raised his head.

'My godson?' said Lukáshka, meaning by that word the
dead Chéchen.

'Your godson won't rise, but the red one is the godson's
brother!'

'Let him thank God that he got off whole himself,' replied
Lukáshka.

'What are you glad about?' asked Olénin. 'Supposing
your brother had been killed; would you be glad?'

The Cossack looked at Olénin with laughing eyes. He
seemed to have understood all that Olénin wished to say to
him, but to be above such considerations.

'Well, that happens too! Don't our fellows get killed
sometimes?'

Chapter XXII

THE CAPTAIN and the head of the village rode away, and
Olénin, to please Lukáshka as well as to avoid going back
alone through the dark forest, asked the corporal to give
Lukáshka leave, and the corporal did so. Olénin thought that
Lukáshka wanted to see Maryánka and he was also glad of
the companionship of such a pleasant-looking and sociable
Cossack. Lukáshka and Maryánka he involuntarily united in
his mind, and he found pleasure in thinking about them. 'He
loves Maryánka,' thought Olénin, 'and I could love her,' and
a new and powerful emotion of tenderness overcame him as
they walked homewards together through the dark forest.
Lukáshka too felt happy; something akin to love made itself
felt between these two very different young men. Every time
they glanced at one another they wanted to laugh.

'By which gate do you enter?' asked Olénin.

'By the middle one. But I'll see you as far as the marsh.
After that you have nothing to fear.'

Olénin laughed.

'Do you think I am afraid? Go back, and thank you. I can
get on alone.'

'It's all right! What have I to do? And how can you help
being afraid? Even we are afraid,' said Lukáshka to set

Olénin's self-esteem at rest, and he laughed too.

'Then come in with me. We'll have a talk and a drink and in the morning you can go back.'

'Couldn't I find a place to spend the night?' laughed Lukáshka. 'But the corporal asked me to go back.'

'I heard you singing last night, and also saw you.'

'Every one ...' and Luke swayed his head.

'Is it true you are getting married?' asked Olénin.

'Mother wants me to marry. But I have not got a horse yet.'

'Aren't you in the regular service?'

'Oh dear no! I've only just joined, and have not got a horse yet, and don't know how to get one. That's why the marriage does not come off.'

'And what would a horse cost?'

'We were bargaining for one beyond the river the other day and they would not take sixty rubles for it, though it is a Nogáy horse.'

'Will you come and be my drabánt?' (A drabánt was a kind of orderly attached to an officer when campaigning.) 'I'll get it arranged and will give you a horse,' said Olénin suddenly. 'Really now, I have two and I don't want both.'

'How – don't want it?' Lukáshka said, laughing. 'Why should you make me a present? We'll get on by ourselves by God's help.'

'No, really! Or don't you want to be a drabánt?' said Olénin, glad that it had entered his head to give a horse to Lukáshka, though, without knowing why, he felt uncomfortable and confused and did not know what to say when he tried to speak.

Lukáshka was the first to break the silence.

'Have you a house of your own in Russia?' he asked.

Olénin could not refrain from replying that he had not only one, but several houses.

'A good house? Bigger than ours?' asked Lukáshka good-naturedly.

'Much bigger; ten times as big and three storeys high,' replied Olénin.

'And have you horses such as ours?'

'I have a hundred horses, worth three or four hundred rubles each, but they are not like yours. They are trotters, you know. ... But still, I like the horses here best.'

'Well, and did you come here of your own free will, or were you sent?' said Lukáshka, laughing at him. 'Look! that's where you lost your way,' he added, 'you should have turned to the right.'

'I came by my own wish,' replied Olénin. 'I wanted to see your parts and to join some expeditions.'

'I would go on an expedition any day,' said Lukáshka. 'D'you hear the jackals howling?' he added, listening.

'I say, don't you feel any horror at having killed a man?' asked Olénin.

'What's there to be frightened about? But I should like to join an expedition,' Lukáshka repeated. 'How I want to! How I want to!'

'Perhaps we may be going together. Our company is going before the holidays, and your "hundred" too.'

'And what did you want to come here for? You've a house and horses and serfs. In your place I'd do nothing but make merry! And what is your rank?'

'I am a cadet, but have been recommended for a commission.'

'Well, if you're not bragging about your home, if I were you I'd never have left it! Yes, I'd never have gone away anywhere. Do you find it pleasant living among us?'

'Yes, very pleasant,' answered Olénin.

It had grown quite dark before, talking in this way, they approached the village. They were still surrounded by the deep gloom of the forest. The wind howled through the tree-tops. The jackals suddenly seemed to be crying close beside them, howling, chuckling, and sobbing; but ahead of them in the village the sounds of women's voices and the barking of dogs could already be heard; the outlines of the huts were clearly to be seen; lights gleamed and the air was filled with the peculiar smell of *kisyak* smoke. Olénin felt keenly, that night especially, that here in this village was his

home, his family, all his happiness, and that he never had and
never would live so happily anywhere as he did in this
Cossack village. He was so fond of everybody and especially
of Lukáshka that night. On reaching home, to Lukáshka's
great surprise, Olénin with his own hands led out of the shed
a horse he had bought in Gróznoe – it was not the one he
usually rode but another – not a bad horse though no longer
young, and gave it to Lukáshka.

'Why should you give me a present?' said Lukáshka, 'I
have not yet done anything for you.'

'Really it is nothing,' answered Olénin. 'Take it, and you
will give me a present, and we'll go on an expedition against
the enemy together.'

Lukáshka became confused.

'But what d'you mean by it? As if a horse were of little
value,' he said without looking at the horse.

'Take it, take it! If you don't you will offend me.
Vanyúsha! Take the grey horse to his house.'

Lukáshka took hold of the halter.

'Well then, thank you! This is something unexpected,
undreamt of.'

Olénin was as happy as a boy of twelve.

'Tie it up here. It's a good horse. I bought it in Gróznoe; it
gallops splendidly! Vanyúsha, bring us some *chikhir*. Come
into the hut.'

The wine was brought. Lukáshka sat down and took the
wine-bowl.

'God willing I'll find a way to repay you,' he said,
finishing his wine. 'How are you called?'

'Dmítri Andréich.'

'Well, 'Mítry Andréich, God bless you. We will be *kunaks*.
Now you must come to see us. Though we are not rich
people still we can treat a *kunak*, and I will tell mother in case
you need anything – clotted cream or grapes – and if you
come to the cordon I'm your servant to go hunting or to go
across the river, anywhere you like! There now, only the
other day, what a boar I killed, and I divided it among the
Cossacks, but if I had only known, I'd have given it to you.'

'That's all right, thank you! But don't harness the horse, it has never been in harness.'

'Why harness the horse? And there is something else I'll tell you if you like,' said Lukáshka, bending his head. 'I have a *kunak*, Giréy Khan. He asked me to lie in ambush by the road where they come down from the mountains. Shall we go together? I'll not betray you. I'll be your *murid*.'

'Yes, we'll go; we'll go some day.'

Lukáshka seemed quite to have quieted down and to have understood Olénin's attitude towards him. His calmness and the ease of his behaviour surprised Olénin, and he did not even quite like it. They talked long, and it was late when Lukáshka, not tipsy (he never was tipsy) but having drunk a good deal, left Olénin after shaking hands.

Olénin looked out of the window to see what he would do. Lukáshka went out, hanging his head. Then, having led the horse out of the gate, he suddenly shook his head, threw the reins of the halter over its head, sprang onto its back like a cat, gave a wild shout, and galloped down the street. Olénin expected that Lukáshka would go to share his joy with Maryánka, but though he did not do so Olénin still felt his soul more at ease than ever before in his life. He was as delighted as a boy, and could not refrain from telling Vanyúsha not only that he had given Lukáshka the horse, but also why he had done it, as well as his new theory of happiness. Vanyúsha did not approve of his theory, and announced that '*l'argent il n'y a pas!*' and that therefore it was all nonsense.

Lukáshka rode home, jumped off the horse, and handed it over to his mother, telling her to let it out with the communal Cossack herd. He himself had to return to the cordon that same night. His deaf sister undertook to take the horse, and explained by signs that when she saw the man who had given the horse, she would bow down at his feet. The old woman only shook her head at her son's story, and decided in her own mind that he had stolen it. She therefore told the deaf girl to take it to the herd before daybreak.

Lukáshka went back alone to the cordon pondering over

Olénin's action. Though he did not consider the horse a good one, yet it was worth at least forty rubles and Lukáshka was very glad to have the present. But why it had been given him he could not at all understand, and therefore he did not experience the least feeling of gratitude. On the contrary, vague suspicions that the cadet had some evil intentions filled his mind. What those intentions were he could not decide, but neither could he admit the idea that a stranger would give him a horse worth forty rubles for nothing, just out of kindness; it seemed impossible. Had he been drunk one might understand it! He might have wished to show off. But the cadet had been sober, and therefore must have wished to bribe him to do something wrong. 'Eh, humbug!' thought Lukáshka. 'Haven't I got the horse and we'll see later on. I'm not a fool myself and we shall see who'll get the better of the other,' he thought, feeling the necessity of being on his guard, and therefore arousing in himself unfriendly feelings towards Olénin. He told no one how he had got the horse. To some he said he had bought it, to others he replied evasively. However, the truth soon got about in the village, and Lukáshka's mother and Maryánka, as well as Elias Vasílich and other Cossacks, when they heard of Olénin's unnecessary gift, were perplexed, and began to be on their guard against the cadet. But despite their fears his action aroused in them a great respect for his simplicity and wealth.

'Have you heard,' said one, 'that the cadet quartered on Elias Vasílich has thrown a fifty-ruble horse at Lukáshka? He's rich! ...'

'Yes, I heard of it,' replied another profoundly, 'he must have done him some great service. We shall see what will come of this cadet. Eh! what luck that Snatcher has!'

'Those cadets are crafty, awfully crafty,' said a third. 'See if he don't go setting fire to a building, or doing something!'

Chapter XXIII

OLÉNIN's life went on with monotonous regularity. He had little intercourse with the commanding officers or with his equals. The position of a rich cadet in the Caucasus was peculiarly advantageous in this respect. He was not sent out to work, or for training. As a reward for going on an expedition he was recommended for a commission, and meanwhile he was left in peace. The officers regarded him as an aristocrat and behaved towards him with dignity. Card-playing and the officers' carousals accompanied by the soldier-singers, of which he had had experience when he was with the detachment, did not seem to him attractive, and he also avoided the society and life of the officers in the village. The life of officers stationed in a Cossack village has long had its own definite form. Just as every cadet or officer when in a fort regularly drinks porter, plays cards, and discusses the rewards given for taking part in the expeditions, so in the Cossack villages he regularly drinks *chikhir* with his hosts, treats the girls to sweet-meats and honey, dangles after the Cossack women, and falls in love, and occasionally marries there. Olénin always took his own path and had an uncon-scious objection to the beaten tracks. And here, too, he did not follow the ruts of a Caucasian officer's life.

It came quite naturally to him to wake up at daybreak. After drinking tea and admiring from his porch the moun-tains, the morning, and Maryánka, he would put on a tattered ox-hide coat, sandals of soaked raw hide, buckle on a dagger, take a gun, put cigarettes and some lunch in a little bag, call his dog, and soon after five o'clock would start for the forest beyond the village. Towards seven in the evening he would return tired and hungry with five or six pheasants hanging from his belt (sometimes with some other animal) and with his bag of food and cigarettes untouched. If the thoughts in his head had lain like the lunch and cigarettes in the bag, one might have seen that during all those fourteen hours not a single thought had moved in it. He returned morally fresh, strong, and perfectly happy, and he could not tell what he had been thinking about all the time. Were they ideas, memories, or dreams that had been flitting through his mind? They were frequently all three. He would rouse himself and ask what he had been thinking about; and would see himself as a Cossack working in a vineyard with his Cossack wife, or an *abrek* in the mountains, or a boar running away from himself. And all the time he kept peering and watching for a pheasant, a boar, or a deer.

In the evening Daddy Eróshka would be sure to be sitting with him. Vanyúsha would bring a jug of *chikhir*, and they would converse quietly, drink, and separate to go quite contentedly to bed. The next day he would again go shooting, again be healthily weary, again they would sit conversing and drink their fill, and again be happy. Sometimes on a holiday or day of rest Olénin spent the whole day at home. Then his chief occupation was watching Maryánka, whose every movement, without realizing it himself, he followed greedily from his window or his porch. He regarded Maryánka and loved her (so he thought) just as he loved the beauty of the mountains and the sky, and he had no thought of entering into any relations with her. It seemed to him that between him and her such relations as there were between her and the Cossack Lukáshka could not exist, and still less such as often existed between rich officers and other Cossack girls. It seemed to him that if he tried to do as his fellow officers did, he would exchange his complete enjoyment of contemplation for an abyss of suffering, disillusionment, and remorse. Besides, he had already achieved a triumph of self-sacrifice in connexion with her which had given him great pleasure, and above all he was in a way afraid of Maryánka and would not for anything have ventured to utter a word of love to her lightly.

Once during the summer, when Olénin had not gone out shooting but was sitting at home, quite unexpectedly a Moscow acquaintance, a very young man whom he had met in society, came in.

'Ah, *mon cher*, my dear fellow, how glad I was when I heard that you were here!' he began in his Moscow French, and he went on intermingling French words in his remarks. 'They said, "Olénin". What Olénin? and I was so pleased. . . . Fancy fate bringing us together here! Well, and how are you? How? Why?' and Prince Belétski told his whole story: how he had temporarily entered the regiment, how the Commander-in-Chief had offered to take him as an adjutant, and how he would take up the post after this campaign although personally he felt quite indifferent about it.

'Living here in this hole one must at least make a career – get a cross – or a rank – be transferred to the Guards. That is quite indispensable, not for myself but for the sake of my relations and friends. The prince received me very well; he is a very decent fellow,' said Belétski, and went on unceasingly. 'I have been recommended for the St. Anna Cross for the expedition. Now I shall stay here a bit until we start on the campaign. It's capital here. What women! Well, and how are you getting on? I was told by our captain, Stártsev you know, a kind-hearted stupid creature. ... Well, he said you were living like an awful savage, seeing no one! I quite understand you don't want to be mixed up with the set of officers we have here. I am so glad now you and I will be able to see something of one another. I have put up at the Cossack corporal's house. There is such a girl there. Ústenka! I tell you she's just charming.'

And more and more French and Russian words came pouring forth from that world which Olénin thought he had left for ever. The general opinion about Belétski was that he was a nice, good-natured fellow. Perhaps he really was; but in spite of his pretty, good-natured face, Olénin thought him extremely unpleasant. He seemed just to exhale that filthiness which Olénin had forsworn. What vexed him most was that he could not – had not the strength – abruptly to repulse this man who came from that world: as if that old world he used to belong to had an irresistible claim on him. Olénin felt angry with Belétski and with himself, yet against his wish he introduced French phrases into his own conversation, was interested in the Commander-in-Chief and in their Moscow acquaintances, and because in this Cossack village he and Belétski both spoke French, he spoke contemptuously of their fellow officers and of the Cossacks, and was friendly with Belétski, promising to visit him and inviting him to drop in to see him. Olénin however did not himself go to see Belétski.

Vanyúsha for his part approved of Belétski, remarking that he was a real gentleman.

Belétski at once adopted the customary life of a rich officer in a Cossack village. Before Olénin's eyes, in one month he came to be like an old resident of the village; he made the old men drunk, arranged evening parties, and himself went to parties arranged by the girls — bragged of his conquests, and even got so far that, for some unknown reason, the women and girls began calling him grandad, and the Cossacks, to whom a man who loved wine and women was clearly understandable, got used to him and even liked him better than they did Olénin, who was a puzzle to them.

Chapter XXIV

IT WAS five in the morning. Vanyúsha was in the porch heating the samovar, and using the leg of a long boot instead of bellows. Olénin had already ridden off to bathe in the Térek. (He had recently invented a new amusement: to swim his horse in the river.) His landlady was in her outhouse, and the dense smoke of the kindling fire rose from the chimney. The girl was milking the buffalo cow in the shed. 'Can't keep quiet, the damned thing!' came her impatient voice, followed by the rhythmical sound of milking.

From the street in front of the house horses' hoofs were heard clattering briskly, and Olénin, riding bareback on a handsome dark-grey horse which was still wet and shining, rode up to the gate. Maryánka's handsome head, tied round with a red kerchief, appeared from the shed and again disappeared. Olénin was wearing a red silk shirt, a white Circassian coat girdled with a strap which carried a dagger, and a tall cap. He sat his well-fed wet horse with a slightly conscious elegance and, holding his gun at his back, stooped to open the gate. His hair was still wet, and his face shone with youth and health. He thought himself handsome, agile, and like a brave; but he was mistaken. To any experienced Caucasian he was still only a soldier. When he noticed that the girl had put out her head he stooped with particular smartness, threw open the gate and, tightening the reins, swished his whip and entered the yard. 'Is tea ready, Vanyúsha?' he cried gaily, not looking at the door of the shed. He felt with pleasure how his fine horse, pressing down its flanks, pulling at the bridle and with every muscle quivering and with each foot ready to leap over the fence, pranced on the hard clay of the yard. '*C'est prêt,*' answered Vanyúsha. Olénin felt as if Maryánka's beautiful head was still looking out of the shed but he did not turn to look at her. As he jumped down from his horse he made an awkward movement and caught his gun against the porch, and turned a frightened look towards the shed, where there was no one to be seen and whence the sound of milking could still be heard.

Soon after he had entered the hut he came out again and sat down with his pipe and a book on the side of the porch which was not yet exposed to the rays of the sun. He meant not to go anywhere before dinner that day, and to write some long-postponed letters; but somehow he felt disinclined to leave his place in the porch, and he was as reluctant to go back into the hut as if it had been a prison. The housewife had heated her oven, and the girl, having driven the cattle, had come back and was collecting *kisyak* and heaping it up along the fence. Olénin went on reading, but did not understand a word of what was written in the book that lay open before him. He kept lifting his eyes from it and looking at the powerful young woman who was moving about. Whether she stepped into the moist morning shadow thrown by the house, or went out into the middle of the yard lit up by the joyous young light, so that the whole of her stately figure in its bright coloured garment gleamed in the sunshine and cast a black shadow – he always feared to lose any one of her movements. It delighted him to see how freely and gracefully her figure bent: into what folds her only garment, a pink smock, draped itself on her bosom and along her shapely legs; how she drew herself up and her tight-drawn smock showed the outline of her heaving bosom, how the soles of her narrow feet in her worn red slippers rested on the ground without altering their shape; how her strong arms with the sleeves rolled up, exerting the muscles, used the spade almost as if in anger, and how her deep dark eyes sometimes glanced at him. Though the delicate brows frowned, yet her eyes expressed pleasure and a knowledge of her own beauty.

'I say, Olénin, have you been up long?' said Belétski as he entered the yard dressed in the coat of a Caucasian officer.

'Ah, Belétski,' replied Olénin, holding out his hand. 'How is it you are out so early?'

'I had to. I was driven out; we are having a ball tonight. Maryánka, of course you'll come to Ústenka's?' he added, turning to the girl.

Olénin felt surprised that Belétski could address this woman so easily. But Maryánka, as though she had not heard him, bent her head, and throwing the spade across her shoulder went with her firm masculine tread towards the outhouse.

'She's shy, the wench is shy,' Belétski called after her. 'Shy of you,' he added as, smiling gaily, he ran up the steps of the porch.

'How is it you are having a ball and have been driven out?'

'It's at Ústenka's, at my landlady's, that the ball is, and you two are invited. A ball consists of a pie and a gathering of girls.'

'What should we do there?'

Belétski smiled knowingly and winked, jerking his head in the direction of the outhouse into which Maryánka had disappeared.

Olénin shrugged his shoulders and blushed.

'Well, really you are a strange fellow!' said he.

'Come now, don't pretend'

Olénin frowned, and Belétski noticing this smiled insinuatingly. 'Oh, come, what do you mean?' he said, 'living in the same house – and such a fine girl, a splendid girl, a perfect beauty'

'Wonderfully beautiful! I never saw such a woman before,' replied Olénin.

'Well then?' said Belétski, quite unable to understand the situation.

'It may be strange,' replied Olénin, 'but why should I not say what is true? Since I have lived here women don't seem to exist for me. And it is so good, really! Now what can there be in common between us and women like these? Eróshka — that's a different matter! He and I have a passion in common — sport.'

'There now! In common! And what have I in common with Amália Ivánovna? It's the same thing! You may say they're not very clean — that's another matter ... *À la guerre, comme à la guerre!* ...'

'But I have never known any Amália Ivánovas, and have never known how to behave with women of that sort,' replied Olénin. 'One cannot respect them, but these I do respect.'

'Well go on respecting them! Who wants to prevent you?'

Olénin did not reply. He evidently wanted to complete what he had begun to say. It was very near his heart.

'I know I am an exception ...' He was visibly confused. 'But my life has so shaped itself that I not only see no necessity to renounce my rules, but I could not live here, let alone live as happily as I am doing, were I to live as you do. Therefore I look for something quite different from what you look for.'

Belétski raised his eyebrows incredulously. 'Anyhow, come to me this evening; Maryánka will be there and I will make you acquainted. Do come, please! If you feel dull you can go away. Will you come?'

'I would come, but to speak frankly I am afraid of being seriously carried away.'

'Oh, oh, oh!' shouted Belétski. 'Only come, and I'll see that you aren't. Will you? On your word?'

'I would come, but really I don't understand what we shall do; what part we shall play!'

'Please, I beg of you. You will come?'

'Yes, perhaps I'll come,' said Olénin.

'Really now! Charming women such as one sees nowhere

else, and to live like a monk! What an idea! Why spoil your life and not make use of what is at hand? Have you heard that our company is ordered to Vozdvízhensk?'

'Hardly. I was told the 8th Company would be sent there,' said Olénin.

'No. I have had a letter from the adjutant there. He writes that the Prince himself will take part in the campaign. I am very glad I shall see something of him. I'm beginning to get tired of this place.'

'I hear we shall start on a raid soon.'

'I have not heard of it; but I have heard that Krinovítsin has received the Order of St. Anna for a raid. He expected a lieutenancy,' said Belétski laughing. 'He was let in! He has set off for headquarters.'

It was growing dusk and Olénin began thinking about the party. The invitation he had received worried him. He felt inclined to go, but what might take place there seemed strange, absurd, and even rather alarming. He knew that neither Cossack men nor older women, nor anyone besides the girls, were to be there. What was going to happen? How was he to behave? What would they talk about? What connexion was there between him and those wild Cossack girls? Belétski had told him of such curious, cynical, and yet rigid relations. It seemed strange to think that he would be there in the same hut with Maryánka and perhaps might have to talk to her. It seemed to him impossible when he remembered her majestic bearing. But Belétski spoke of it as if it were all perfectly simple. 'Is it possible that Belétski will treat Maryánka in the same way? That is interesting,' thought he. 'No, better not go. It's all so horrid, so vulgar, and above all – it leads to nothing!' But again he was worried by the question of what would take place; and besides he felt as if bound by a promise. He went out without having made up his mind one way or the other, but he walked as far as Belétski's, and went in there.

The hut in which Belétski lived was like Olénin's. It was raised nearly five feet from the ground on wooden piles, and had two rooms. In the first (which Olénin entered by the steep flight of steps) feather beds, rugs, blankets, and cushions were tastefully and handsomely arranged, Cossack fashion, along the main wall. On the side wall hung brass basins and weapons, while on the floor, under a bench, lay water-melons and pumpkins. In the second room there was a big brick oven, a table, and sectarian icons. It was here that Belétski was quartered, with his camp-bed and his pack and trunks. His weapons hung on the wall with a little rug behind them, and on the table were his toilet appliances and some portraits. A silk dressing-gown had been thrown on the bench. Belétski himself, clean and good-looking, lay on the bed in his underclothing, reading *Les Trois Mousquetaires*.

He jumped up.

'There, you see how I have arranged things. Fine! Well, it's good that you have come. They are working furiously. Do you know what the pie is made of? Dough with a stuffing of pork and grapes. But that's not the point. You just look at the commotion out there!'

And really, on looking out of the window they saw an unusual bustle going on in the hut. Girls ran in and out, now for one thing and now for another.

'Will it soon be ready?' cried Belétski.

'Very soon! Why? Is Grandad hungry?' and from the hut came the sound of ringing laughter.

Ústenka, plump, small, rosy, and pretty, with her sleeves turned up, ran into Belétski's hut to fetch some plates.

'Get away or I shall smash the plates!' she squeaked, escaping from Belétski. 'You'd better come and help,' she shouted to Olénin, laughing. 'And don't forget to get some refreshments for the girls.' ('Refreshments' meaning spice-bread and sweets.)

'And has Maryánka come?'

'Of course! She brought some dough.'

'Do you know,' said Belétski, 'if one were to dress Ústenka up and clean and polish her up a bit, she'd be better than all our beauties. Have you ever seen that Cossack woman who married a colonel; she was charming! Bór-sheva? What dignity! Where do they get it . . .'

'I have not seen Bórsheva, but I think nothing could be better than the costume they wear here.'

'Ah, I'm first-rate at fitting into any kind of life,' said Belétski with a sigh of pleasure. 'I'll go and see what they are up to.'

He threw his dressing-gown over his shoulders and ran out, shouting, 'And you look after the "refreshments".'

Olénin sent Belétski's orderly to buy spice-bread and honey; but it suddenly seemed to him so disgusting to give money (as if he were bribing someone) that he gave no definite reply to the orderly's question: 'How much spice-bread with peppermint, and how much with honey?'

'Just as you please.'

'Shall I spend all the money,' asked the old soldier impressively. 'The peppermint is dearer. It's sixteen kopeks.'

'Yes, yes, spend it all,' answered Olénin and sat down by the window, surprised that his heart was thumping as if he were preparing himself for something serious and wicked.

He heard screaming and shrieking in the girls' hut when Belétski went there, and a few moments later saw how he jumped out and ran down the steps, accompanied by shrieks, bustle, and laughter.

'Turned out,' he said.

A little later Ústenka entered and solemnly invited her visitors to come in: announcing that all was ready.

When they came into the room they saw that everything was really ready. Ústenka was rearranging the cushions along the wall. On the table, which was covered by a disproportionately small cloth, was a decanter of *chikhir* and some dried fish. The room smelt of dough and grapes. Some half dozen girls in smart tunics, with their heads not covered as usual with kerchiefs, were huddled together in a corner behind the oven, whispering, giggling, and spluttering with laughter.

'I humbly beg you to do honour to my patron saint,' said Ústenka, inviting her guests to the table.

Olénin noticed Maryánka among the group of girls, who without exception were all handsome, and he felt vexed and hurt that he met her in such vulgar and awkward circumstances. He felt stupid and awkward, and made up his mind to do what Belétski did. Belétski stepped to the table somewhat solemnly yet with confidence and ease, drank a glass of wine to Ústenka's health, and invited the others to do the same. Ústenka announced that girls don't drink.

'We might with a little honey,' exclaimed a voice from among the group of girls.

The orderly, who had just returned with the honey and spice-cakes, was called in. He looked askance (whether with envy or with contempt) at the gentlemen, who in his opinion were on the spree; and carefully and conscientiously handed over to them a piece of honeycomb and the cakes wrapped up in a piece of greyish paper, and began explaining circumstantially all about the price and the change, but Belétski sent him away.

Having mixed honey with wine in the glasses, and having lavishly scattered the three pounds of spice-cakes on the table, Belétski dragged the girls from their corners by force, made them sit down at the table, and began distributing the cakes among them. Olénin involuntarily noticed how Maryánka's sunburnt but small hand closed on two round peppermint nuts and one brown one, and that she did not know what to do with them. The conversation was halting and constrained, in spite of Ústenka's and Belétski's free and easy manner and their wish to enliven the company. Olénin faltered, and tried to think of something to say, feeling that he was exciting curiosity and perhaps provoking ridicule and infecting the others with his shyness. He blushed, and it seemed to him that Maryánka in particular was feeling uncomfortable. 'Most likely they are expecting us to give them some money,' thought he. 'How are we to do it? And how can we manage quickest to give it and get away?'

Chapter XXV

'How is it you don't know your own lodger?' said Belétski, addressing Maryánka.

'How is one to know him if he never comes to see us?' answered Maryánka, with a look at Olénin.

Olénin felt frightened, he did not know of what. He flushed and, hardly knowing what he was saying, remarked: 'I'm afraid of your mother. She gave me such a scolding the first time I went in.'

Maryánka burst out laughing.

'And so you were frightened?' she said, and glanced at him and turned away.

It was the first time Olénin had seen the whole of her beautiful face. Till then he had seen her with her kerchief covering her to the eyes. It was not for nothing that she was reckoned the beauty of the village. Ústenka was a pretty girl, small, plump, rosy, with merry brown eyes, and red lips which were perpetually smiling and chattering. Maryánka on the contrary was certainly not pretty but beautiful. Her features might have been considered too masculine and almost harsh had it not been for her tall stately figure, her powerful chest and shoulders, and especially the severe yet tender expression of her long dark eyes which were darkly shadowed beneath their black brows, and for the gentle expression of her mouth and smile. She rarely smiled, but her smile was always striking. She seemed to radiate virginal strength and health. All the girls were good-looking, but they themselves and Belétski, and the orderly when he brought in the spice-cakes, all involuntarily gazed at Maryánka, and anyone addressing the girls was sure to address her. She seemed a proud and happy queen among them.

Belétski, trying to keep up the spirit of the party, chattered incessantly, made the girls hand round *chikhir*, fooled about with them, and kept making improper remarks in French about Maryánka's beauty to Olénin, calling her 'yours' (*la vôtre*), and advising him to behave as he did himself. Olénin felt more and more uncomfortable. He was devising an excuse to get out and run away when Belétski announced that Ústenka, whose saint's day it was, must offer *chikhir* to everybody with a kiss. She consented on condition that they should put money on her plate, as is the custom at weddings.

'What fiend brought me to this disgusting feast?' thought Olénin, rising to go away.

'Where are you off to?'

'I'll fetch some tobacco,' he said, meaning to escape, but Belétski seized his hand.

'I have some money,' he said to him in French.

'One can't go away, one has to pay here,' thought Olénin bitterly, vexed at his own awkwardness. 'Can't I really behave like Belétski? I ought not to have come, but once I am here I must not spoil their fun. I must drink like a Cossack,' and taking the wooden bowl (holding about eight tumblers) he almost filled it with *chikhir* and drank it almost all. The girls looked at him, surprised and almost frightened, as he drank. It seemed to them strange and not right. Ústenka brought them another glass each, and kissed them both. 'There girls, now we'll have some fun,' she said, clinking on the plate the four rubles the men had put there.

Olénin no longer felt awkward, but became talkative.

'Now, Maryánka, it's your turn to offer us wine and a kiss,' said Belétski, seizing her hand.

'Yes, I'll give you such a kiss!' she said playfully, preparing to strike at him.

'One can kiss Grandad without payment,' said another girl.

'There's a sensible girl,' said Belétski, kissing the struggling girl. 'No, you must offer it,' he insisted, addressing Maryánka. 'Offer a glass to your lodger.'

And taking her by the hand he led her to the bench and sat her down beside Olénin.

'What a beauty,' he said, turning her head to see it in profile.

Maryánka did not resist but proudly smiling turned her long eyes towards Olénin.

'A beautiful girl,' repeated Belétski.

'Yes, see what a beauty I am,' Maryánka's look seemed to endorse. Without considering what he was doing Olénin embraced Maryánka and was going to kiss her, but she suddenly extricated herself, upsetting Belétski and pushing the top off the table, and sprang away towards the oven. There was much shouting and laughter. Then Belétski whispered something to the girls and suddenly they all ran out into the passage and locked the door behind them.

'Why did you kiss Belétski and won't kiss me?' asked Olénin.

'Oh, just so. I don't want to, that's all!' she answered, pouting and frowning. 'He's Grandad,' she added with a smile. She went to the door and began to bang at it. 'Why have you locked the door, you devils?'

'Well, let them be there and us here,' said Olénin, drawing closer to her.

She frowned, and sternly pushed him away with her hand. And again she appeared so majestically handsome to Olénin that he came to his senses and felt ashamed of what he was doing. He went to the door and began pulling at it himself.

'Belétski! Open the door! What a stupid joke!'

Maryánka again gave a bright happy laugh. 'Ah, you're afraid of me?' she said.

'Yes, you know you're as cross as your mother.'

'Spend more of your time with Eróshka; that will make the girls love you!' And she smiled, looking straight and close into his eyes.

He did not know what to reply. 'And if I were to come to see you – ' he let fall.

'That would be a different matter,' she replied, tossing her head.

At that moment Belétski pushed the door open, and Maryánka sprang away from Olénin and in doing so her thigh struck his leg.

'It's all nonsense what I have been thinking about – love and self-sacrifice and Lukáshka. Happiness is the one thing. He who is happy is right,' flashed through Olénin's mind, and with a strength unexpected to himself he seized and kissed the beautiful Maryánka on her temple and her cheek. Maryánka was not angry, but only burst into a loud laugh and ran out to the other girls.

That was the end of the party. Ústenka's mother, returned

from her work, gave all the girls a scolding, and turned them all out.

Chapter XXVI

'YES,' thought Olénin, as he walked home. 'I need only slacken the reins a bit and I might fall desperately in love with this Cossack girl.' He went to bed with these thoughts, but expected it all to blow over and that he would continue to live as before.

But the old life did not return. His relations to Maryánka were changed. The wall that had separated them was broken down. Olénin now greeted her every time they met.

The master of the house having returned to collect the rent, on hearing of Olénin's wealth and generosity invited him to his hut. The old woman received him kindly, and from the day of the party onwards Olénin often went in of an evening and sat with them till late at night. He seemed to be living in the village just as he used to, but within him everything had changed. He spent his days in the forest, and towards eight o'clock, when it began to grow dusk, he would go to see his hosts, alone or with Daddy Eróshka. They grew so used to him that they were surprised when he stayed away. He paid well for his wine and was a quiet fellow. Vanyúsha would bring him his tea and he would sit down in a corner near the oven. The old woman did not mind him but went on with her work, and over their tea or their *chikhir* they talked about Cossack affairs, about the neighbours, or about Russia: Olénin relating and the others inquiring. Sometimes he brought a book and read to himself. Maryánka crouched like a wild goat with her feet drawn up under her, sometimes on the top of the oven, sometimes in a dark corner. She did not take part in the conversations, but Olénin saw her eyes and face and heard her moving or cracking sunflower seeds, and he felt that she listened with her whole being when he spoke, and was aware of his presence while he silently read to himself. Sometimes he thought her eyes were fixed on him, and meeting their radiance he involuntarily became silent and gazed at her. Then she would instantly hide her face and he would pretend to be deep in conversation with the old woman, while he listened all the time to her breathing and to her every movement and waited for her to look at him again. In the presence of others she was generally bright and friendly with him, but when they were alone together she was shy and rough. Sometimes he came in before Maryánka had returned home. Suddenly he would hear her firm footsteps and catch a glimmer of her blue cotton smock at the open door. Then she would step into the middle of the hut, catch sight of him, and her eyes would give a scarcely perceptible kindly smile, and he would feel happy and frightened.

He neither sought for nor wished for anything from her, but every day her presence became more and more necessary to him.

Olénin had entered into the life of the Cossack village so fully that his past seemed quite foreign to him. As to the future, especially a future outside the world in which he was now living, it did not interest him at all. When he received letters from home, from relatives and friends, he was offended by the evident distress with which they regarded him as a lost man, while he in his village considered those as lost who did not live as he was living. He felt sure he would never repent of having broken away from his former surroundings and of having settled down in this village to such a solitary and original life. When out on expeditions, and when quartered at one of the forts, he felt happy too; but it was here, from under Daddy Eróshka's wing, from the forest and from his hut at the end of the village, and especially when he thought of Maryánka and Lukáshka, that he seemed to see the falseness of his former life. That falseness used to rouse his indignation even before, but now it seemed inexpressibly vile and ridiculous. Here he felt freer and freer every day and more and more of a man. The Caucasus now appeared entirely different to what his imagination had painted it. He had found nothing at all like his dreams, nor like the descriptions of the Caucasus he had heard and read.

'There are none of all those chestnut steeds, precipices, Amalet Beks, heroes or villains,' thought he. 'The people live as nature lives: they die, are born, unite, and more are born – they fight, eat and drink, rejoice and die, without any restrictions but those that nature imposes on sun and grass, on animal and tree. They have no other laws.' Therefore these people, compared to himself, appeared to him beautiful, strong, and free, and the sight of them made him feel ashamed and sorry for himself. Often it seriously occurred to him to throw up everything, to get registered as a Cossack, to buy a hut and cattle and marry a Cossack woman (only not Maryánka, whom he conceded to Lukáshka), and to live with Daddy Eróshka and go shooting and fishing with him, and go with the Cossacks on their expeditions. 'Why ever don't I do it? What am I waiting for?' he asked himself, and he egged himself on and shamed himself. 'Am I afraid of doing what I hold to be reasonable and right? Is the wish to be a simple Cossack, to live close to nature, not to injure anyone but even to do good to others, more stupid than my former dreams, such as those of becoming a minister of state or a colonel?' but a voice seemed to say that he should wait, and not take any decision. He was held back by a dim consciousness that he could not live altogether like Eróshka and Lukáshka because he had a different idea of happiness – he was held back by the thought that happiness lies in self-sacrifice. What he had done for Lukáshka continued to give him joy. He kept looking for occasions to sacrifice himself for others, but did not meet with them. Sometimes he forgot this newly discovered recipe for happiness and considered himself capable of identifying his life with Daddy Eróshka's, but then he quickly bethought himself and promptly clutched at the idea of conscious self-sacrifice, and from that basis looked calmly and proudly at all men and at their happiness.

Chapter XXVII

JUST BEFORE the vintage Lukáshka came on horseback to see Olénin. He looked more dashing than ever.

'Well? Are you getting married?' asked Olénin, greeting him merrily.

Lukáshka gave no direct reply.

'There, I've exchanged your horse across the river. This *is* a horse! A Kabardá horse from the Lov stud. I know horses.'

They examined the new horse and made him caracole about the yard. The horse really was an exceptionally fine one, a broad and long gelding, with glossy coat, thick silky tail, and the soft fine mane and crest of a thoroughbred. He was so well fed that 'you might go to sleep on his back' as Lukáshka expressed it. His hoofs, eyes, teeth, were exquisitely shaped and sharply outlined, as one only finds them in very pure-bred horses. Olénin could not help admiring the horse, he had not yet met with such a beauty in the Caucasus.

'And how it goes!' said Lukáshka, patting its neck. 'What a step! And so clever – he simply runs after his master.'

'Did you have to add much to make the exchange?' asked Olénin.

'I did not count it,' answered Lukáshka with a smile. 'I got him from a *kunak*.'

'A wonderfully beautiful horse! What would you take for it?' asked Olénin.

'I have been offered a hundred and fifty rubles for it, but I'll give it you for nothing,' said Lukáshka, merrily. 'Only say the word and it's yours. I'll unsaddle it and you may take it. Only give me some sort of a horse for my duties.'

'No, on no account.'

'Well then, here is a dagger I've brought you,' said Lukáshka, unfastening his girdle and taking out one of the two daggers which hung from it. 'I got it from across the river.'

'Oh, thank you!'

'And mother has promised to bring you some grapes herself.'

'That's quite unnecessary. We'll balance up some day. You see I don't offer you any money for the dagger!'

'How could you? We are *kunaks*. It's just the same as when Giréy Khan across the river took me into his home and said,

"Choose what you like!" So I took this sword. It's our custom.'

They went into the hut and had a drink.

'Are you staying here awhile?' asked Olénin.

'No, I have come to say good-bye. They are sending me from the cordon to a company beyond the Térek. I am going to-night with my comrade Nazárka.'

'And when is the wedding to be?'

'I shall be coming back for the betrothal, and then I shall return to the company again,' Lukáshka replied reluctantly.

'What, and see nothing of your betrothed?'

'Just so – what is the good of looking at her? When you go on campaign ask in our company for Lukáshka the Broad. But what a lot of boars there are in our parts! I've killed two. I'll take you.'

'Well, good-bye! Christ save you.'

Lukáshka mounted his horse, and without calling on Maryánka, rode caracoling down the street, where Nazárka was already awaiting him.

'I say, shan't we call round?' asked Nazárka, winking in the direction of Yámka's house.

'That's a good one!' said Lukáshka. 'Here, take my horse to her and if I don't come soon give him some hay. I shall reach the company by the morning anyway.'

'Hasn't the cadet given you anything more?'

'I am thankful to have paid him back with a dagger – he was going to ask for the horse,' said Lukáshka, dismounting and handing over the horse to Nazárka.

He darted into the yard past Olénin's very window, and came up to the window of the cornet's hut. It was already quite dark. Maryánka, wearing only her smock, was combing her hair preparing for bed.

'It's I – ' whispered the Cossack.

Maryánka's look was severely indifferent, but her face suddenly brightened up when she heard her name. She opened the window and leant out, frightened and joyous.

'What – what do you want?' she said.

'Open!' uttered Lukáshka. 'Let me in for a minute. I am so sick of waiting! It's awful!'

He took hold of her head through the window and kissed her.

'Really, do open!'

'Why do you talk nonsense? I've told you I won't! Have you come for long?'

He did not answer but went on kissing her, and she did not ask again.

'There, through the window one can't even hug you properly,' said Lukáshka.

'Maryánka dear!' came the voice of her mother, 'who is that with you?'

Lukáshka took off his cap, which might have been seen, and crouched down by the window.

'Go, be quick!' whispered Maryánka.

'Lukáshka called round,' she answered; 'he was asking for Daddy.'

'Well then send him here!'

'He's gone; said he was in a hurry.'

In fact, Lukáshka, stooping, as with big strides he passed under the windows, ran out through the yard and towards Yámka's house unseen by anyone but Olénin. After drinking two bowls of *chikhir* he and Nazárka rode away to the outpost. The night was warm, dark, and calm. They rode in silence, only the footfall of their horses was heard. Lukáshka started a song about the Cossack, Mingál, but stopped before he had finished the first verse, and after a pause, turning to Nazárka, said:

'I say, she wouldn't let me in!'

'Oh?' rejoined Nazárka. 'I knew she wouldn't. D'you know what Yámka told me? The cadet has begun going to their house. Daddy Eróshka brags that he got a gun from the cadet for getting him Maryánka.'

'He lies, the old devil!' said Lukáshka, angrily. 'She's not such a girl. If he does not look out I'll wallop that old devil's sides,' and he began his favourite song:

'From the village of Izmáylov,
  From the master's favourite garden,
  Once escaped a keen-eyed falcon.
Soon after him a huntsman came a-riding,
  And he beckoned to the falcon that had strayed,
  But the bright-eyed bird thus answered:
"In gold cage you could not keep me,
On your hand you could not hold me,
  So now I fly to blue seas far away.
There a white swan I will kill,
Of sweet swan-flesh have my fill." '

Chapter XXVIII

THE BETROTHAL was taking place in the cornet's hut. Lukáshka had returned to the village, but had not been to see Olénin, and Olénin had not gone to the betrothal though he had been invited. He was sad as he had never been since he settled in this Cossack village. He had seen Lukáshka earlier in the evening and was worried by the question why Lukáshka was so cold towards him. Olénin shut himself up in his hut and began writing in his diary as follows:

'Many things have I pondered over lately and much have I changed,' wrote he, 'and I have come back to the copybook maxim: The one way to be happy is to love, to love self-denyingly, to love everybody and everything; to spread a web of love on all sides and to take all who come into it. In this way I caught Vanyúsha, Daddy Eróshka, Lukáshka, and Maryánka.'

As Olénin was finishing this sentence Daddy Eróshka entered the room.

Eróshka was in the happiest frame of mind. A few evenings before this, Olénin had gone to see him and had found him with a proud and happy face deftly skinning the carcass of a boar with a small knife in the yard. The dogs (Lyam his pet among them) were lying close by watching what he was doing and gently wagging their tails. The little boys were respectfully looking at him through the fence and not even teasing him as was their wont. His women neighbours, who were as a rule not too gracious towards him, greeted him and brought him, one a jug of *chikhir*, another some clotted cream, and a third a little flour. The next day Eróshka sat in his store-room all covered with blood, and distributed pounds of boar-flesh, taking in payment money from some and wine from others. His face clearly expressed, 'God has sent me luck. I have killed a boar, so now I am wanted.' Consequently, he naturally began to drink, and had gone on for four days never leaving the village. Besides which he had had something to drink at the betrothal.

He came to Olénin quite drunk: his face red, his beard tangled, but wearing a new *beshmet* trimmed with gold braid; and he brought with him a *balaláyka* which he had obtained beyond the river. He had long promised Olénin this treat, and felt in the mood for it, so that he was sorry to find Olénin writing.

'Write on, write on, my lad,' he whispered, as if he thought that a spirit sat between him and the paper and must not be frightened away, and he softly and silently sat down on the floor. When Daddy Eróshka was drunk his favourite position was on the floor. Olénin looked round, ordered some wine to be brought, and continued to write. Eróshka found it dull to drink by himself and he wished to talk.

'I've been to the betrothal at the cornet's. But there! They're shwine! – Don't want them! – Have come to you.'

'And where did you get your *balaláyka*?' asked Olénin, still writing.

'I've been beyond the river and got it there, brother mine,' he answered, also very quietly. 'I'm a master at it. Tartar or Cossack, squire or soldiers' songs, any kind you please.'

Olénin looked at him again, smiled, and went on writing.

That smile emboldened the old man.

'Come, leave off, my lad, leave off!' he said with sudden firmness.

'Well, perhaps I will.'

'Come, people have injured you but leave them alone, spit

at them! Come, what's the use of writing and writing, what's the good?'

And he tried to mimic Olénin by tapping the floor with his thick fingers, and then twisted his big face to express contempt.

'What's the good of writing quibbles. Better have a spree and show you're a man!'

No other conception of writing found place in his head except that of legal chicanery.

Olénin burst out laughing and so did Eróshka. Then, jumping up from the floor, the latter began to show off his skill on the *balaláyka* and to sing Tartar songs.

'Why write, my good fellow! You'd better listen to what I'll sing to you. When you're dead you won't hear any more songs. Make merry now!'

First he sang a song of his own composing accompanied by a dance:

> 'Ah, dee, dee, dee, dee, dee, dim,
> Say where did they last see him?
> In a booth, at the fair,
> He was selling pins, there.'

Then he sang a song he had learnt from his former sergeant-major:

> 'Deep I fell in love on Monday,
> Tuesday nothing did but sigh,
> Wednesday I popped the question,
> Thursday waited her reply.
> Friday, late, it came at last,
> Then all hope for me was past!
> Saturday my life to take
> I determined like a man,
> But for my salvation's sake
> Sunday morning changed my plan!'

Then he sang again:

> 'Oh dee, dee, dee, dee, dee, dim,
> Say where did they last see him?'

And after that, winking, twitching his shoulders, and footing it to the tune, he sang:

> 'I will kiss you and embrace,
> Ribbons red twine round you;
> And I'll call you little Grace.
> Oh, you little Grace now do
> Tell me, do you love me true?'

And he became so excited that with a sudden dashing movement he started dancing around the room accompanying himself the while.

Songs like 'Dee, dee, dee' – 'gentlemen's songs' – he sang for Olénin's benefit, but after drinking three more tumblers of *chikhir* he remembered old times and began singing real Cossack and Tartar songs. In the midst of one of his favourite songs his voice suddenly trembled and he ceased singing, and only continued strumming on the *balaláyka*.

'Oh, my dear friend!' he said.

The peculiar sound of his voice made Olénin look round.

The old man was weeping. Tears stood in his eyes and one tear was running down his cheek.

'You are gone, my young days, and will never come back!' he said, blubbering and halting. 'Drink, why don't you drink!' he suddenly shouted with a deafening roar, without wiping away his tears.

There was one Tartar song that specially moved him. It had few words, but its charm lay in the sad refrain. 'Ay day, dalalay!' Eróshka translated the words of the song: 'A youth drove his sheep from the *aoul* to the mountains: the Russians came and burnt the *aoul*, they killed all the men and took all the women into bondage. The youth returned from the mountains. Where the *aoul* had stood was an empty space; his mother not there, nor his brothers, nor his house; one tree alone was left standing. The youth sat beneath the tree and wept. "Alone like thee, alone am I left,"' and Eróshka began singing: 'Ay day, dalalay!' and the old man repeated several times this wailing, heart-rending refrain.

When he had finished the refrain Eróshka suddenly seized

a gun that hung on the wall, rushed hurriedly out into the yard and fired off both barrels into the air. Then again he began, more dolefully, his 'Ay day, dalalay – ah, ah, ' and ceased.

Olénin followed him into the porch and looked up into the starry sky in the direction where the shots had flashed. In the cornet's house there were lights and the sound of voices. In the yard girls were crowding round the porch and the windows, and running backwards and forwards between the hut and the outhouse. Some Cossacks rushed out of the hut and could not refrain from shouting, re-echoing the refrain of Daddy Eróshka's song and his shots.

'Why are you not at the betrothal?' asked Olénin.

'Never mind them! Never mind them!' muttered the old man, who had evidently been offended by something there. 'Don't like them, I don't. Oh, those people! Come back into the hut! Let them make merry by themselves and we'll make merry by ourselves.'

Olénin went in.

'And Lukáshka, is he happy? Won't he come to see me?' he asked.

'What, Lukáshka? They've lied to him and said I am getting his girl for you,' whispered the old man. 'But what's the girl? She will be ours if we want her. Give enough money – and she's ours. I'll fix it up for you. Really!'

'No, Daddy, money can do nothing if she does not love me. You'd better not talk like that!'

'We are not loved, you and I. We are forlorn,' said Daddy Eróshka suddenly, and again he began to cry.

Listening to the old man's talk Olénin had drunk more than usual. 'So now my Lukáshka is happy,' thought he; yet he felt sad. The old man had drunk so much that evening that he fell down on the floor and Vanyúsha had to call soldiers in to help, and spat as they dragged the old man out. He was so angry with the old man for his bad behaviour that he did not even say a single French word.

Chapter XXIX

IT WAS August. For days the sky had been cloudless, the sun scorched unbearably and from early morning the warm wind raised a whirl of hot sand from the sand-drifts and from the road, and bore it in the air through the reeds, the trees, and the village. The grass and the leaves on the trees were covered with dust, the roads and dried-up salt marshes were baked so hard that they rang when trodden on. The water had long since subsided in the Térek and rapidly vanished and dried up in the ditches. The slimy banks of the pond near the village were trodden bare by the cattle and all day long you could hear the splashing of water and the shouting of girls and boys bathing. The sand-drifts and the reeds were already drying up in the steppes, and the cattle, lowing, ran into the fields in the day-time. The boars migrated into the distant reed-beds and to the hills beyond the Térek. Mosquitoes and gnats swarmed in thick clouds over the low lands and villages. The snow-peaks were hidden in grey mist. The air was rarefied and smoky. It was said that *abreks* had crossed the now shallow river and were prowling on this side of it. Every night the sun set in a glowing red blaze. It was the busiest time of the year. The villagers all swarmed in the melon-fields and the vineyards. The vineyards thickly overgrown with twining verdure lay in cool, deep shade. Everywhere between the broad translucent leaves, ripe, heavy, black clusters peeped out. Along the dusty road from the vineyards the creaking carts moved slowly, heaped up with black grapes. Clusters of them, crushed by the wheels, lay in the dirt. Boys and girls in smocks stained with grape-juice, with grapes in their hands and mouths, ran after their mothers. On the road you continually came across tattered labourers with baskets of grapes on their powerful shoulders; Cossack maidens, veiled with kerchiefs to their eyes, drove bullocks harnessed to carts laden high with grapes. Soldiers who happened to meet these carts asked for grapes, and the maidens, clambering up without stopping their carts, would take an armful of grapes and drop them into the skirts of the soldiers' coats. In some homesteads they had already begun pressing the grapes; and the smell of the emptied skins filled the air. One saw the blood-red troughs in the pent-houses in the yards and Nogáy labourers with their trousers rolled up and their legs stained with the juice. Grunting pigs gorged themselves with the empty skins and rolled about in them. The flat roofs of the outhouses were all spread over with the dark amber clusters drying in the sun. Daws and magpies crowded round the roofs, picking the seeds and fluttering from one place to another.

The fruits of the year's labour were being merrily gathered in, and this year the fruit was unusually fine and plentiful.

In the shady green vineyards amid a sea of vines, laughter, songs, merriment, and the voices of women were to be heard on all sides, and glimpses of their bright-coloured garments could be seen.

Just at noon Maryánka was sitting in their vineyard in the shade of a peach-tree, getting out the family dinner from under an unharnessed cart. Opposite her, on a spread-out horse-cloth, sat the cornet (who had returned from the school) washing his hands by pouring water on them from a little jug. Her little brother, who had just come straight out of the pond, stood wiping his face with his wide sleeves, and gazed anxiously at his sister and his mother and breathed deeply, awaiting his dinner. The old mother, with her sleeves rolled up over her strong sunburnt arms, was arranging grapes, dried fish, and clotted cream on a little low, circular Tartar table. The cornet wiped his hands, took off his cap, crossed himself, and moved nearer to the table. The boy seized the jug and eagerly began to drink. The mother and daughter crossed their legs under them and sat down by the table. Even in the shade it was intolerably hot. The air above the vineyard smelt unpleasant: the strong warm wind passing amid the branches brought no coolness, but only monotonously bent the tops of the pear, peach, and mulberry trees with which the vineyard was sprinkled. The cornet, having crossed himself once more, took a little jug of *chikhir* that stood behind him covered with a vine-leaf, and having had a drink from the mouth of the jug passed it to the old woman. He had nothing on over his shirt, which was unfastened at the neck and showed his shaggy muscular chest. His fine-featured cunning face looked cheerful; neither in his attitude nor in his words was his usual wiliness to be seen; he was cheerful and natural.

'Shall we finish the bit beyond the shed to-night?' he asked, wiping his wet beard.

'We'll manage it,' replied his wife, 'if only the weather does not hinder us. The Dëmkins have not half finished yet,' she added. 'Only Ústenka is at work there, wearing herself out.'

'What can you expect of them?' said the old man proudly.

'Here, have a drink, Maryánka dear!' said the old woman, passing the jug to the girl. 'God willing we'll have enough to pay for the wedding feast,' she added.

'That's not yet awhile,' said the cornet with a slight frown.

The girl hung her head.

'Why shouldn't we mention it?' said the old woman. 'The affair is settled, and the time is drawing near too.'

'Don't make plans beforehand,' said the cornet. 'Now we have the harvest to get in.'

'Have you seen Lukáshka's new horse?' asked the old woman. 'That which Dmítri Andréich Olénin gave him is gone – he's exchanged it.'

'No, I have not; but I spoke with the servant to-day,' said the cornet, 'and he said his master has again received a thousand rubles.'

'Rolling in riches, in short,' said the old woman.

The whole family felt cheerful and contented.

The work was progressing successfully. The grapes were more abundant and finer than they had expected.

After dinner Maryánka threw some grass to the oxen, folded her *beshmet* for a pillow, and lay down under the wagon on the juicy down-trodden grass. She had on only a red kerchief over her head and a faded blue print smock, yet she felt unbearably hot. Her face was burning, and she did not know where to put her feet, her eyes were moist with sleepiness and weariness, her lips parted involuntarily, and her chest heaved heavily and deeply.

The busy time of year had begun a fortnight ago and the continuous heavy labour had filled the girl's life. At dawn she jumped up, washed her face with cold water, wrapped herself in a shawl, and ran out barefoot to see to the cattle. Then she hurriedly put on her shoes and her *beshmet* and, taking a small bundle of bread, she harnessed the bullocks and drove away to the vineyards for the whole day. There she cut the grapes and carried the baskets with only an hour's interval for rest, and in the evening she returned to the village, bright and not tired, dragging the bullocks by a rope or driving them with a long stick. After attending to the cattle, she took some sunflower seeds in the wide sleeve of her smock and went to the corner of the street to crack them and have some fun with the other girls. But as soon as it was dusk she returned home, and after having supper with her parents and her brother in the dark outhouse, she went into the hut, healthy and free from care, and climbed onto the oven, where half drowsing she listened to their lodger's conversation. As soon as he went away she would throw herself down on her bed and sleep soundly and quietly till morning. And so it went on day after day. She had not seen Lukáshka since the day of their betrothal, but calmly awaited the wedding. She had got used to their lodger and felt his intent looks with pleasure.

Chapter XXX

ALTHOUGH there was no escape from the heat and the mosquitoes swarmed in the cool shadow of the wagons, and her little brother tossing about beside her kept pushing her, Maryánka having drawn her kerchief over her head was just falling asleep, when suddenly their neighbour Ústenka came running towards her and, diving under the wagon, lay down beside her.

'Sleep, girls, sleep!' said Ústenka, making herself comfortable under the wagon. 'Wait a bit,' she exclaimed, 'this won't do!'

She jumped up, plucked some green branches, and stuck them through the wheels on both sides of the wagon and hung her *beshmet* over them.

'Let me in,' she shouted to the little boy as she again crept under the wagon. 'Is this the place for a Cossack – with the girls? Go away!'

When alone under the wagon with her friend, Ústenka suddenly put both her arms round her, and clinging close to her began kissing her cheeks and neck.

'Darling, sweetheart,' she kept repeating, between bursts of shrill, clear laughter.

'Why, you've learnt it from Grandad,' said Maryánka, struggling. 'Stop it!'

And they both broke into such peals of laughter that Maryánka's mother shouted to them to be quiet.

'Are you jealous?' asked Ústenka in a whisper.

'What humbug! Let me sleep. What have you come for?'

But Ústenka kept on, 'I say! But I wanted to tell you such a thing.'

Maryánka raised herself on her elbow and arranged the kerchief which had slipped off.

'Well, what is it?'

'I know something about your lodger!'

'There's nothing to know,' said Maryánka.

'Oh, you rogue of a girl!' said Ústenka, nudging her with her elbow and laughing. 'Won't tell anything. Does he come to you?'

'He does. What of that?' said Maryánka with a sudden blush.

'Now I'm a simple lass. I tell everybody. Why should I pretend?' said Ústenka, and her bright rosy face suddenly became pensive. 'Whom do I hurt? I love him, that's all about it.'

'Grandad, do you mean?'

'Well, yes!'

'And the sin?'

'Ah, Maryánka! When is one to have a good time if not while one's still free? When I marry a Cossack I shall bear children and shall have cares. There now, when you get married to Lukáshka not even a thought of joy will enter your head: children will come, and work!'

'Well? Some who are married live happily. It makes no difference!' Maryánka replied quietly.

'Do tell me just this once what has passed between you and Lukáshka?'

'What has passed? A match was proposed. Father put it off for a year, but now it's been settled and they'll marry us in autumn.'

'But what did he say to you?' Maryánka smiled.

'What should he say? He said he loved me. He kept asking me to come to the vineyards with him.'

'Just see what pitch! But you didn't go, did you? And what a dare-devil he has become: the first among the braves. He makes merry out there in the army too! The other day our Kírka came home; he says: "What a horse Lukáshka's got in exchange!" But all the same I expect he frets after you. And what else did he say?'

'Must you know everything?' said Maryánka laughing. 'One night he came to my window tipsy, and asked me to let him in.'

'And you didn't let him?'

'Let him, indeed! Once I have said a thing I keep to it firm as a rock,' answered Maryánka seriously.

'A fine fellow! If he wanted her, no girl would refuse him.'

'Well, let him go to the others,' replied Maryánka proudly.

'You don't pity him?'

'I do pity him, but I'll have no nonsense. It is wrong.' Ústenka suddenly dropped her head on her friend's breast, seized hold of her, and shook with smothered laughter. 'You silly fool!' she exclaimed, quite out of breath. 'You don't want to be happy,' and she began tickling Maryánka.

'Oh, leave off!' said Maryánka, screaming and laughing. 'You've crushed Lazútka.'

'Hark at those young devils! Quite frisky! Not tired yet!' came the old woman's sleepy voice from the wagon.

'Don't want happiness,' repeated Ústenka in a whisper, insistently. 'But you are lucky, that you are! How they love you! You are so crusty, and yet they love you. Ah, if I were in your place I'd soon turn the lodger's head! I noticed him when you were at our house. He was ready to eat you with his eyes. What things Grandad has given me! And yours they say is the richest of the Russians. His orderly says they have serfs of their own.'

Maryánka raised herself, and after thinking a moment, smiled.

'Do you know what he once told me: the lodger I mean?' she said, biting a bit of grass. 'He said, "I'd like to be Lukáshka the Cossack, or your brother Lazútka – ." What do you think he meant?'

'Oh, just chattering what came into his head,' answered Ústenka. 'What does mine not say! Just as if he was possessed!'

Maryánka dropped her hand on her folded *beshmet*, threw her arm over Ústenka's shoulder, and shut her eyes.

'He wanted to come and work in the vineyard to-day: father invited him,' she said, and after a short silence she fell asleep.

Chapter XXXI

THE SUN had come out from behind the pear-tree that had shaded the wagon, and even through the branches that Ústenka had fixed up it scorched the faces of the sleeping girls. Maryánka woke up and began arranging the kerchief on her head. Looking about her, beyond the pear-tree she noticed their lodger, who with his gun on his shoulder stood talking to her father. She nudged Ústenka and smilingly pointed him out to her.

'I went yesterday and didn't find a single one,' Olénin was saying as he looked about uneasily, not seeing Maryánka through the branches.

'Ah, you should go out there in that direction, go right as by compasses, there in a disused vineyard denominated as the Waste, hares are always to be found,' said the cornet, having at once changed his manner of speech.

'A fine thing to go looking for hares in these busy times! You had better come and help us, and do some work with the girls,' the old woman said merrily. 'Now then, girls, up with you!' she cried.

Maryánka and Ústenka under the cart were whispering and could hardly restrain their laughter.

Since it had become known that Olénin had given a horse worth fifty rubles to Lukáshka, his hosts had become more amiable and the cornet in particular saw with pleasure his daughter's growing intimacy with Olénin.

'But I don't know how to do the work,' replied Olénin, trying not to look through the green branches under the wagon where he had now noticed Maryánka's blue smock and red kerchief.

'Come, I'll give you some peaches,' said the old woman.

'It's only according to the ancient Cossack hospitality. It's her old woman's silliness,' said the cornet, explaining and apparently correcting his wife's words. 'In Russia, I expect, it's not so much peaches as pineapple jam and preserves you have been accustomed to eat at your pleasure.'

'So you say hares are to be found in the disused vineyard?' asked Olénin. 'I will go there,' and throwing a hasty glance through the green branches he raised his cap and disappeared between the regular rows of green vines.

The sun had already sunk behind the fence of the vineyards, and its broken rays glittered through the translucent leaves when Olénin returned to his host's vineyard. The wind was falling and a cool freshness was beginning to spread around. By some instinct Olénin recognized from afar Maryánka's blue smock among the rows of vine, and, picking grapes on his way, he approached her. His highly excited dog also now and then seized a low-hanging cluster of grapes in his slobbering mouth. Maryánka, her face flushed, her sleeves rolled up, and her kerchief down below her chin, was rapidly cutting the heavy clusters and laying them in a basket. Without letting go of the vine she had hold of, she stopped to smile pleasantly at him and resumed her work. Olénin drew near and threw his gun behind his back to have his hands free. 'Where are your people? May God aid you! Are you alone?' he meant to say but did not say, and only raised his cap in silence.

He was ill at ease alone with Maryánka, but as if purposely to torment himself he went up to her.

'You'll be shooting the women with your gun like that,' said Maryánka.

'No, I shan't shoot them.'

They were both silent.

Then after a pause she said: 'You should help me.'

He took out his knife and began silently to cut off the clusters. He reached from under the leaves low down a thick bunch weighing about three pounds, the grapes of which grew so close that they flattened each other for want of space. He showed it to Maryánka.

'Must they all be cut? Isn't this one too green?'

'Give it here.'

Their hands touched. Olénin took her hand, and she looked at him smiling.

'Are you going to be married soon?' he asked.

She did not answer, but turned away with a stern look.

'Do you love Lukáshka?'

'What's that to you?'

'I envy him!'

'Very likely!'

'No really. You are so beautiful!'

And he suddenly felt terribly ashamed of having said it, so commonplace did the words seem to him. He flushed, lost control of himself, and seized both her hands.

'Whatever I am, I'm not for you. Why do you make fun of me?' replied Maryánka, but her look showed how certainly she knew he was not making fun.

'Making fun? If you only knew how I –'

The words sounded still more commonplace, they accorded still less with what he felt, but yet he continued, 'I don't know what I would not do for you –'

'Leave me alone, you pitch!'

But her face, her shining eyes, her swelling bosom, her shapely legs, said something quite different. It seemed to him that she understood how petty were all things he had said, but that she was superior to such considerations. It seemed to him she had long known all he wished and was not able to tell her, but wanted to hear how he would say it. 'And how can she help knowing,' he thought, 'since I only want to tell her all that she herself is? But she does not wish to understand, does not wish to reply.'

'Hallo!' suddenly came Ústenka's high voice from behind the vine at no great distance, followed by her shrill laugh. 'Come and help me, Dmítri Andréich. I am all alone,' she cried, thrusting her round, naïve little face through the vines.

Olénin did not answer nor move from his place.

Maryánka went on cutting and continually looked up at Olénin. He was about to say something, but stopped, shrugged his shoulders and, having jerked up his gun, walked out of the vineyard with rapid strides.

Chapter XXXII

HE STOPPED once or twice, listening to the ringing laughter of Maryánka and Ústenka who, having come together, were shouting something. Olénin spent the whole evening hunting in the forest and returned home at dusk without having killed anything. When crossing the road he noticed her open the door of the outhouse, and her blue smock showed through it. He called to Vanyúsha very loud so as to let her know that he was back, and then sat down in the porch in his usual place. His hosts now returned from the vineyard; they came out of the outhouse and into their hut, but did not ask him in. Maryánka went twice out of the gate. Once in the twilight it seemed to him that she was looking at him. He eagerly followed her every movement, but could not make up his mind to approach her. When she disappeared into the hut he left the porch and began pacing up and down the yard, but Maryánka did not come out again. Olénin spent the whole sleepless night out in the yard listening to every sound in his hosts' hut. He heard them talking early in the evening, heard them having their supper and pulling out their cushions, and going to bed; he heard Maryánka laughing at something, and then heard everything growing gradually quiet. The cornet and his wife talked a while in whispers, and someone was breathing. Olénin re-entered his hut. Vanyúsha lay asleep in his clothes. Olénin envied him, and again went out to pace the yard, always expecting something, but no one came, no one moved, and he only heard the regular breathing of three people. He knew Maryánka's breathing and listened to it and to the beating of his own heart. In the village everything was quiet. The waning moon rose late, and the deep-breathing cattle in the yard became more visible as they lay down and slowly rose. Olénin angrily asked himself, 'What is it I want?' but could not tear himself away from the enchantment of the night. Suddenly he thought he distinctly heard the floor creak and the sound of footsteps in his hosts' hut. He rushed to the door, but all was silent again except for the sound of regular breathing, and in the yard the buffalo-cow, after a deep sigh, again moved, rose on her foreknees and then on her feet, swished her tail, and something splashed steadily on the dry clay ground; then she lay down again in the dim moonlight. He asked himself: 'What am I to do?' and definitely decided to go to bed, but again he heard a sound, and in his imagination there arose the image of Maryánka coming out into this moonlit misty night, and again he rushed to her window and again heard the sound of footsteps. Not till just before dawn did he go up to her window and push at the shutter and then run to the door, and this time he really heard Maryánka's deep breathing and her footsteps. He took hold

of the latch and knocked. The floor hardly creaked under the
bare cautious footsteps which approached the door. The
latch clicked, the door creaked, and he noticed a faint smell
of marjoram and pumpkin, and Maryánka's whole figure
appeared in the doorway. He saw her only for an instant in
the moonlight. She slammed the door and, muttering something, ran lightly back again. Olénin began rapping softly
but nothing responded. He ran to the window and listened.
Suddenly he was startled by a shrill, squeaky man's voice.

'Fine!' exclaimed a rather small young Cossack in a white
cap, coming across the yard close to Olénin. 'I saw ... fine!'

Olénin recognized Nazárka, and was silent, not knowing
what to do or say.

'Fine! I'll go and tell them at the office, and I'll tell her
father! That's a fine cornet's daughter! One's not enough for
her.'

'What do you want of me, what are you after?' uttered
Olénin.

'Nothing; only I'll tell them at the office.'

Nazárka spoke very loud, and evidently did so intentionally, adding: 'Just see what a clever cadet!'

Olénin trembled and grew pale.

'Come here, here!' He seized the Cossack firmly by the
arm and drew him towards his hut.

'Nothing happened, she did not let me in, and I too mean
no harm. She is an honest girl –'

'Eh, discuss –'

'Yes, but all the same I'll give you something now. Wait a
bit!'

Nazárka said nothing. Olénin ran into his hut and brought
out ten rubles, which he gave to the Cossack.

'Nothing happened, but still I was to blame, so I give this!
– Only for God's sake don't let anyone know, for nothing
happened ... '

'I wish you joy,' said Nazárka laughing, and went away.

Nazárka had come to the village that night at Lukáshka's
bidding to find a place to hide a stolen horse, and now,
passing by on his way home, had heard the sound of

footsteps. When he returned next morning to his company he bragged to his chum, and told him how cleverly he had got ten rubles. Next morning Olénin met his hosts and they knew nothing about the events of the night. He did not speak to Maryánka, and she only laughed a little when she looked at him. Next night he also passed without sleep, vainly wandering about the yard. The day after he purposely spent shooting, and in the evening he went to see Belétski to escape from his own thoughts. He was afraid of himself, and promised himself not to go to his hosts' hut any more.

That night he was roused by the sergeant-major. His company was ordered to start at once on a raid. Olénin was glad this had happened, and thought he would not again return to the village.

The raid lasted four days. The commander, who was a relative of Olénin's, wished to see him and offered to let him remain with the staff, but this Olénin declined. He found that he could not live away from the village, and asked to be allowed to return to it. For having taken part in the raid he received a soldier's cross, which he had formerly greatly desired. Now he was quite indifferent about it, and even more indifferent about his promotion, the order for which had still not arrived. Accompanied by Vanyúsha he rode back to the cordon without any accident several hours in advance of the rest of the company. He spent the whole evening in his porch watching Maryánka, and he again walked about the yard, without aim or thought, all night.

Chapter XXXIII

IT WAS late when he awoke the next day. His hosts were no longer in. He did not go shooting, but now took up a book, and now went out into the porch, and now again re-entered the hut and lay down on the bed. Vanyúsha thought he was ill.

Towards evening Olénin got up, resolutely began writing, and wrote on till late at night. He wrote a letter, but did not post it because he felt that no one would have understood what he wanted to say, and besides it was not necessary that anyone but himself should understand it. This is what he wrote:

'I receive letters of condolence from Russia. They are afraid that I shall perish, buried in these wilds. They say about me: "He will become coarse; he will be behind the times in everything; he will take to drink, and who knows but that he may marry a Cossack girl." It was not for nothing, they say, that Ermólov declared: "Anyone serving in the Caucasus for ten years either becomes a confirmed drunkard or marries a loose woman." How terrible! Indeed it won't do for me to ruin myself when I might have the great happiness of even becoming the Countess B——'s husband, or a Court chamberlain, or a *Maréchal de noblesse* of my district. Oh, how repulsive and pitiable you all seem to me! You do not know what happiness is and what life is! One must taste life once in all its natural beauty, must see and understand what I see every day before me – those eternally unapproachable snowy peaks, and a majestic woman in that primitive beauty in which the first woman must have come from her creator's hands – and then it becomes clear who is ruining himself and who is living truly or falsely – you or I. If you only knew how despicable and pitiable you, in your delusions, seem to me! When I picture to myself – in place of my hut, my forests, and my love – those drawing-rooms, those women with their pomatum-greased hair eked out with false curls, those unnaturally grimacing lips, those hidden, feeble, distorted limbs, and that chatter of obligatory drawing-room conversation which has no right to the name – I feel unendurably revolted. I then see before me those obtuse faces, those rich eligible girls whose looks seem to say: "It's all right, you may come near though I am rich and eligible" – and that arranging and rearranging of seats, that shameless match-making and that eternal tittle-tattle and pretence; those rules – with whom to shake hands, to whom only to nod, with whom to converse (and all this done deliberately with a conviction of its inevitability), that continual ennui in the blood passing on from generation to generation. Try to understand or believe just this one thing: you need only see and comprehend what truth and beauty are, and all that you now say and think and all your wishes for me and for yourselves will fly to atoms! Happiness is being with nature, seeing her, and conversing with her. "He may even (God forbid) marry a common Cossack girl, and be quite lost socially" I can imagine them saying of me with sincere pity! Yet the one thing I desire is to be quite "lost" in your sense of the word. I wish to marry a Cossack girl, and dare not because it would be a height of happiness of which I am unworthy.

'Three months have passed since I first saw the Cossack girl, Maryánka. The views and prejudices of the world I had left were still fresh in me. I did not then believe that I could love that woman. I delighted in her beauty just as I delighted in the beauty of the mountains and the sky, nor could I help delighting in her, for she is as beautiful as they. I found that the sight of her beauty had become a necessity of my life and I began asking myself whether I did not love her. But I could find nothing within myself at all like love as I had imagined it to be. Mine was not the restlessness of loneliness and desire for marriage, nor was it platonic, still less a carnal love such as I have experienced. I needed only to see her, to hear her, to know that she was near – and if I was not happy, I was at peace.

'After an evening gathering at which I met her and touched her, I felt that between that woman and myself there existed an indissoluble though unacknowledged bond against which I could not struggle, yet I did struggle. I asked myself: "Is it possible to love a woman who will never understand the profoundest interests of my life? Is it possible to love a woman simply for her beauty, to love the statue of a woman?" But I was already in love with her, though I did not yet trust to my feelings.

'After that evening when I first spoke to her our relations changed. Before that she had been to me an extraneous but majestic object of external nature: but since then she has become a human being. I began to meet her, to talk to her, and sometimes to go to work for her father and to spend whole evenings with them, and in this intimate intercourse she remained still in my eyes just as pure, inaccessible, and majestic. She always responded with equal calm, pride, and cheerful equanimity. Sometimes she was friendly, but generally her every look, every word, and every movement expressed equanimity – not contemptuous, but crushing and bewitching. Every day with a feigned smile on my lips I tried to play a part, and with torments of passion and desire in my heart I spoke banteringly to her. She saw that I was dissembling, but looked straight at me cheerfully and simply. This position became unbearable. I wished not to deceive her but to tell her all I thought and felt. I was extremely agitated. We were in the vineyard when I began to tell her of my love, in words I am now ashamed to remember. I am ashamed because I ought not to have dared to speak so to her because she stood far above such words and above the feeling they were meant to express. I said no more, but from that day my position has been intolerable. I did not wish to demean myself by continuing our former flippant relations, and at the same time I felt that I had not yet reached the level of straight and simple relations with her. I asked myself despairingly, "What am I to do?" In foolish dreams I imagined her now as my mistress and now as my wife, but rejected both ideas with disgust. To make her a wanton woman would be dreadful. It would be murder. To turn her into a fine lady, the wife of Dmítri Andréich Olénin, like a Cossack woman here who is married to one of our officers, would be still worse. Now could I turn Cossack like Lukáshka, and steal horses, get drunk on *chikhir*, sing rollicking songs, kill people, and when drunk climb in at her window for the night without a thought of who and what I am, it would be different: then we might understand one another and I might be happy.

'I tried to throw myself into that kind of life but was still more conscious of my own weakness and artificiality. I cannot forget myself and my complex, distorted past, and my future appears to me still more hopeless. Every day I have before me the distant snowy mountains and this majestic, happy woman. But not for me is the only happiness possible in the world; I cannot have this woman! What is most terrible and yet sweetest in my condition is that I feel that I understand her but that she will never understand me; not because she is inferior: on the contrary she ought not to understand me. She is happy, she is like nature: consistent, calm, and self-contained; and I, a weak distorted being, want her to understand my deformity and my torments! I have not slept at night, but have aimlessly passed under her windows not rendering account to myself of what was happening to me. On the 18th our company started on a raid, and I spent three days away from the village. I was sad and apathetic, the usual songs, cards, drinking-bouts, and talk of rewards in the regiment, were more repulsive to me than usual. Yesterday I returned home and saw her, my hut, Daddy Eróshka, and the snowy mountains, from my porch, and was seized by such a strong, new feeling of joy that I understood it all. I love this woman; I feel real love for the first and only time in my life. I know what has befallen me. I do not fear to be degraded by this feeling, I am not ashamed of my love, I am proud of it. It is not my fault that I love. It has come about against my will. I tried to escape from my love by self-renunciation, and tried to devise a joy in the Cossack Lukáshka's and Maryánka's love, but thereby only stirred up my own love and jealousy. This is not the ideal, the so-called exalted love which I have known before; not that sort of attachment in which you admire your own love and feel that the source of your emotion is within yourself and do everything yourself. I have felt that too. It is still less a desire for enjoyment: it is something different. Perhaps in her I love nature: the person-ification of all that is beautiful in nature; but yet I am not acting by my own will, but some elemental force loves through me; the whole of God's world, all nature, presses this love into my soul and says, "Love her." I love her not with my mind or my imagination, but with my whole being. Loving her I feel myself to be an integral part of all

God's joyous world. I wrote before about the new convictions to which my solitary life had brought me, but no one knows with what labour they shaped themselves within me and with what joy I realized them and saw a new way of life opening out before me; nothing was dearer to me than those convictions ... Well! ... love has come and neither they nor any regrets for them remain! It is even difficult for me to believe that I could prize such a one-sided, cold, and abstract state of mind. Beauty came and scattered to the winds all that laborious inward toil, and no regret remains for what has vanished! Self-renunciation is all nonsense and absurdity! That is pride, a refuge from well-merited unhappiness, and salvation from the envy of others' happiness: "Live for others, and do good!" – Why? when in my soul there is only love for myself and the desire to love her and to live her life with her? Not for others, not for Lukáshka, I now desire happiness. I do not now love those others. Formerly I should have told myself that this is wrong. I should have tormented myself with the questions: What will become of her, of me, and of Lukáshka? Now I don't care. I do not live my own life, there is something stronger than me which directs me. I suffer; but formerly I was dead and only now do I live. To-day I will go to their house and tell her everything.'

Chapter XXXIV

LATE THAT evening, after writing this letter, Olénin went to his hosts' hut. The old woman was sitting on a bench behind the oven unwinding cocoons. Maryánka with her head uncovered sat sewing by the light of a candle. On seeing Olénin she jumped up, took her kerchief and stepped to the oven.

'Maryánka dear,' said her mother, 'won't you sit here with me a bit?'

'No, I'm bareheaded,' she replied, and sprang up on the oven.

Olénin could only see a knee, and one of her shapely legs hanging down from the oven. He treated the old woman to tea. She treated her guest to clotted cream which she sent Maryánka to fetch. But having put a plateful on the table Maryánka again sprang on the oven from whence Olénin felt her eyes upon him. They talked about household matters. Granny Ulítka became animated and went into raptures of hospitality. She brought Olénin preserved grapes and a grape tart and some of her best wine, and pressed him to eat and drink with the rough yet proud hospitality of country folk, only found among those who produce their bread by the labour of their own hands. The old woman, who had at first struck Olénin so much by her rudeness, now often touched him by her simple tenderness towards her daughter.

'Yes, we need not offend the Lord by grumbling! We have enough of everything, thank God. We have pressed sufficient *chikhir* and have preserved and shall sell three or four barrels of grapes and have enough left to drink. Don't be in a hurry to leave us. We will make merry together at the wedding.'

'And when is the wedding to be?' asked Olénin, feeling his blood suddenly rush to his face while his heart beat irregularly and painfully.

He heard a movement on the oven and the sound of seeds being cracked.

'Well, you know, it ought to be next week. We are quite ready,' replied the old woman, as simply and quietly as though Olénin did not exist. 'I have prepared and have procured everything for Maryánka. We will give her away properly. Only there's one thing not quite right. Our Lukáshka has been running rather wild. He has been too much on the spree! He's up to tricks! The other day a Cossack came here from his company and said he had been to Nogáy.'

'He must mind he does not get caught,' said Olénin.

'Yes, that's what I tell him. "Mind, Lukáshka, don't you get into mischief. Well, of course, a young fellow naturally wants to cut a dash. But there's a time for everything. Well, you've captured or stolen something and killed an *abrek*! Well, you're a fine fellow! But now you should live quietly for a bit, or else there'll be trouble."'

'Yes, I saw him a time or two in the division, he was always merry-making. He has sold another horse,' said Olénin, and glanced towards the oven.

A pair of large, dark, and hostile eyes glittered as they gazed severely at him.

He became ashamed of what he had said. 'What of it? He does no one any harm,' suddenly remarked Maryánka. 'He makes merry with his own money,' and lowering her legs she jumped down from the oven and went out banging the door.

Olénin followed her with his eyes as long as she was in the hut, and then looked at the door and waited, understanding nothing of what Granny Ulítka was telling him.

A few minutes later some visitors arrived: an old man, Granny Ulítka's brother, with Daddy Eróshka, and following them came Maryánka and Ústenka.

'Good evening,' squeaked Ústenka. 'Still on holiday?' she added, turning to Olénin.

'Yes, still on holiday,' he replied, and felt, he did not know why, ashamed and ill at ease.

He wished to go away but could not. It also seemed to him impossible to remain silent. The old man helped him by asking for a drink, and they had a drink. Olénin drank with Eróshka, with the other Cossack, and again with Eróshka, and the more he drank the heavier was his heart. But the two old men grew merry. The girls climbed onto the oven, where they sat whispering and looking at the men, who drank till it was late. Olénin did not talk, but drank more than the others. The Cossacks were shouting. The old woman would not let them have any more *chikhir*, and at last turned them out. The girls laughed at Daddy Eróshka, and it was past ten when they all went out into the porch. The old men invited themselves to finish their merry-making at Olénin's. Ústenka ran off home and Eróshka led the old Cossack to Vanyúsha. The old woman went out to tidy up the shed. Maryánka remained alone in the hut. Olénin felt fresh and joyous, as if he had only just woke up. He noticed everything, and having let the old men pass ahead he turned back to the hut where Maryánka was preparing for bed. He went up to her and wished to say something, but his voice broke. She moved away from him, sat down cross-legged on her bed in the corner, and looked at him silently with wild and frightened eyes. She was evidently afraid of him. Olénin felt this. He felt sorry and ashamed of himself, and at the same time proud and pleased that he aroused even that feeling in her.

'Maryánka!' he said. 'Will you never take pity on me? I can't tell you how I love you.'

She moved still farther away.

'Just hear how the wine is speaking! . . . You'll get nothing from me!'

'No, it is not the wine. Don't marry Lukáshka. I will marry you.' ('What am I saying,' he thought as he uttered these words. 'Shall I be able to say the same to-morrow?' 'Yes, I shall, I am sure I shall, and I will repeat them now,' replied an inner voice.)

'Will you marry me?'

She looked at him seriously and her fear seemed to have passed.

'Maryánka, I shall go out of my mind! I am not myself. I will do whatever you command,' and madly tender words came from his lips of their own accord.

'Now then, what are you drivelling about?' she interrupted, suddenly seizing the arm he was stretching towards her. She did not push his arm away but pressed it firmly with her strong hard fingers. 'Do gentlemen marry Cossack girls? Go away!'

'But will you? Everything . . .'

'And what shall we do with Lukáshka?' said she, laughing.

He snatched away the arm she was holding and firmly embraced her young body, but she sprang away like a fawn and ran barefoot into the porch: Olénin came to his senses and was terrified at himself. He again felt himself inexpressibly vile compared to her, yet not repenting for an instant of what he had said he went home, and without even glancing at the old men who were drinking in his room he lay down and fell asleep more soundly than he had done for a long time.

Chapter XXXV

THE NEXT day was a holiday. In the evening all the villagers, their holiday clothes shining in the sunset, were out in the street. That season more wine than usual had been produced, and the people were now free from their labours. In a month the Cossacks were to start on a campaign and in many families preparations were being made for weddings.

Most of the people were standing in the square in front of the Cossack Government Office and near the two shops, in one of which cakes and pumpkin seeds were sold, in the other kerchiefs and cotton prints. On the earth-embankment of the office-building sat or stood the old men in sober grey, or black coats without gold trimmings or any kind of ornament. They conversed among themselves quietly in measured tones, about the harvest, about the young folk, about village affairs, and about old times, looking with dignified equanimity at the younger generation. Passing by them, the women and girls stopped and bent their heads. The young Cossacks respectfully slackened their pace and raised their caps, holding them for a while over their heads. The old men then stopped speaking. Some of them watched the passers-by severely, others kindly, and in their turn slowly took off their caps and put them on again.

The Cossack girls had not yet started dancing their *khorovóds*, but having gathered in groups, in their bright-coloured *beshmets* with white kerchiefs on their heads pulled down to their eyes, they sat either on the ground or on the earth-banks about the huts sheltered from the oblique rays of the sun, and laughed and chattered in their ringing voices. Little boys and girls playing in the square sent their balls high up into the clear sky, and ran about squealing and shouting. The half-grown girls had started dancing their *khorovóds*, and were timidly singing in their thin shrill voices. Clerks, lads not in the service, or home for the holiday, bright-faced and wearing smart white or new red Circassian gold-trimmed coats, went about arm in arm in twos or threes from one group of women or girls to another, and stopped to joke and chat with the Cossack girls. The Armenian shopkeeper, in a gold-trimmed coat of fine blue cloth, stood at the open door through which piles of folded bright-coloured kerchiefs were visible and, conscious of his own importance and with the pride of an Oriental tradesman, waited for customers. Two red-bearded, barefooted Chéchens, who had come from beyond the Térek to see the fête, sat on their heels outside the house of a friend, negligently smoking their little pipes and occasionally spitting, watching the villagers and exchanging remarks with one another in their rapid guttural speech. Occasionally a workaday-looking soldier in an old overcoat passed across the square among the bright-clad girls. Here and there the songs of tipsy Cossacks who were merry-making could already be heard. All the huts were closed; the porches had been scrubbed clean the day before. Even the old women were out in the street, which was everywhere sprinkled with pumpkin and melon seed-shells. The air was warm and still, the sky deep and clear. Beyond the roofs the dead-white mountain range, which seemed very near, was turning rosy in the glow of the evening sun. Now and then from the other side of the river came the distant roar of a cannon, but above the village, mingling with one another, floated all sorts of merry holiday sounds.

Olénin had been pacing the yard all that morning hoping to see Maryánka. But she, having put on holiday clothes, went to Mass at the chapel and afterwards sat with the other girls on an earth-embankment cracking seeds; sometimes again, together with her companions, she ran home, and each time gave the lodger a bright and kindly look. Olénin felt afraid to address her playfully or in the presence of others. He wished to finish telling her what he had begun to say the night before, and to get her to give him a definite answer. He waited for another moment like that of yesterday evening, but the moment did not come, and he felt that he could not remain any longer in this uncertainty. She went out into the street again, and after waiting awhile he too went out and without knowing where he was going he followed her. He passed by the corner where she was sitting in her shining blue satin *beshmet*, and with an aching heart he heard behind him the girls laughing.

Belétski's hut looked out onto the square. As Olénin was passing it he heard Belétski's voice calling to him, 'Come in,' and in he went.

After a short talk they both sat down by the window and were soon joined by Eróshka, who entered dressed in a new *beshmet* and sat down on the floor beside them.

'There, that's the aristocratic party,' said Belétski, pointing with his cigarette to a brightly coloured group at the corner. 'Mine is there too. Do you see her? in red. That's a new *beshmet*. Why don't you start the *khorovód*?' he shouted, leaning out of the window. 'Wait a bit, and then when it grows dark let us go too. Then we will invite them to Ústenka's. We must arrange a ball for them!'

'And I will come to Ústenka's,' said Olénin in a decided tone. 'Will Maryánka be there?'

'Yes, she'll be there. Do come!' said Belétski, without the least surprise. 'But isn't it a pretty picture?' he added, pointing to the motley crowds.

'Yes, very!' Olénin assented, trying to appear indifferent. 'Holidays of this kind,' he added, 'always make me wonder why all these people should suddenly be contented and jolly. To-day for instance, just because it happens to be the fifteenth of the month, everything is festive. Eyes and faces and voices and movements and garments, and the air and the sun, are all in a holiday mood. And we no longer have any holidays!'

'Yes,' said Belétski, who did not like such reflections.

'And why are you not drinking, old fellow?' he said, turning to Eróshka.

Eróshka winked at Olénin, pointing to Belétski. 'Eh, he's a proud one that *kunak* of yours,' he said.

Belétski raised his glass. '*Allah birdy*' he said, emptying it. (*Allah birdy*, 'God has given!' – the usual greeting of Caucasians when drinking together.)

'*Sau bul*' ('Your health'), answered Eróshka smiling, and emptied his glass.

'Speaking of holidays!' he said, turning to Olénin as he rose and looked out of the window, 'What sort of holiday is that! You should have seen them make merry in the old days! The women used to come out in their gold-trimmed *sarafáns*. Two rows of gold coins hanging round their necks and gold-cloth diadems on their heads, and when they passed they made a noise, "flu, flu," with their dresses. Every woman looked like a princess. Sometimes they'd come out, a whole herd of them, and begin singing songs so that the air seemed to rumble, and they went on making merry all night. And the Cossacks would roll out a barrel into the yards and sit down and drink till break of day, or they would go hand-in-hand sweeping the village. Whoever they met they seized and took along with them, and went from house to house. Sometimes they used to make merry for three days on end. Father used to come home – I still remember it – quite red and swollen, without a cap, having lost everything: he'd come and lie down. Mother knew what to do: she would bring him some fresh caviar and a little *chikhir* to sober him up, and would herself run about in the village looking for his cap. Then he'd sleep for two days! That's the sort of fellows they were then! But now what are they?'

'Well, and the girls in the *sarafáns*, did they make merry all by themselves?' asked Belétski.

'Yes, they did! Sometimes Cossacks would come on foot or on horse and say, "Let's break up the *khorovóds*," and they'd go, but the girls would take up cudgels. Carnival week, some young fellow would come galloping up, and they'd cudgel his horse and cudgel him too. But he'd break through, seize the one he loved, and carry her off. And his sweetheart would love him to his heart's content! Yes, the girls in those days, they were regular queens!'

Chapter XXXVI

JUST THEN two men rode out of the side street into the

square. One of them was Nazárka. The other, Lukáshka, sat slightly sideways on his well-fed bay Kabardá horse which stepped lightly over the hard road jerking its beautiful head with its fine glossy mane. The well-adjusted gun in its cover, the pistol at his back, and the cloak rolled up behind his saddle showed that Lukáshka had not come from a peaceful place or from one near by. The smart way in which he sat a little sideways on his horse, the careless motion with which he touched the horse under its belly with his whip, and especially his half-closed black eyes, glistening as he looked proudly around him, all expressed the conscious strength and self-confidence of youth. 'Ever seen as fine a lad?' his eyes, looking from side to side, seemed to say. The elegant horse with its silver ornaments and trappings, the weapons, and the handsome Cossack himself attracted the attention of everyone in the square. Nazárka, lean and short, was much less well dressed. As he rode past the old men, Lukáshka paused and raised his curly white sheepskin cap above his closely cropped black head.

'Well, have you carried off many Nogáy horses?' asked a lean old man with a frowning, lowering look.

'Have you counted them, Grandad, that you ask?' replied Lukáshka, turning away.

'That's all very well, but you need not take my lad along with you,' the old man muttered with a still darker frown.

'Just see the old devil, he knows everything,' muttered Lukáshka to himself, and a worried expression came over his face; but then, noticing a corner where a number of Cossack girls were standing, he turned his horse towards them.

'Good evening, girls!' he shouted in his powerful, resonant voice, suddenly checking his horse. 'You've grown old without me, you witches!' and he laughed.

'Good evening, Lukáshka! Good evening, laddie!' the merry voices answered. 'Have you brought much money? Buy some sweets for the girls! ... Have you come for long? True enough, it's long since we saw you....'

'Nazárka and I have just flown across to make a night of

it,' replied Lukáshka, raising his whip and riding straight at the girls.

'Why, Maryánka has quite forgotten you,' said Ústenka, nudging Maryánka with her elbow and breaking into a shrill laugh.

Maryánka moved away from the horse and throwing back her head calmly looked at the Cossack with her large sparkling eyes.

'True enough, you have not been home for a long time! Why are you trampling us under your horse?' she remarked dryly, and turned away.

Lukáshka had appeared particularly merry. His face shone with audacity and joy. Obviously staggered by Maryánka's cold reply he suddenly knitted his brow.

'Step up on my stirrup and I'll carry you away to the mountains, Mammy!' he suddenly exclaimed, and as if to disperse his dark thoughts he caracoled among the girls. Stooping down towards Maryánka, he said, 'I'll kiss, oh, how I'll kiss you! . . .'

Maryánka's eyes met his and she suddenly blushed and stepped back.

'Oh, bother you! you'll crush my feet,' she said, and bending her head looked at her well-shaped feet in their tightly fitting light blue stockings with clocks and her new red slippers trimmed with narrow silver braid.

Lukáshka turned towards Ústenka, and Maryánka sat down next to a woman with a baby in her arms. The baby stretched his plump little hands towards the girl and seized a necklace string that hung down onto her blue *beshmet*. Maryánka bent towards the child and glanced at Lukáshka from the corner of her eyes. Lukáshka just then was getting out from under his coat, from the pocket of his black *beshmet*, a bundle of sweetmeats and seeds.

'There, I give them to all of you,' he said, handing the bundle to Ústenka and smiling at Maryánka.

A confused expression again appeared on the girl's face. It was as though a mist gathered over her beautiful eyes. She drew her kerchief down below her lips, and leaning her head over the fair-skinned face of the baby that still held her by her coin necklace she suddenly began to kiss it greedily. The baby pressed his little hands against the girl's high breasts, and opening his toothless mouth screamed loudly.

'You're smothering the boy!' said the little one's mother, taking him away; and she unfastened her *beshmet* to give him the breast. 'You'd better have a chat with the young fellow.'

'I'll only go and put up my horse and then Nazárka and I will come back; we'll make merry all night,' said Lukáshka, touching his horse with his whip and riding away from the girls.

Turning into a side street, he and Nazárka rode up to two huts that stood side by side.

'Here we are all right, old fellow! Be quick and come soon!' called Lukáshka to his comrade, dismounting in front of one of the huts; then he carefully led his horse in at the gate of the wattle fence of his own home.

'How d'you do, Stëpka?' he said to his dumb sister, who, smartly dressed like the others, came in from the street to take his horse; and he made signs to her to take the horse to the hay, but not to unsaddle it.

The dumb girl made her usual humming noise, smacked her lips as she pointed to the horse and kissed it on the nose, as much as to say that she loved it and that it was a fine horse.

'How d'you do, Mother? How is it that you have not gone out yet?' shouted Lukáshka, holding his gun in place as he mounted the steps of the porch.

His old mother opened the door.

'Dear me! I never expected, never thought, you'd come,' said the old woman. 'Why, Kírka said you wouldn't be here.'

'Go and bring some *chikhir*, Mother. Nazárka is coming here and we will celebrate the feast day.'

'Directly, Lukáshka, directly!' answered the old woman. 'Our women are making merry. I expect our dumb one has gone too.'

She took her keys and hurriedly went to the outhouse.

Nazárka, after putting up his horse and taking the gun off his shoulder, returned to Lukáshka's house and went in.

Chapter XXXVII

'YOUR HEALTH!' said Lukáshka, taking from his mother's hands a cup filled to the brim with *chikhir* and carefully raising it to his bowed head.

'A bad business!' said Nazárka. 'You heard how Daddy Burlák said, "Have you stolen many horses?" He seems to know!'

'A regular wizard!' Lukáshka replied shortly. 'But what of it!' he added, tossing his head. 'They are across the river by now. Go and find them!'

'Still it's a bad lookout.'

'What's a bad lookout? Go and take some *chikhir* to him to-morrow and nothing will come of it. Now let's make merry. Drink!' shouted Lukáshka, just in the tone in which old Eróshka uttered the word. 'We'll go out into the street and make merry with the girls. You go and get some honey; or no, I'll send our dumb wench. We'll make merry till morning.'

Nazárka smiled.

'Are we stopping here long?' he asked.

'Till we've had a bit of fun. Run and get some vodka. Here's the money.'

Nazárka ran off obediently to get the vodka from Yámka's.

Daddy Eróshka and Ergushóv, like birds of prey, scenting where the merry-making was going on, tumbled into the hut one after the other, both tipsy.

'Bring us another half-pail,' shouted Lukáshka to his mother, by way of reply to their greeting.

'Now then, tell us where did you steal them, you devil?' shouted Eróshka. 'Fine fellow, I'm fond of you!'

'Fond indeed ...' answered Lukáshka laughing, 'carrying sweets from cadets to lasses! Eh, you old ...'

'That's not true, not true! ... Oh, Mark,' and the old man

burst out laughing. 'And how that devil begged me. "Go,"
he said, "and arrange it." He offered me a gun! But no. I'd
have managed it, but I feel for you. Now tell us where have
you been?' And the old man began speaking in Tartar.

Lukáshka answered him promptly.

Ergushóv, who did not know much Tartar, only occasionally put in a word in Russian:

'What I say is he's driven away the horses. I know it for a
fact,' he chimed in.

'Giréy and I went together.' (His speaking of Giréy Khan
as 'Giréy' was, to the Cossack mind, evidence of his bold-
ness.) 'Just beyond the river he kept bragging that he knew
the whole of the steppe and would lead the way straight, but
we rode on and the night was dark, and my Giréy lost his
way and began wandering in a circle without getting
anywhere: couldn't find the village, and there we were. We
must have gone too much to the right. I believe we
wandered about well-nigh till midnight. Then, thank goodness, we heard dogs howling.'

'Fools!' said Daddy Eróshka. 'There now, we too used to
lose our way in the steppe. (Who the devil can follow it?)
But I used to ride up a hillock and start howling like the
wolves, like this!' He placed his hands before his mouth, and
howled like a pack of wolves, all on one note. 'The dogs
would answer at once. . . . Well, go on – so you found them?'

'We soon led them away! Nazárka was nearly caught by
some Nogáy women, he was!'

'Caught indeed,' Nazárka, who had just come back, said in
an injured tone.

'We rode off again, and again Giréy lost his way and
almost landed us among the sand-drifts. We thought we
were just getting to the Térek but we were riding away from
it all the time!'

'You should have steered by the stars,' said Daddy
Eróshka.

'That's what I say,' interjected Ergushóv,

'Yes, steer when all is black; I tried and tried all about. . .
and at last I put the bridle on one of the mares and let my

own horse go free – thinking he'll lead us out, and what do you think! he just gave a snort or two with his nose to the ground, galloped ahead, and led us straight to our village. Thank goodness! It was getting quite light. We barely had time to hide them in the forest. Nagím came across the river and took them away.'

Ergushóv shook his head. 'It's just what I said. Smart. Did you get much for them?'

'It's all here,' said Lukáshka, slapping his pocket.

Just then his mother came into the room, and Lukáshka did not finish what he was saying.

'Drink!' he shouted.

'We too, Gírich and I, rode out late one night . . .' began Eróshka.

'Oh bother, we'll never hear the end of you!' said Lukáshka. 'I am going.' And having emptied his cup and tightened the strap of his belt he went out.

Chapter XXXVIII

IT WAS already dark when Lukáshka went out into the street. The autumn night was fresh and calm. The full golden moon floated up behind the tall dark poplars that grew on one side of the square. From the chimneys of the outhouses smoke rose and spread above the village, mingling with the mist. Here and there lights shone through the windows, and the air was laden with the smell of *kisyak*, grape-pulp, and mist. The sounds of voices, laughter, songs, and the cracking of seeds mingled just as they had done in the daytime, but were now more distinct. Clusters of white kerchiefs and caps gleamed through the darkness near the houses and by the fences.

In the square, before the shop door which was lit up and open, the black and white figures of Cossack men and maids showed through the darkness, and one heard from afar their loud songs and laughter and talk. The girls, hand in hand, went round and round in a circle stepping lightly in the dusty square. A skinny girl, the plainest of them all, set the tune:

'From beyond the wood, from the forest dark,
From the garden green and the shady park,
There came out one day two young lads so gay.
Young bachelors, hey! brave and smart were they!
And they walked and walked, then stood still, each man,
And they talked and soon to dispute began!
Then a maid came out; as she came along,
Said, "To one of you I shall soon belong!"
'Twas the fair-faced lad got the maiden fair,
Yes, the fair-faced lad with the golden hair!
Her right hand so white in his own took he,
And he led her round for his mates to see!
And said, "Have you ever in all your life,
Met a lass as fair as my sweet little wife?" '

The old women stood round listening to the songs. The little boys and girls ran about chasing one another in the dark. The men stood by, catching at the girls as the latter moved round, and sometimes breaking the ring and entering it. On the dark side of the doorway stood Belétski and Olénin, in their Circassian coats and sheepskin caps, and talked together in a style of speech unlike that of the Cossacks, in low but distinct tones, conscious that they were attracting attention. Next to one another in the *khorovód* circle moved plump little Ústenka in her red *beshmet* and the stately Maryánka in her new smock and *beshmet*. Olénin and Belétski were discussing how to snatch Ústenka and Maryánka out of the ring. Belétski thought that Olénin wished only to amuse himself, but Olénin was expecting his fate to be decided. He wanted at any cost to see Maryánka alone that very day and to tell her everything, and ask her whether she could and would be his wife. Although that question had long been answered in the negative in his own mind, he hoped he would be able to tell her all he felt, and that she would understand him.

'Why did you not tell me sooner?' said Belétski. 'I would have got Ústenka to arrange it for you. You are such a queer fellow! ...'

'What's to be done! ... Some day, very soon, I'll tell you

all about it. Only now, for Heaven's sake, arrange so that she should come to Ústenka's.'

'All right, that's easily done! Well, Maryánka, will you belong to the "fair-faced lad", and not to Lukáshka?' said Belétski, speaking to Maryánka first for propriety's sake, but having received no reply he went up to Ústenka and begged her to bring Maryánka home with her. He had hardly time to finish what he was saying before the leader began another song and the girls started pulling each other round in the ring by the hand.

They sang:

'Past the garden, by the garden,
A young man came strolling down,
Up the street and through the town.
And the first time as he passed
He did wave his strong right hand.
As the second time he passed
Waved his hat with silken band.
But the third time as he went
He stood still: before her bent.

"How is it that thou, my dear,
My reproaches dost not fear?
In the park don't come to walk
That we there might have a talk?
Come now, answer me, my dear,
Dost thou hold me in contempt?
Later on, thou knowest, dear,
Thou'lt get sober and repent.
Soon to woo thee I will come,
And when we shall married be
Thou wilt weep because of me!"

"Though I knew what to reply,
Yet I dared not him deny,
No, I dared not him deny!
So into the park went I,
In the park my lad to meet,
There my dear one I did greet."

"Maiden dear, I bow to thee!
Take this handkerchief from me.

In thy white hand take it, see!
Say I am beloved by thee.
I don't know at all, I fear,
What I am to give thee, dear!
To my dear I think I will
Of a shawl a present make —
And five kisses for it take."'

Lukáshka and Nazárka broke into the ring and started walking about among the girls. Lukáshka joined in the singing, taking seconds in his clear voice as he walked in the middle of the ring swinging his arms. 'Well, come in, one of you!' he said. The other girls pushed Maryánka, but she would not enter the ring. The sound of shrill laughter, slaps, kisses, and whispers mingled with the singing.

As he went past Olénin, Lukáshka gave a friendly nod.

'Dmítri Andréich! Have you too come to have a look?' he said.

'Yes,' answered Olénin dryly.

Belétski stooped and whispered something into Ústenka's ear. She had not time to reply till she came round again, when she said:

'All right, we'll come.'

'And Maryánka too?'

Olénin stooped towards Maryánka. 'You'll come? Please do, if only for a minute. I must speak to you.'

'If the other girls come, I will.'

'Will you answer my question?' said he, bending towards her. 'You are in good spirits to-day.'

She had already moved past him. He went after her.

'Will you answer?'

'Answer what?'

'The question I asked you the other day,' said Olénin, stooping to her ear. 'Will you marry me?'

Maryánka thought for a moment.

'I'll tell you,' said she, 'I'll tell you to-night.'

And through the darkness her eyes gleamed brightly and kindly at the young man.

He still followed her. He enjoyed stooping closer to her.

But Lukáshka, without ceasing to sing, suddenly seized her firmly by the hand and pulled her from her place in the ring of girls into the middle. Olénin had only time to say, 'Come to Ústenka's,' and stepped back to his companion. The song came to an end. Lukáshka wiped his lips, Maryánka did the same, and they kissed. 'No, no, kisses five!' said Lukáshka. Chatter, laughter, and running about, succeeded to the rhythmic movements and sound. Lukáshka, who seemed to have drunk a great deal, began to distribute sweetmeats to the girls.

'I offer them to everyone!' he said with proud, comically pathetic self-admiration. 'But anyone who goes after soldiers goes out of the ring!' he suddenly added, with an angry glance at Olénin.

The girls grabbed his sweetmeats from him, and, laughing, struggled for them among themselves. Belétski and Olénin stepped aside.

Lukáshka, as if ashamed of his generosity, took off his cap and wiping his forehead with his sleeve came up to Maryánka and Ústenka.

'Answer me, my dear, dost thou hold me in contempt?' he said in the words of the song they had just been singing, and turning to Maryánka he angrily repeated the words: 'Dost thou hold me in contempt? When we shall married be thou wilt weep because of me!' he added, embracing Ústenka and Maryánka both together.

Ústenka tore herself away, and swinging her arm gave him such a blow on the back that she hurt her hand.

'Well, are you going to have another turn?' he asked.

'The other girls may if they like,' answered Ústenka, 'but I am going home and Maryánka was coming to our house too.'

With his arm still round her, Lukáshka led Maryánka away from the crowd to the darker corner of a house.

'Don't go, Maryánka,' he said, 'let's have some fun for the last time. Go home and I will come to you!'

'What am I to do at home? Holidays are meant for merrymaking. I am going to Ústenka's,' replied Maryánka.

'I'll marry you all the same, you know!'

'All right,' said Maryánka, 'we shall see when the time comes.'

'So you are going,' said Lukáshka sternly, and, pressing her close, he kissed her on the cheek.

'There, leave off! Don't bother,' and Maryánka, wrenching herself from his arms, moved away.

'Ah my girl, it will turn out badly,' said Lukáshka reproachfully and stood still, shaking his head. 'Thou wilt weep because of me ...' and turning away from her he shouted to the other girls:

'Now then! Play away!'

What he had said seemed to have frightened and vexed Maryánka. She stopped, 'What will turn out badly?'

'Why, that!'

'That what?'

'Why, that you keep company with a soldier-lodger and no longer care for me!'

'I'll care just as long as I choose. You're not my father, nor my mother. What do you want? I'll care for whom I like!'

'Well, all right ...' said Lukáshka, 'but remember!' He moved towards the shop. 'Girls!' he shouted, 'why have you stopped? Go on dancing. Nazárka, fetch some more *chikhir*.'

'Well, will they come?' asked Olénin, addressing Belétski.

'They'll come directly,' replied Belétski. 'Come along, we must prepare the ball.'

Chapter XXXIX

IT WAS already late in the night when Olénin came out of Belétski's hut following Maryánka and Ústenka. He saw in the dark street before him the gleam of the girl's white kerchief. The golden moon was descending towards the steppe. A silvery mist hung over the village. All was still; there were no lights anywhere and one heard only the receding footsteps of the young women. Olénin's heart beat fast. The fresh moist atmosphere cooled his burning face. He glanced at the sky and turned to look at the hut he had just come out of: the candle was already out. Then he again peered through the darkness at the girls' retreating shadows. The white kerchief disappeared in the mist. He was afraid to remain alone, he was so happy. He jumped down from the porch and ran after the girls.

'Bother you, someone may see ...' said Ústenka.

'Never mind!'

Olénin ran up to Maryánka and embraced her.

Maryánka did not resist.

'Haven't you kissed enough yet?' said Ústenka. 'Marry and then kiss, but now you'd better wait.'

'Good-night, Maryánka. To-morrow I will come to see your father and tell him. Don't you say anything.'

'Why should I!' answered Maryánka.

Both the girls started running. Olénin went on by himself thinking over all that had happened. He had spent the whole evening alone with her in a corner by the oven. Ústenka had not left the hut for a single moment, but had romped about with the other girls and with Belétski all the time. Olénin had talked in whispers to Maryánka.

'Will you marry me?' he had asked.

'You'd deceive me and not have me,' she replied cheerfully and calmly.

'But do you love me? Tell me for God's sake!'

'Why shouldn't I love you? You don't squint,' answered Maryánka, laughing and with her hard hands squeezing his. ...

'What whi–ite, whi–i–ite, soft hands you've got – so like clotted cream,' she said.

'I am in earnest. Tell me, will you marry me?'

'Why not, if father gives me to you?'

'Well then remember, I shall go mad if you deceive me. To-morrow I will tell your mother and father. I shall come and propose.'

Maryánka suddenly burst out laughing.

'What's the matter?'

'It seems so funny!'

'It's true! I will buy a vineyard and a house and will enroll myself as a Cossack.'

'Mind you don't go after other women then. I am severe about that.'

Olénin joyfully repeated all these words to himself. The memory of them now gave him pain and now such joy that it took away his breath. The pain was because she had remained as calm as usual while talking to him. She did not seem at all agitated by these new conditions. It was as if she did not trust him and did not think of the future. It seemed to him that she only loved him for the present moment, and that in her mind there was no future with him. He was happy because her words sounded to him true, and she had consented to be his. 'Yes,' thought he to himself, 'we shall only understand one another when she is quite mine. For such love there are no words. It needs life – the whole of life. To-morrow everything will be cleared up. I cannot live like this any longer; to-morrow I will tell everything to her father, to Belétski, and to the whole village.'

Lukáshka, after two sleepless nights, had drunk so much at the fête that for the first time in his life his feet would not carry him, and he slept in Yámka's house.

Chapter XL

THE NEXT day Olénin awoke earlier than usual, and immediately remembered what lay before him, and he joyfully recalled her kisses, the pressure of her hard hands, and her words, 'What white hands you have!' He jumped up and wished to go at once to his hosts' hut to ask for their consent to his marriage with Maryánka. The sun had not yet risen, but it seemed that there was an unusual bustle in the street and side-street: people were moving about on foot and on horseback, and talking. He threw on his Circassian coat and hastened out into the porch. His hosts were not yet up. Five Cossacks were riding past and talking loudly together. In front rode Lukáshka on his broad-backed Kabardá horse.

The Cossacks were all speaking and shouting so that it was impossible to make out exactly what they were saying.

'Ride to the Upper Post,' shouted one.

'Saddle and catch us up, be quick,' said another.

'It's nearer through the other gate!'

'What are you talking about?' cried Lukáshka. 'We must go through the middle gates, of course.'

'So we must, it's nearer that way,' said one of the Cossacks who was covered with dust and rode a perspiring horse. Lukáshka's face was red and swollen after the drinking of the previous night and his cap was pushed to the back of his head. He was calling out with authority as though he were an officer.

'What is the matter? Where are you going?' asked Olénin, with difficulty attracting the Cossacks' attention.

'We are off to catch *abreks*. They're hiding among the sand-drifts. We are just off, but there are not enough of us yet.'

And the Cossacks continued to shout, more and more of them joining as they rode down the street. It occurred to Olénin that it would not look well for him to stay behind; besides he thought he could soon come back. He dressed, loaded his gun with bullets, jumped onto his horse which Vanyúsha had saddled more or less well, and overtook the Cossacks at the village gates. The Cossacks had dismounted, and filling a wooden bowl with *chikhir* from a little cask which they had brought with them, they passed the bowl round to one another and drank to the success of their expedition. Among them was a smartly dressed young cornet, who happened to be in the village and who took command of the group of nine Cossacks who had joined for the expedition. All these Cossacks were privates, and although the cornet assumed the airs of a commanding officer, they only obeyed Lukáshka. Of Olénin they took no notice at all, and when they had all mounted and started, and Olénin rode up to the cornet and began asking him what was taking place, the cornet, who was usually quite friendly, treated him with marked condescension. It was with great difficulty that Olénin managed to find out from him what was happening. Scouts who had been sent out to search for *abreks* had come upon several hillsmen some six miles from the village. These *abreks* had taken shelter in pits and had fired at the scouts, declaring they would not surrender. A corporal who had been scouting with two Cossacks had remained to watch the *abreks*, and had sent one Cossack back to get help.

The sun was just rising. Three miles beyond the village the steppe spread out and nothing was visible except the dry, monotonous, sandy, dismal plain covered with the foot-marks of cattle, and here and there with tufts of withered grass, with low reeds in the flats, and rare, little-trodden footpaths, and the camps of the nomad Nogáy tribe just visible far away. The absence of shade and the austere aspect of the place were striking. The sun always rises and sets red in the steppe. When it is windy whole hills of sand are carried by the wind from place to place.

When it is calm, as it was that morning, the silence, uninterrupted by any movement or sound, is peculiarly striking. That morning in the steppe it was quiet and dull, though the sun had already risen. It all seemed specially soft and desolate. The air was hushed, the footfalls and the snorting of the horses were the only sounds to be heard, and even they quickly died away.

The men rode almost silently. A Cossack always carries his weapons so that they neither jingle nor rattle. Jingling weapons are a terrible disgrace to a Cossack. Two other Cossacks from the village caught the party up and exchanged a few words. Lukáshka's horse either stumbled or caught its foot in some grass, and became restive – which is a sign of bad luck among the Cossacks, and at such a time was of special importance. The others exchanged glances and turned away, trying not to notice what had happened. Lukáskha pulled at the reins, frowned sternly, set his teeth, and flourished his whip above his head. His good Kabardá horse, prancing from one foot to another not knowing with which to start, seemed to wish to fly upwards on wings. But

Lukáshka hit its well-fed sides with his whip once, then again, and a third time, and the horse, showing its teeth and spreading out its tail, snorted and reared and stepped on its hind legs a few paces away from the others.

'Ah, a good steed that!' said the cornet.

That he said steed instead of *horse* indicated special praise.

'A lion of a horse,' assented one of the others, an old Cossack.

The Cossacks rode forward silently, now at a footpace, then at a trot, and these changes were the only incidents that interrupted for a moment the stillness and solemnity of their movements.

Riding through the steppe for about six miles, they passed nothing but one Nogáy tent, placed on a cart and moving slowly along at a distance of about a mile from them. A Nogáy family was moving from one part of the steppe to another. Afterwards they met two tattered Nogáy women with high cheekbones, who with baskets on their backs were gathering dung left by the cattle that wandered over the steppe. The cornet, who did not know their language well, tried to question them, but they did not understand him and, obviously frightened, looked at one another.

Lukáshka rode up to them both, stopped his horse, and promptly uttered the usual greeting. The Nogáy women were evidently relieved, and began speaking to him quite freely as to a brother.

'*Ay-ay, kop abrek!*' they said plaintively, pointing in the direction in which the Cossacks were going. Olénin understood that they were saying, 'Many *abreks.*'

Never having seen an engagement of that kind, and having formed an idea of them only from Daddy Eróshka's tales, Olénin wished not to be left behind by the Cossacks, but wanted to see it all. He admired the Cossacks, and was on the watch, looking and listening and making his own observations. Though he had brought his sword and a loaded gun with him, when he noticed that the Cossacks avoided him he decided to take no part in the action, as in his opinion his courage had already been sufficiently proved when he was with his detachment, and also because he was very happy.

Suddenly a shot was heard in the distance.

The cornet became excited, and began giving orders to the Cossacks as to how they should divide and from which side they should approach. But the Cossacks did not appear to pay any attention to these orders, listening only to what Lukáshka said and looking to him alone. Lukáshka's face and figure were expressive of calm solemnity. He put his horse to a trot with which the others were unable to keep pace, and screwing up his eyes kept looking ahead.

'There's a man on horseback,' he said, reining in his horse and keeping in line with the others.

Olénin looked intently, but could not see anything. The Cossacks soon distinguished two riders and quietly rode straight towards them.

'Are those the *abreks*?' asked Olénin.

The Cossacks did not answer his question, which appeared quite meaningless to them. The *abreks* would have been fools to venture across the river on horseback.

'That's friend Ródka waving to us, I do believe,' said Lukáshka, pointing to the two mounted men who were now clearly visible. 'Look, he's coming to us.'

A few minutes later it became plain that the two horsemen were the Cossack scouts. The corporal rode up to Lukáshka.

Chapter XLI

'ARE THEY FAR?' was all Lukáshka said.

Just then they heard a sharp shot some thirty paces off. The corporal smiled slightly.

'Our Gúrka is having shots at them,' he said, nodding in the direction of the shot.

Having gone a few paces farther they saw Gúrka sitting behind a sand-hillock and loading his gun. To while away the time he was exchanging shots with the *abreks*, who were behind another sand-heap. A bullet came whistling from their side.

The cornet was pale and grew confused. Lukáshka dismounted from his horse, threw the reins to one of the other Cossacks, and went up to Gúrka. Olénin also dismounted and, bending down, followed Lukáshka. They had hardly reached Gúrka when two bullets whistled above them. Lukáshka looked around laughing at Olénin and stooped a little.

'Look out or they will kill you, Dmítri Andréich,' he said. 'You'd better go away – you have no business here.' But Olénin wanted absolutely to see the *abreks*.

From behind the mound he saw caps and muskets some two hundred paces off. Suddenly a little cloud of smoke appeared from thence, and again a bullet whistled past. The *abreks* were hiding in a marsh at the foot of the hill. Olénin was much impressed by the place in which they sat. In reality it was very much like the rest of the steppe, but because the *abreks* sat there it seemed to detach itself from all the rest and to have become distinguished. Indeed it appeared to Olénin that it was the very spot for *abreks* to occupy. Lukáshka went back to his horse and Olénin followed him.

'We must get a hay-cart,' said Lukáshka, 'or they will be killing some of us. There behind that mound is a Nogáy cart with a load of hay.'

The cornet listened to him and the corporal agreed. The cart of hay was fetched, and the Cossacks, hiding behind it, pushed it forward. Olénin rode up a hillock from whence he could see everything. The hay-cart moved on and the Cossacks crowded together behind it. The Cossacks advanced, but the Chéchens, of whom there were nine, sat with their knees in a row and did not fire.

All was quiet. Suddenly from the Chéchens arose the sound of a mournful song, something like Daddy Eróshka's 'Ay day, dalalay.' The Chéchens knew that they could not escape, and to prevent themselves from being tempted to take to flight they had strapped themselves together, knee to knee, had got their guns ready, and were singing their death-song.

The Cossacks with their hay-cart drew closer and closer,

and Olénin expected the firing to begin at any moment, but the silence was only broken by the *abreks'* mournful song. Suddenly the song ceased; there was a sharp report, a bullet struck the front of the cart, and Chéchen curses and yells broke the silence and shot followed on shot and one bullet after another struck the cart. The Cossacks did not fire and were now only five paces distant.

Another moment passed and the Cossacks with a whoop rushed out on both sides from behind the cart – Lukáshka in front of them. Olénin heard only a few shots, then shouting and moans. He thought he saw smoke and blood, and abandoning his horse and quite beside himself he ran towards the Cossacks. Horror seemed to blind him. He could not make out anything, but understood that all was over. Lukáshka, pale as death, was holding a wounded Chéchen by the arms and shouting, 'Don't kill him. I'll take him alive!' The Chéchen was the red-haired man who had fetched his brother's body away after Lukáshka had killed him. Lukáshka was twisting his arms. Suddenly the Chéchen wrenched himself free and fired his pistol. Lukáshka fell, and blood began to flow from his stomach. He jumped up, but fell again, swearing in Russian and in Tartar. More and more blood appeared on his clothes and under him. Some Cossacks approached him and began loosening his girdle. One of them, Nazárka, before beginning to help, fumbled for some time, unable to put his sword in its sheath: it would not go the right way. The blade of the sword was blood-stained.

The Chéchens with their red hair and clipped moustaches lay dead and hacked about. Only the one we know of, who had fired at Lukáshka, though wounded in many places was still alive. Like a wounded hawk all covered with blood (blood was flowing from a wound under his right eye), pale and gloomy, he looked about him with wide-open excited eyes and clenched teeth as he crouched, dagger in hand, still prepared to defend himself. The cornet went up to him as if intending to pass by, and with a quick movement shot him in the ear. The Chéchen started up, but it was too late, and he fell.

The Cossacks, quite out of breath, dragged the bodies aside and took the weapons from them. Each of the red-haired Chéchens had been a man, and each one had his own individual expression. Lukáshka was carried to the cart. He continued to swear in Russian and in Tartar.

'No fear, I'll strangle him with my hands. *Anna seni!*' he cried, struggling. But he soon became quiet from weakness.

Olénin rode home. In the evening he was told that Lukáshka was at death's door, but that a Tartar from beyond the river had undertaken to cure him with herbs.

The bodies were brought to the village office. The women and the little boys hastened to look at them.

It was growing dark when Olénin returned, and he could not collect himself after what he had seen. But towards night memories of the evening before came rushing to his mind. He looked out of the window, Maryánka was passing to and fro from the house to the cowshed, putting things straight. Her mother had gone to the vineyard and her father to the office. Olénin could not wait till she had quite finished her work, but went out to meet her. She was in the hut standing with her back towards him. Olénin thought she felt shy.

'Maryánka,' said he, 'I say, Maryánka! May I come in?' She suddenly turned. There was a scarcely perceptible trace of tears in her eyes and her face was beautiful in its sadness. She looked at him in silent dignity.

Olénin again said:

'Maryánka, I have come —'

'Leave me alone!' she said. Her face did not change but the tears ran down her cheeks.

'What are you crying for? What is it?'

'What?' she repeated in a rough voice. 'Cossacks have been killed, that's what for.'

'Lukáshka?' said Olénin.

'Go away! What do you want?'

'Maryánka!' said Olénin, approaching her.

'You will never get anything from me!'

'Maryánka, don't speak like that,' Olénin entreated.

'Get away. I'm sick of you!' shouted the girl, stamping her

foot, and moved threateningly towards him. And her face expressed such abhorrence, such contempt, and such anger that Olénin suddenly understood that there was no hope for him, and that his first impression of this woman's inaccessibility had been perfectly correct.

Olénin said nothing more, but ran out of the hut.

Chapter XLII

FOR TWO hours after returning home he lay on his bed motionless. Then he went to his company commander and obtained leave to visit the staff. Without taking leave of anyone, and sending Vanyúsha to settle his accounts with his landlord, he prepared to leave for the fort where his regiment was stationed. Daddy Eróshka was the only one to see him off. They had a drink, and then a second, and then yet another. Again as on the night of his departure from Moscow, a three-horsed conveyance stood waiting at the door. But Olénin did not confer with himself as he had done then, and did not say to himself that all he had thought and done here was 'not it'. He did not promise himself a new life. He loved Maryánka more than ever, and knew that he could never be loved by her.

'Well, good-bye, my lad!' said Daddy Eróshka. 'When you go on an expedition, be wise and listen to my words – the words of an old man. When you are out on a raid or the like (you know I'm an old wolf and have seen things), and when they begin firing, don't get into a crowd where there are many men. When you fellows get frightened you always try to get close together with a lot of others. You think it is merrier to be with others, but that's where it is worst of all! They always aim at a crowd. Now I used to keep farther away from the others and went alone, and I've never been wounded. Yet what things haven't I seen in my day?'

'But you've got a bullet in your back,' remarked Vanyúsha, who was clearing up the room.

'That was the Cossacks fooling about,' answered Eróshka.

'Cossacks? How was that?' asked Olénin.

'Oh, just so. We were drinking. Vánka Sítkin, one of the Cossacks, got merry, and puff! he gave me one from his pistol just here.'

'Yes, and did it hurt?' asked Olénin. 'Vanyúsha, will you soon be ready?' he added.

'Ah, where's the hurry! Let me tell you. When he banged into me, the bullet did not break the bone but remained here. And I say: "You've killed me, brother. Eh! What have you done to me? I won't let you off! You'll have to stand me a pailful!"'

'Well, but did it hurt?' Olénin asked again, scarcely listening to the tale.

'Let me finish. He stood a pailful, and we drank it, but the blood went on flowing. The whole room was drenched and covered with blood. Grandad Burlák, he says, "The lad will give up the ghost. Stand a bottle of the sweet sort, or we shall have you taken up!" They bought more drink, and boozed and boozed –'

'Yes, but did it hurt you much?' Olénin asked once more.

'Hurt, indeed! Don't interrupt: I don't like it. Let me finish. We boozed and boozed till morning, and I fell asleep on the top of the oven, drunk. When I woke in the morning I could not unbend myself anyhow –'

'Was it very painful?' repeated Olénin, thinking that now he would at last get an answer to his question.

'Did I tell you it was painful? I did not say it was painful, but I could not bend and could not walk.'

'And then it healed up?' said Olénin, not even laughing, so heavy was his heart.

'It healed up, but the bullet is still there. Just feel it!' And lifting his shirt he showed his powerful back, where just near the bone a bullet could be felt and rolled about.

'Feel how it rolls,' he said, evidently amusing himself with the bullet as with a toy. 'There now, it has rolled to the back.'

'And Lukáshka, will he recover?' asked Olénin.

'Heaven only knows! There's no doctor. They've gone for one.'

'Where will they get one? From Gróznoe?' asked Olénin.

'No, my lad. Were I the Tsar I'd have hung all your Russian doctors long ago. Cutting is all they know! There's our Cossack Bakláshka, no longer a real man now that they've cut off his leg! That shows they're fools. What's Bakláshka good for now? No, my lad, in the mountains there are real doctors. There was my chum, Vórchik, he was on an expedition and was wounded just here in the chest. Well, your doctors gave him up, but one of theirs came from the mountains and cured him! They understand herbs, my lad!'

'Come, stop talking rubbish,' said Olénin. 'I'd better send a doctor from head-quarters.'

'Rubbish!' the old man said mockingly. 'Fool, fool! Rubbish. You'll send a doctor! – If yours cured people, Cossacks and Chéchens would go to you for treatment, but as it is your officers and colonels send to the mountains for doctors. Yours are all humbugs, all humbugs.'

Olénin did not answer. He agreed only too fully that all was humbug in the world in which he had lived and to which he was now returning.

'How is Lukáshka? You've been to see him?' he asked.

'He just lies as if he were dead. He does not eat nor drink. Vodka is the only thing his soul accepts. But as long as he drinks vodka it's well. I'd be sorry to lose the lad. A fine lad – a brave, like me. I too lay dying like that once. The old women were already wailing. My head was burning. They had already laid me out under the holy icons. So I lay there, and above me on the oven little drummers, no bigger than this, beat the tattoo. I shout at them and they drum all the harder.' (The old man laughed.) 'The women brought our church elder. They were getting ready to bury me. They said, "He defiled himself with worldly unbelievers; he made merry with women; he ruined people; he did not fast, and he played the *balaláyka*. Confess," they said. So I began to confess. "I've sinned!" I said. Whatever the priest said, I always answered "I've sinned." He began to ask me about the *balaláyka*. "Where is the accursed thing," he says. "Show it me and smash it." But I say, "I've not got it." I'd hidden it myself in a net in the outhouse. I knew they could not find it. So they left me. Yet after all I recovered. When I went for my *balaláyka* – What was I saying?' he continued. 'Listen to me, and keep farther away from the other men or you'll get killed foolishly. I feel for you, truly: you are a drinker – I love you! And fellows like you like riding up the mounds. There was one who lived here who had come from Russia, he always would ride up the mounds (he called the mounds so funnily, "hillocks"). Whenever he saw a mound, off he'd gallop. Once he galloped off that way and rode to the top quite pleased, but a Chéchen fired at him and killed him! Ah, how well they shoot from their gun-rests, those Chéchens! Some of them shoot even better than I do. I don't like it when a fellow gets killed so foolishly! Sometimes I used to look at your soldiers and wonder at them. There's foolishness for you! They go, the poor fellows, all in a clump, and even sew red collars to their coats! How can they help being hit! One gets killed, they drag him away and another takes his place! What foolishness!' the old man repeated, shaking his head. 'Why not scatter, and go one by one? So you just go like that and they won't notice you. That's what you must do.'

'Well, thank you! Good-bye, Daddy. God willing we may meet again,' said Olénin, getting up and moving towards the passage.

The old man, who was sitting on the floor, did not rise.

'Is that the way one says "Good-bye"? Fool, fool!' he began. 'Oh dear, what has come to people? We've kept company, kept company for well-nigh a year, and now "Good-bye!" and off he goes! Why, I love you, and how I pity you! You are so forlorn, always alone, always alone. You're somehow so unsociable. At times I can't sleep for thinking about you. I am so sorry for you. As the song has it:

> "It is very hard, dear brother,
> In a foreign land to live."

So it is with you.'

'Well, good-bye,' said Olénin again.

The old man rose and held out his hand. Olénin pressed it and turned to go.

'Give us your mug, your mug!'

And the old man took Olénin by the head with both hands and kissed him three times with wet moustaches and lips, and began to cry.

'I love you, good-bye!'

Olénin got into the cart.

'Well, is that how you're going? You might give me something for a remembrance. Give me a gun! What do you want two for?' said the old man, sobbing quite sincerely.

Olénin got out a musket and gave it to him.

'What a lot you've given the old fellow,' murmured Vanyúsha, 'he'll never have enough! A regular old beggar. They are all such irregular people,' he remarked, as he wrapped himself in his overcoat and took his seat on the box.

'Hold your tongue, swine!' exclaimed the old man, laughing. 'What a stingy fellow!'

Maryánka came out of the cowshed, glanced indifferently at the cart, bowed and went towards the hut.

'La fille!' said Vanyúsha, with a wink, and burst out into a silly laugh.

'Drive on!' shouted Olénin, angrily.

'Good-bye, my lad! Good-bye. I won't forget you!' shouted Eróshka.

Olénin turned round. Daddy Eróshka was talking to Maryánka, evidently about his own affairs, and neither the old man nor the girl looked at Olénin.

ABOUT THE INTRODUCER

Formerly Thomas Warton Professor of English Literature in the University of Oxford and Fellow of St Catherine's College, JOHN BAYLEY is the author of *Tolstoy and the Novel* and books about Hardy, Shakespeare and Housman.

ABOUT THE TRANSLATORS

LOUISE and AYLMER MAUDE spent much of their lives in Russia. Their Quaker background led them to share many of Tolstoy's views on spiritual life, moral obligation and passive resistance to violence, and they helped him to organize the Doukhobor migration to Canada in 1893. Aylmer Maude, whose business activities left him time to write a biography of his friend, also translated most of Tolstoy's major works in partnership with his wife. These translations, which were commended by the author himself, are still widely regarded as the best.

CHINUA ACHEBE
Things Fall Apart

THE ARABIAN NIGHTS
(tr. Husain Haddawy)

MARCUS AURELIUS
Meditations

JANE AUSTEN
Emma
Mansfield Park
Northanger Abbey
Persuasion
Pride and Prejudice
Sense and Sensibility

HONORÉ DE BALZAC
Cousin Bette
Eugénie Grandet
Old Goriot

SIMONE DE BEAUVOIR
The Second Sex

WILLIAM BLAKE
Poems and Prophecies

JORGE LUIS BORGES
Ficciones

JAMES BOSWELL
The Life of Samuel Johnson

CHARLOTTE BRONTË
Jane Eyre
Villette

EMILY BRONTË
Wuthering Heights

MIKHAIL BULGAKOV
The Master and Margarita

SAMUEL BUTLER
The Way of all Flesh

ITALO CALVINO
If on a winter's night a traveler

ALBERT CAMUS
The Stranger

WILLA CATHER
Death Comes for the Archbishop

MIGUEL DE CERVANTES
Don Quixote

GEOFFREY CHAUCER
Canterbury Tales

ANTON CHEKHOV
The Steppe and Other Stories
My Life and Other Stories

KATE CHOPIN
The Awakening

CARL VON CLAUSEWITZ
On War

SAMUEL TAYLOR COLERIDGE
Poems

WILKIE COLLINS
The Moonstone
The Woman in White

JOSEPH CONRAD
Heart of Darkness
Lord Jim
Nostromo
The Secret Agent
Typhoon and Other Stories
Under Western Eyes

DANIEL DEFOE
Moll Flanders
Robinson Crusoe

CHARLES DICKENS
Bleak House
David Copperfield
Great Expectations
Hard Times
Little Dorrit
Nicholas Nickleby
Oliver Twist
Our Mutual Friend
A Tale of Two Cities

DENIS DIDEROT
Memoirs of a Nun

JOHN DONNE
The Complete English Poems

Everyman's Library, founded in 1906 and relaunched in 1991, aims to offer the most complete library in the English language of the world's classics. Each volume is printed in a classic typeface on acid-free, cream-wove paper with a sewn full cloth binding.